IN HER DREAMS

WRITTEN BY OLIVIA PELAR

Chapter 1

"Who are you?" I whispered to myself in frustration. After relentlessly scouring the internet for clues, I had yet to find the identity of the man whose murder I witnessed.

The bell above the door jingled, distracting me from my hunt. I temporarily shifted my attention from the screen of my laptop to the source of the jingles. Olivia, my older sister, was returning from taking out the trash. I eagerly returned my attention back to the screen.

Olivia approached the counter where I was perched on a tattered, counter height stool. I felt her cast a concerned look my way. "Are you still looking for him?"

"Yes," I scoffed, turning my attention back to my sister. "Did you think I would just give up looking for him?"

"I had hoped you would. It was just a bad dream, Heidi. Besides, you have spent the last week looking for obituaries and news articles to back up your claims." Her hand rested sassily on her hip and her eyebrow arched, "Have you found any?"

Okay, so, maybe I didn't witness a murder in real life. But I'm convinced something bad happened to the John Doe in my dream that night. The terror felt too real.

That night, I walked alone through a field of vibrant purple flowers, until I heard a chilling bellow from behind me. There stood a man, clenching his chest, and screaming at the top of his lungs. I ran to him to see if I could help but once I reached him, he was gasping for breath. He looked me in my eyes and mouthed the word "*help.*" Tears and terror filled his bright blue eyes as he watched me do absolutely nothing. I didn't know what to do. There was no one around us. My own cries for help went unanswered. Once he stopped breathing, he fell face down in the field of purple flowers, leaving me alone.

Or at least I thought I was alone.

I couldn't shake the feeling that someone was watching me. All I could think to do was run. Run as fast and as far as I could in the opposite direction. That's when I noticed I wasn't alone. Just on the edge of my dream, among the smear of purple left behind from my desperate departure, stood an obscure figure. When I woke up, I was covered in sweat and felt sick to my stomach. My mind raced with too many questions, then emotions, to sort through all at once.

"No. Not yet," I admitted. Olivia shook her head in disbelief at me and headed toward the back office. Before she could reach the door, I reaffirmed my thoughts, "I'm telling you, something just didn't feel right about it, Olivia."

She turned to me and held a hand up for me to stop. "Enough already, Heidi. I'm starting to worry about you."

I suppressed my eyes' need to narrow. "What is there to worry about?"

Olivia let out a sigh. "You've always had an

active imagination and allowed your thoughts to run wild. Even as a kid, you'd tell us stories of dreams you had, convinced that they weren't dreams at all."

She wasn't wrong. But I was a kid. What kid doesn't have an active imagination?

"I know you get bored, doing the same thing day in and day out, but you can't allow your imagination to take over like you're allowing it to."

Again, she wasn't wrong on either count. But still, I couldn't shake the feeling that that dream was different.

"You need to find a hobby. Or a boyfriend," she teased trying to lighten the mood. We've never stayed irritated with each other for long.

That time, I let the pull of my eyes win. They rolled disapprovingly at her suggestion of a boyfriend. Before I could get in the last word, she turned and disappeared into the back office.

I did have hobbies though. This whole town was a one stop shop for outdoor hobbies, and I enjoy them all.

My home, Mount Hopewell, is a small tourist town nestled in the mountains that host visitors all year round. This rural, idyllic town has been popular for its hiking trails in the warm months and ski slopes in the winter months. I love the outdoors, and there has always been plenty to do. Still, a change of scenery from time to time would be appreciated.

I have tried to convince Olivia to take a trip with me, to get out of town for a while and experience and new adventure together. Her answer was always "no." Except for the one time I changed my mind because I had a nightmare about our plane crashing. But she would have still said no because if we left, my parents would have had to tend to the store.

The General Store has been in our family for three generations. My Grams and Pops built and ran this store, for almost forty years, when they first moved to Mount Hopewell way back when. They eventually left the store to Mom. She started to work here as soon as she was old enough to reach the cash register and count back change. Even back then, she hoped she'd be able to pass the store to her own children one day. That day has approached quickly now that my parents were nearing their seventies.

Not wanting to sound ungrateful, my family was fortunate that the store remained up and running all these years. Being the only store in town, the residents and tourists depend on us for their everyday necessities. With that said, there's no adventure being tied to the store.

To combat my boredom and fulfil my longing to have different experiences, I'd ask tourists about their travels any opportunity I got. I'd be lying if I said that I didn't fantasize about the stories they shared with me. Their stories would often carry over in my dreams, allowing me to live vicariously through them.

So, Olivia wasn't wrong about my imagination getting the best of me, but that doesn't mean what I felt in that dream wasn't real.

Olivia appeared from the back office with her belongings. "I'm going to get out of here. Ronny just got back home and I'm going to cook supper for us. We'd love it if you could join us too." Ronny Johnson, Olivia's boyfriend, returned home tonight from his latest trip. He's the owner of Mountain

Wood and Transportation, where the majority of his days are spent traveling for work.

I narrowed my eyes at her. She was up to something.

"Duncan will be there too," she finally confessed.

"Ah, there it is," I said, staring at her unamused. Duncan Johnson was Ronny's adopted younger brother. Ever since Olivia and Ronny started dating a few years back, my family has had it in their heads that Duncan and I should date too.

We went out a few times before Ronny and Olivia started dating officially, which was maybe three years ago. We enjoyed ourselves on those few dates, but that didn't mean either of us were going to jump into a steady relationship. Not then, and not now.

"What?" she grinned. "You need to eat. He needs to eat. I'm cooking…"

"Right. And it has nothing to do with the fact that you've been trying to set Duncan and me up?" I crossed my arms waiting for her to answer.

"Pshh," she flicked her wrist at me, "no."

"Uh-huh." I shook my head at her poor attempt to be subtle. She definitely had ulterior motives, but I could eat. I wouldn't mind the company either. "But yes, I'll be there. Thank you."

"Great…"

"But," I interrupted, as I wagged my finger at her. "No funny business from you tonight. I don't need you, or anyone else, meddling in Duncan's and my relationship." I used air quotes for the word relationship.

She smiled innocently at me. "I can't make any promises. See you in a bit."

Olivia practically skipped out the door, leaving me alone in the store. I closed my laptop and looked around, surveying all that needed to be done before I could leave too.

I first noticed spilled coffee under our fairly new register, which I thoroughly cleaned underneath, leaving no traces of the sticky brown liquid behind. Earlier today, one of our customers spilled her coffee when checking out. I wiped it up off the counter when it happened but hadn't noticed that the spill ran under the register. If anything were to happen to it, Mom would never let us spend money to update anything again.

It took months for Olivia and me to convince our parents to let us upgrade the register. And about four months ago, they finally agreed. Our previous register was bulky and looked like an oversized printing calculator. It was terribly outdated, and we had to ring up each item individually by keying in the prices. This new one was digital and was equipped with a convenient barcode scanner.

There were several things around the store that needed to be upgraded. The floors, for starters, were the original wooden floors that my grandparents built. They've been warped and worn for years now, and my mom has not budged on letting us redo them.

The aisle shelving wasn't in bad shape, but they're short with only three shelves on all four sides. Olivia and I could see right over them. If my mom would let us get taller shelves, we would have more space to hold more products. We only have three aisles as of now, all holding the basics. Things like cleaning products, detergents, paper products,

feminine products, and over-the-counter medicines are stocked down one aisle. The other two aisles are used to hold various food and produce items with an end cap reserved for beer and wine.

The coolers along the wall held perishable items like milk, eggs, and frozen foods.

In the back of the store, a small four-tier round shelf sat unevenly and held Mrs. Trudy's homemade goodies. The shelf was nearly empty tonight. I made a mental note to stop by her house tomorrow to pick up more.

Keeping the four-tiered shelf company in the back of the store was a wall of antique-looking P.O. Boxes. The houses around here didn't have mailboxes at the end of the driveways. Instead, our mailman, Tim, delivered mail to the P.O. boxes here in the store. Technically, there's nothing wrong with the boxes, they're just the same ones that went in after my grandparents built this place. Any time Olivia or I brought up any of these issues to my mom, we're met with a resounding "no."

I busied myself with dusting the shelves and P.O. Boxes before retrieving the broom and dustpan. All that I had left to do was sweep the warped floors.

The General Store wasn't the only resident-owned business in Mount Hopewell. Most of the residents of this town owned a small business that helped promote and maintain tourist attraction year-round. In addition to the store, there were six different lodging locations, Ed and Margie rented out hiking and ski gear, and Tammy and Stan owned a small car rental lot where they also offered transportation services. Mrs. Trudy didn't have a storefront, but all of her homemade pastries and candies, in addition to her fresh vegetables and beautiful flowers, were sold in the store.

If a resident didn't own a business but still lived here, it was usually for one of two reasons. They were either elderly and couldn't be bothered to move away or they preferred to be secluded from the surrounding cities. Residents that were similar in age to Olivia and I had mostly all moved away after graduating high school. The majority moved away to attend college; others left just to leave. Olivia and I were some of the few who stayed since we had to help our parents run the store.

Olivia, who is six years older than me, didn't have the desire to move away or attend college. She's content with working here at the store. I didn't want to leave just to leave, but for me, not being able to attend college was another lost experience.

I had begged my parents to let me go to college, but the answer was always no. My parents didn't have the money to send me off on a traditional college experience. Since I was guaranteed a job here at the store, they didn't see a need for me to take on mountains of debt.

Three years ago, though, as a gift to myself for my twenty-third birthday, I started taking online classes and have since graduated with my associates degree. I had planned to continue my education afterwards, but it *is* expensive and not something I can afford. Ironically enough, the jobs that would pay me enough to be able to afford school required a degree. There was a time, thanks to a dream I had after watching a documentary on marine life, where I said, "to hell with it" and almost started taking zoology classes. The thought of it sounded fun and exciting. I would talk my family's ear off about it. That was, until I read a story about a whale attacking a fisherman. Then my dreams were also tainted with the story, which consumed my thoughts, and freaked me out. I decided then that zoology wasn't for me.

Just another example of my active imagination, I guessed.

After I finished sweeping the floors, I emptied the dustpan into the trashcan in the office and turned out the light. The two rocking chairs between the office door and checkout counter were crooked. I straightened them up so they were facing the direction of the television hanging on the wall above the coolers. Olivia and I bought these rocking chairs for our parents a few years ago. We wanted them to have somewhere to sit and relax when the store was slow. The two backless stools behind the counter were no longer suitable for when they wanted to rest their legs. We thought it would be nice if they could rest their backs too. My parents are in fairly great shape to be knocking on the door of their seventies, but standing on your feet all day can be taxing.

I scanned the store one last time before heading off to Olivia's. Satisfied that everything was in its place, I grabbed my purse, turned out the main overhead light, and locked the door of the store behind me.

Chapter 2

My keys clanked and clattered as I dropped them on my console table by the front door. I kicked off my shoes and carried my leftovers from Olivia's to the kitchen and placed them in the fridge. The cabinet groaned as I opened it and retrieved a glass before filling it with water and taking a sip. I had a good time tonight at Oliva's for supper. She and Ronny were too cute. I'm happy they've found each other.

Conversation with Duncan was light and pleasant as always, although he did seem to be a bit more reserved than usual. Almost like he was shy. But that didn't make any sense so maybe it was just me. Thankfully, Olivia didn't make the evening more awkward by pushing the subject of Duncan and I dating.

Don't get me wrong, there's not anything wrong with Duncan. He was intelligent, hardworking, and ruggedly handsome. From what I gathered on the few dates we've been on, Duncan was content with working at his and his brother's lumber yard and staying in Mount Hopewell for the rest of his life. Which was fine. Unless you were me and wanted to experience some sense of adventure from time to time. We've ultimately agreed that we're better as friends. Friends with benefits, that is.

Heading back to the living room, I took a seat on the couch in front of the tv. I wanted to catch up on one of my shows. This one was about people who, on paper are perfectly compatible, get married the first time they meet each other. The couples then live a married life for a few months before they have to decide to stay married or get divorced. It's a real nail biter.

My phone buzzed, alerting me to a message. I unlocked the screen to see who it was from. Duncan Johnson.

Duncan: It was good to see you tonight.

Then another message came immediately after:

Duncan: It's been a while since we last saw each other.

Nine days actually, but I wasn't counting. And by *saw each other*, what he meant was *had sex*.

Mmm. That was a good night.

The two of us hiked to Marshall's Point that evening. It's not an easy hike for the elderly residents and tourists wouldn't attempt to hike it in the evening, so Duncan and I had the trail to ourselves.

On our way up, we didn't talk about anything in particular, just small talk mostly. Once we got to the rest area with picnic tables, we sat to catch our breaths. I remembered looking over at him, his black tee shirt stretching across his expanding chest, and thinking impure thoughts.

He either read my mind or my face said everything I was thinking in that moment because he pulled his shirt off, walked over to me, bent down, and pressed his lips against mine. Standing up to meet him, he walked me to the side of table and sat me on top of it. His lips feverishly kissed mine as his hands quickly pushed my thighs apart. His right hand moved between my thighs, pressing hard and rubbing up and down against the seam of my athletic pants.

Finally, he pulled me to the edge of the table, and pulled my pants down from under my ass, removing the barrier between us. Once he freed his cock from behind his sweatpants, he slid himself into my slick folds, baring our asses to no one but the birds.

I typed my response:

Heidi: It was good to see you too. And you're right, it has been a while.

My phone buzzed again. Another text from Duncan.

Duncan: I'm surprised Ronny and Olivia didn't try to push their agenda tonight. I assumed that's why they invited us both over for dinner.

Heidi: I'm not so sure they didn't. Do you think they were more affectionate with each other tonight than they normally were? It felt like to me they were trying to show us what it'd be like to have someone to come home to.

Duncan: Huh. Now that you mention it, I think you might be right.

Heidi: I normally am ;). But hey, I'm beat, and I need to get to bed. Talk to you soon?

Duncan: Talk soon. Sweet dreams, Heidi.

I locked my phone screen, stood from the couch, and turned off the tv. As it turned out, I was too tired to finish an episode tonight. I headed down the hall, to my bedroom, then the master bathroom to start my shower.

I really need to get to bed, but I needed to wash the day away first. It has been a long one and I have been looking forward to getting some rest. Mostly because I'll get to dream. I've always dreamed. For as long as I can remember, I've experienced vivid dreams. They feel real in a way that feels like I'm able to experience life beyond Mount Hopewell. Sometimes that's an amazing feeling, being so alive and in the moment while dreaming, but sometimes it was terrifying.

Amazing in the way that I could have experiences without leaving home, or stressing about the money it took to have those experiences. One night, I dreamed I was hang gliding in Switzerland. I could feel the wind rush past my face and push against my sail. The views of the small mountain town below me were stunning as the wind carried me closer to the ground.

However, my dreams could feel terrifying, like watching a stranger die in front of you knowing there was absolutely nothing you could do to stop it.

Letting the shower warm up, I recalled the night that made me believe in the power of my dreams. I was maybe ten or eleven years old, and my family and I went up to the slopes for the day. It was my first time skiing and I wasn't doing too well. No matter what I did, I couldn't stay upright. Any time I got ready to head down the slope I'd fall right on my butt. I got so frustrated and decided to save myself from the embarrassment, and bruises, and called it a day. I spent the rest of the afternoon building snowmen and playing with some of the other children who had decided to give up too. Later that night though, I learned to ski in my dreams.

I was back at the top of those slopes, with my skis on and the instructor was there giving lessons. He'd say "Pie to stop. The bigger the pie, the slower you go. Don't cross your skis, and if you fall, sit on your high hip and walk to the tips until you're ready to stand." He kept repeating it over and over before I realized I could move down the slope. There wasn't anyone else on the slope and I was free to fall without feeling embarrassed. I fell repeatedly until suddenly, I didn't. I was skiing!

I remembered waking up the next morning feeling confident. I knew I could ski and was ready to prove it. I begged my parents to take me back to the slopes to show them what I had learned while I was sleeping. They gave in, mostly so they could just enjoy a peaceful Sunday, but they also didn't want to crush my spirit. When we got to the top of those slopes, I skied like it was what I was born to do. I didn't fall, not even once! My parents were surprised. They convinced themselves that I was just being stubborn the day before. But I knew, I knew from then on out that my dreams were special. I have since used my dreams to help me experience life without the financial ability to do so.

My dreams excite me. It's hard not to share the details of some of them with my parents and Oliva. As much as I wish I could share them all, I have learned that doing so just fuels their worry for me. They've said that I spend too much time in a fantasy land and not enough time here in reality. Olivia was especially critical this evening about my dream with John Doe.

I washed away the doubts Olivia had about me witnessing his murder. She's my sister and best friend. I knew she only wanted what's best for me, which made it hard not to take her words into consideration – that maybe it was just a dream after all.

The water ran over me, removing the suds from my body, as I tried to convince myself that Olivia was right. But ultimately, I decided that she's not right, she can't be. Not even a little. I had to figure out what happened to him.

I have only told Olivia about my dream with John Doe. If her reaction was any indication to how my parents would react, I think it's safe to say I won't share that specific dream with my them. Their reaction would be far worse than Olivia's. Especially my mom's.

Freshly showered and dressed in fresh pajamas, I slid into my bed ready for sleep. As soon as my head hit the pillow, I drifted off to my sweetest escape.

I'm at the store. Mom was here too. She's sitting in her rocking chair near the end of the checkout counter. I walked over and sat in the empty rocking chair next to hers.

"How are you doing, Mom?"

"I'm doing good sweetheart. How are you?" She reached over to grab my hand.

"I'm doing good. I've had a lot on my mind lately though."

She squeezed my hand lovingly. "What about?"

I decided to be brave and tell her about the dream. It's not like I'm actually talking to her. "I had a terrible dream. About a man dying."

"That does sound terrible. Thankfully, it's just a dream."

"That's just it. I don't think it was. I think he really did die."

She eyed me suspiciously, "What do you mean,

Heidi?"

"I mean, I think he's a real person and I've been trying to find him."

Mom let go of my hand and took a breath. "Heidi. You're too old to be chasing foolish ideas like this. You're not a kid anymore. We've been over this. Your dreams are just that. Dreams. There's nothing real about them." She stood as she scolded me, "All the times you've tried to convince us that your dreams are special was just a way for you to feel like you have purpose. You hate working at the store so much that you'd rather make up dramatic tales and call them dreams."

I was shocked at her tone. I didn't expect her to have such a strong reaction in my dream. This is what I imagine it'd be like if I actually told her.

That's not true at all!" I stood to meet her gaze. "I can't believe that's what you think."

"Or maybe you spend so much time in your head because Duncan has moved on. You blew your chance at happiness and now you regret it."

Okay, that took a turn I didn't expect. What the hell is going on here?

My hands slapped my sides in exasperation, "What does Duncan have to do with any of this?"

"I hear he's dating someone. Someone in the city."

I turned my back to her and huffed in frustration. I couldn't stand here and argue with the dream version of my mom. Through the glass pane of the door, something out of place caught my eye. I noticed a man staring at me from the parking lot. With my mom still ranting about Duncan behind me, I head to the door and opened it. "Hey," I yelled to him, not in the mood for anything else unexpected. "Can I help you?"

He looked surprised but didn't respond. He looked off in the distance and took off running. I followed behind him.

Suddenly, I was no longer in the parking lot of the store. I'm now in a dim, grey room. I looked around at the change of my surroundings and that's when I saw him again.

I caught his dark eyes staring into me. He looked at me as if he knew me.

But that can't be right. I don't know him. Do I?

A familiar feeling caught in my chest.

Ever since I saw John Doe die in front of me in the field of purple flowers, I've scrutinized every detail of every dream. This was the same feeling I felt then, when it felt like I was being watched. I had a feeling that his presence now wasn't a coincidence. I'm certain he's not some character my mind has made up.

His lips part, making room for words to flow through. His eyes searched my body before landing on my face. His expression relaxed. He looked almost relieved as a smile began to curve from his lips.

Wow.

My knees nearly buckled from the sight of him. His brand of handsome didn't exist in Mount Hopewell. Each tooth, perfectly in place, pressed behind full lips. The contrast of his white teeth against his warm colored skin appeared to be too perfect to exist. I was fixated on him. A mix of butterflies and ecstasy stirred in my stomach as his *eyes became busy scanning my face, like he's trying to memorize every feature.*

I wanted to reach out and touch him. I need to feel his skin beneath my fingers. I need to run my hands through his dark short hair. Except, when I try to extend my arm toward him, I'm unable to move. I tried again. But nothing. No movement. I looked at him, trying to understand why I couldn't move, but his expression sent an unexplainable chill down my spine.

The feeling was back. Someone is watching us.

His eyes grew wide with fear. His forehead crinkled with subtle wrinkles and his grin had morphed from an upright crescent to a tight line.

He looked scared. But, scared of what?
Of me?

Chapter 3

The soft rays of the sun peaked through the curtains of my bedroom window, nudging me awake, removing me from my dream.

Dammit.

I rubbed my hands over my face in frustration.

Why did his expression change? I wondered. Why couldn't I move? That's never happened to me before.

I didn't understand why the dark eyed man appeared in my dream, or why that familiar feeling returned, but if I had to take a guess, I'd guess that he was somehow connected to John Doe.

Was he the one watching me in the field of purple flowers? *I sound like I'm losing my mind.*

Rolling over to check the time from the clock on my bedside table, I learned that the sun beat my alarm by thirteen minutes. Waking up at 6:30 each morning was just another impact of this monotonous life. As much as I'd like to sit at home, continuing my search for John Doe, and now this dark eyed man, I had to get to the store.

Dragging myself out of my bed and into my bathroom, I'm jarred by my reflection in the mirror. My long brown hair was tangled at its ends and an impression of my wrinkled pillowcase was impressed across my cheek. Evidence that I slept hard last night.

Once I've brushed out all the tangles, I pulled my hair back into a ponytail for the day. I also added a coat of mascara to the lashes of my hazel eyes. With the weather being so nice outside, I opted for a pair of jean shorts and a tee shirt. Sliding the neck of my tee shirt down over my head, I remembered that I need to stop by Mrs. Trudy's before I got to the store. I grabbed my purse and headed out the door in a hurry.

The bell above the door jingled as I entered the store with a couple of boxes of Mrs. Trudy's homemade goodies. Olivia and Mom were both behind the counter. Mom's back was to me as she put on a pot of coffee and set out the breakfast sandwiches she made for us and the store's daily regulars.

"Good morning, Mom. Good morning, Olivia," I chirped and shut the door behind me.

"Good morning, Heidi," Olivia said before she shot me a wary look. A look I'm all too familiar with. It's the look she gives me when Mom is in a mood, a warning that I should tread lightly. I wondered what's got her goose this early in the morning as I waited for her to turn around and greet me.

She doesn't.

"Mom? Is everything okay?"

She finally turned around and said, "I have news. You might want to sit down for this."

Fear and curiosity roamed my thoughts. I sat the homemade treats I just brought in on the counter next to the register. My body stiffened, preparing for devastating news. Before I could even consider the thought of if I wanted to sit down or not, she blurted out, "Duncan is seeing someone. Esther, from my knitting group, said she and her daughter went out to Easton City for lunch yesterday. When they got up to leave their table, she saw Duncan near the back of the restaurant having lunch with another woman."

I blinked in confusion. I looked to Oliva for a clue as to why Mom was so upset by this. Oliva shrugged her shoulders. "Okay. And this is upsetting because…" I trailed off, hoping that she would finish my sentence.

"Because he's clearly seeing another woman behind your back!"

"Behind my back?" I asked confused. "Mom, Duncan and I are not together. We are friends. We will only ever be friends."

"Well, who else do you expect to settle down with," she huffed. She turned her back to me, bussing herself with a meaningless task before finally saying, "He's your best chance at getting married."

My eyes rolled and shoulders sagged, "for the last time, I'm *not* worried about getting married right now." I was annoyed. She pushed this subject too often.

"Why?" she asked, turning back to face me with her hands on her hips. "Because you're worried about that silly dream you had?" she said almost absent-mindedly. "You're always stuck in your head about one thing or another."

I looked at her stunned. She can't be talking about *the* dream could she? I glanced quickly at Olivia, asking her with my eyes if she had told Mom about it. I saw her shake her head no before I returned my expression back to Mom. "Mom, what *silly* dream?"

"About that poor man dying. He didn't really die, Heidi. It was just a dream."

If Olivia didn't tell her, how does she know about

it?

"So, are you going to live in your head all day and let that hussy steal away with your man? Or are you going to come down to reality and do something about it?"

I rolled my eyes at her again, "Mom, *hussy* is a bit much, don't you think?" Mom flicked her hand at me, brushing off my question, before she grabbed the boxes and carried them off to the office. "And I won't be talking to Duncan because it's not any of my business." She stopped to face me. "Regardless of the reasons, we're *not* together."

"I can't have this conversation with you when you're being irrational. Eat your breakfast and we'll talk about this later." She disappeared for a moment into the office before she came back out with her purse in hand. "I'm going to head home now. I love you both." And out the door, she went.

Well, that was not a conversation I expected to have with my mom. I can't believe she said Duncan was my only chance at getting married. What a shitty thing to say to me. I looked at Olivia, "You promise you didn't say anything to her about my dream?"

"I promise I didn't," she held her hands up in front of her defensively. "Did you maybe tell her and forget?"

Did I? The only time I brought it up to her was...

I thought about the conversations I've had with my mom since that dream and only one conversation came to mind. The one we had in last night's dream.

But I couldn't tell Olivia that, she's worried about me enough as it is. I shrugged my shoulders at her and lied. "I can't remember."

"Maybe she overheard us talking about it before."

I doubt it. But I can't confront that thought just yet. "Yeah. Maybe."

I walked behind the counter for the breakfast Mom left for me. I propped myself up on the stool next to Olivia and began to eat. Carefully replaying each time Olivia and I talked about my dream, I searched for an explanation of how Mom could know about it.

By the time I'd finished my breakfast and my coffee, I still hadn't come up with an explanation. Instead of dwelling on the thought, I made myself busy with restocking the tiered shelf with Mrs. Trudy's goodies.

Oliva headed back to her house for lunch, which left me to man the store alone. It was almost noon and the only customers we had were Ronny and Tim, the mailman. Except, Tim doesn't technically count as a customer. He had to stop in every weekday morning to drop off mail for the residents. He also picked up the breakfast that Mom made for him each morning.

My parents and Tim grew up together, they're more like family than friends. Actually, the majority of the residents were considered family. Since neither of my parents had siblings, starting and having a big family had always been important to them. That's probably why my mom made such a big deal about me settling down. Because having a large family has always been a dream of *hers*.

I get it, I do, but I can't focus on settling down when my thoughts are constantly running me in different directions. When my dreams dictate my every aspiration on a whim.

I wanted more – no, I *needed* more out of life. Being stuck in a job that's mostly mind-numbing, and didn't pay more than needed, didn't prevent me from becoming engrossed in my literal dreams. A recap of my work week usually went like this: sit in the store, every day. Talked to the same few faces, every day. Restocked the same items on the same shelves, every day. Just about every day is left on repeat. And sure, we got tourists in here frequently that help break up the dullness to the day, but not all tourists liked to stop and talk with a chatty local. Unless they're asking for directions or recommendations, people are generally in and out so they can get on with their plans. And I'm here, stuck in my plans, dreaming about the adventures other people get to experience. Adding a spouse to the mix wouldn't make anything better.

Wanting to occupy my thoughts with anything other than my current frustration, I decided to resume my search for John Doe.

I've spent the last forty-five minutes in the back office on my laptop, continuing my search for the blue-eyed man from the field of purple flowers, when the bell above the door jingled and pulled me away from my search.

"Welcome in!" I called as I exit the threshold of the office into the store. It's Dad. "Oh, hey Dad!"

He met me in front of the rocking chairs and gave me a hug. "How are you, sweetheart?" His expression and tone told me he has an agenda.

"I'm doing okay, Dad." He took a seat in one of the chairs, and I did the same.

"Want to talk about this morning? Your mom told

me the two of you got into a tiff."

I knew it. She always does this. Mom and I argue. She tells Dad. He comes and tries to fix things, so she doesn't have to. "Did we?" I asked sarcastically, arching my eyebrow and looking away as if I'm searching for the memory.

Dad chuckled at my response. "She only wants what's best for you. We both do."

"And marriage is what's best for me?"

"No. It's not just about marriage, Heidi." He paused to gather his words. "We sometimes worry that you don't have any direction in life. Or, let me rephrase that – have too much direction in your life."

"What does that mean, too much direction? All I do is sit in this store, day after day, doing the same thing. That seems to be only one direction to me."

"Well, you know, you do spend a lot of time in that head of yours. You place a lot of stock in your dreams. It's…" he paused again, carefully searching for his words, "childish."

"That sounds like Mom, not you. Did she tell you to tell me that?"

"That's not the point. The point is that I have to agree with her on this one."

I blew out a frustrated sigh and crossed my arms.

"You've always had such an active imagination that played out heavily in your dreams. And I'll admit, when you were younger, we thought it would serve you in a positive way, but all you let it do is distract you from what's important in life."

"Yeah? And what's that?" My harsh tone took me and my dad by surprise.

"Your family. I don't mean just us, but the family

you'll one day have. You spend too much time pursuing these fantasies," he held the palm of his left hand out and pointed to a finger with his right as he mentioned each example, "First it was some extravagant trip you tried to talk Olivia into taking with you. You spent so much time planning it, just to change your mind at a moment's notice when you had a nightmare about the plane crashing. You wanted to become a zoologist. Again, spent so much time researching schools and classes and pestering your mom and me for money for tuition, just to change your mind because of yet another nightmare. Now, you're convinced someone has died... because of a nightmare you had?"

My eyes went wide when he mentioned the last example. Now they both knew about it.

"Has that started to consume your thoughts now too?" he asked kindly but concerned.

When I didn't respond, because I didn't know how to, he continued with his speech.

"If you would put that much effort into your life, here," he pointed his finger to the floor, "you could build yourself something wonderful. And that is what your mom and I want for you. That is why we worry so much about you."

Aggravated, I shot to my feet, causing the rocking chair to rock back and forth violently, as I paced the floor in front of it. "Okay, Dad. Let's say I do that. Let's say I do settle down and have kids. What happens when Olivia and I both have young kids at home when we're supposed to be here instead?"

"Well, your mother and I would watch them of course."

Shit, bad example.

"Okay, how do you propose we support them? We make just enough to cover the bills, Dad."

He stared at me, unable to respond.

"So yeah. I might spend a lot of time in my head, and allow my dreams to *sometimes* dictate those thoughts, but it's better than just sitting around here all day doing nothing. And, when I get an idea that might help me improve my life, our life," my hands gestured between the two of us to emphasize that I do think about my family, "it's immediately met with skepticism and doubt."

Still, my dad didn't speak. He stayed rocking in his chair. I'm not sure if he's tuned me out or if he's processing what I said. In case it was the latter, I kept going.

"And never did I once say I never wanted to get married. It's just not what I want right now." A moment of silence passed between us and I sat back down. "Dad. Please say something."

Finally, he turned to me with a reminiscent smile. "When your mom and I were in high school, we loved each other so much that we knew we would be married someday. Your mom thought it best that I learned how to help operate the store since one day we would be running it together. When she asked her parents to hire me, they flat-out told her no. Not because they didn't like me, but because they weren't convinced that we were serious about the plans we had for our life. Our plans to get married, run the store, and raise our family here. She dreamed that her own kids would get to run this store someday too. But, your grandparents didn't want your mom to invest so much time into something that might not pan out. Fast forward to a few days after she turned eighteen. We drove, what was just fifty miles at the time, to City Hall and got married to prove them wrong."

My eyes softened with unexpected delight. I've never heard that story before.

My dad reached across the arms of our rocking chairs and rested his hand on mine, "After that, Grams and Pops didn't have a good reason not to take our relationship seriously and allowed me to work at the store too. And here we are, almost fifty years later."

I didn't know Mom had it in her, to wildly go against her parents like that. And while I liked learning new things about my parents, I didn't understand where he was going with this.

"Sometimes, we have to invest our time into our thoughts, or our *dreams*," he squeezed my hand and smiled at me, "that could make us happy. Even if other people don't believe in it." He nodded his head slightly, "I'll talk to your mom, try and remind her that everything starts with a dream."

Chapter 4

It's almost six and Oliva has already left for home this evening. Ronny has to leave for another delivery tomorrow and they're spending the evening together before he's gone for the next few days. I just needed to finish this inventory and I'd be on my way too.

I'm crouched down near the shelf of paper products finishing up inventory when the bell above the door jingled. I'm unable to see who's entered so I yelled out, "We're closing up, but we'll be opened tomorrow morning at six a.m."

"I know," a familiar and husky voice responded. "But I thought it'd be best to come by when no one else was here."

I stood and saw Duncan's tall, sturdy build standing near the door. I'll admit, the sight of him burns my cheeks. He had the most alluring green eyes I had ever seen; I felt lost, yet seen, anytime I looked into them. His brown hair was wild and thick on top and longer than the sides, but not so much so that he had to style it to keep it out of his face. His thick and neatly trimmed beard covered his lower cheeks, the space between his nose and around his kissable lips, finally spreading down his strong chin and stopping right above his Adam's apple. "Oh hey, Duncan. How can I help you this evening?"

"I was wondering if you'd like to take a walk with me when you finish up here."

"Sure, give me just a few minutes to lock up. I'll

meet you out front?"

"I'll be waiting." He flashed me a grin before turning to head back outside.

I fanned myself with my clipboard before I returned my focus on the inventory sheet. I made a few updates and set the clipboard on the desk in the office. I grab my keys and sweater, turned out the lights and headed out the door. Locking it behind me, I gave it a few good pushes for good measure. Once I felt certain the door was locked, I turned on my heels and searched for Duncan.

The gravel in the parking lot crunched beneath my feet as I headed to the clearing beside the store where I was sure Duncan was waiting. I had an idea of why he stopped by, and I hoped I was right. Duncan isn't one to just stop by for a chat. We generally kept our conversations on the surface. He has always had a wall built around him. Not that I could blame him for it.

I found him leaning up against the outside of the store with his hands in his pockets. "All locked up now. Where did you want to go?"

He stood up straight. "I thought we could walk Kingsman trail. You up for it?"

I smiled at him, I hoped he'd say Kingsman Trail. "Yeah, I'm up for it. It'll be nice to stretch my legs too after being in the store all day."

We drove our cars to my house where I parked mine before getting in Duncan's truck. The trailhead was just around the bend from my house and made it less suspicious to go in one car. The inside of his truck cab was always clean and always smelled like sawdust despite the lack of it. "How have things at the store been?" he asked as we pulled out of my driveway.

"Oh, you know, the same old same old. The most exciting thing that happened today was when a bird flew into the store." His eye brows raised in amusement. "One of the customers was hollering from the door of the store to the passenger of his car. It sounded like the passenger couldn't make up her mind on which flavor of soda to get. But while the door was being held open, a bird flew right on in."

He laughed and put the truck in park after he pulled into the parking lot of the trailhead. "How'd you get the bird out of there?"

"Bread," I said as I hopped out of his truck. Duncan got out too and we walked toward the trail entrance. "I didn't finish my pulled pork sandwich from lunch today, so I pulled some pieces of bread off and made a trail that led out the door."

"Cleaver thinking. I hope he doesn't go back and tell all his bird buddies about your generosity."

"You and me both." I giggled at the idea of a flock of birds lining up outside the store. "How have things been going at the lumber yard? Olivia was telling me that Ronny has another long haul tomorrow."

Squirrels rustled and shook the tree limbs above us, causing Duncan and I both to look up and briefly watch them. It looked like they were playing follow the leader. The second squirrel mimicked every movement of the first squirrel. "Business is good. We've been in negotiations for a new account this week. The developer is just over in Easton City and if we get their business, Ronny will have consistent deliveries that are closer to home."

"That's wonderful," I said. "Olivia hadn't told me."

"Maybe Ronny hasn't told her yet?"

"Oh?" I looked at him concerned. "You think so?"

"Maybe," he shrugged his wide shoulders. "He's mentioned he didn't want to get her hopes up. If we get this contract, he won't have to make any overnight runs for at least the next three years."

I nodded my head in understanding. "Yeah, I get that. Olivia would be over the moon to have Ronny home every night. Any idea of when a decision is supposed to be made?"

Duncan tilted his head slightly, "Kathrine, the contract broker, said we should hear something within two weeks. I only just met with her yesterday and I understand that there are several companies bidding for this contract. They need time to hear all the companies out.

"Ah," I smiled, looking down at the ground in front of me as we continued to walk. "She's a broker." I chuckled. "That's funny."

Esther apparently doesn't know what she's talking about.

He looked at me with a quizzical expression. "What is?"

"Nothing really, but my mom is convinced that we should be together. This morning she told me that she heard from Esther that you were having lunch with some woman in Easton City." He looked down at me, preparing to speak, but I waved away his words. "Don't worry. I told her that we were only friends and that's all we would ever be. It wasn't the answer she had hoped to hear though. She sent my dad over a few hours later to *fix* things."

He stopped and reached up to touch my chin with his thumb and finger. "Just friends, huh?" A flirtatious grin slipped from his lips.

Dammit. How does he do that to me? I could feel the heat rise to my cheeks as I grinned. "Yes, as far as anyone is concerned, we are just friends. If anyone catches wind of anything more, our families will plan our wedding for us." I took a step forward, signaling that we should keep moving. "We've got to keep walking. I don't want anyone to see us lingering."

"You're right. There aren't many kept secrets between the residents of Mount Hopewell. And apparently, I'm seeing some woman in Easton City."

We both laughed.

We walked in silence for a bit, enjoying the nature around us. Even with my mind focused on not tripping over a root and embarrassing myself, I felt my curiosity growing. "So," I said, preparing myself to ask this next question, which wasn't any of my business, "Are you dating anyone?"

"Nope." He answered quickly.

I stared at the ground to hide my grin from him, "Good." I stopped and looked up at him, "Does that mean you're up for some company again tonight?"

"I'm so glad you asked. Your place or mine?" he asked with a grin.

I looked around to see where we were on the trail and noticed we were already in my neck of the woods. Kingsman trail cut through the woods located behind my backyard. It made for a convenient way to get my *friend* to and from my house on occasion. I bit my lower lip, looked into his green eyes, and said, "Mine."

He grabbed my hand and we cut from the trail and into the woods. Careful not to trip on any tree roots, or downed branches, we finally arrived at my back porch. By now, the sun was starting to set. It was the perfect time of day to sneak Duncan inside. None of my neighbors appeared to be outside, but their houses were so far apart, they wouldn't be able to see us even if they were.

He leaned down and kissed me on the back of my neck as I unlocked and opened the door. He shut it behind him as we entered the kitchen. As his hands found their place on my hips, he turned me around to face him. I perched up on the tips of my toes and threw my arms around his neck. He lifted me up and set me on the counter as our lips collided. His kisses were slow and gentle at first. He held me steady with his left hand as his right traveled from my side to the base of my neck. He fisted his hand in my hair and tugged at it.

A breathy moan escaped from my lips. I peeled the sweater off my shoulders and tossed it on the floor. Our lips separated long enough for Duncan to pull my shirt up over my head. Picking me back up, he carried me to the bedroom and tossed me on my bed. I leaned up against my headboard and watched as he began to undress himself, but he stopped just before removing his boxers.

Tease.

Duncan then began to unbutton my shorts and slid them down the length of my legs before tossing them onto the floor. He kneeled between my spread legs and started to kiss my inner thighs. My skin pebbled in the wake of the sensation his facial hair left as he pressed his lips to my skin. The heat I felt in my cheeks during our walk has now moved between my thighs. His hands moved quickly up my belly and behind my back to unclasp my bra. He slid the bra straps off my shoulders, finally freeing my breast. He moved his lips swiftly over my nipple and flicked it with his strong tongue. Wet with desperation, I pushed down at my panties to let him know I was ready for him. He ripped the flimsy material away from my body before finally removing his own underwear, freeing his impressive cock. He grabbed my thighs and pulled my body closer to his, causing me to lay completely flat on the bed. My chest heaved with anticipation.

Using his knee to force my legs wider apart, he positioned himself between them and greedily buried himself inside me, eliciting a gratifying bolt of ecstasy from my center. He skillfully ravished my body, slamming harder and harder into my slit. My body hummed beneath him as he caught my moans with his mouth. I swelled around his cock, squeezing myself tighter around him until finally, I felt the sweet release of my climax. Duncan released my lips from his and let out a satisfied growl as he pulled out and unloaded his cum on my belly.

Duncan was still upright but sat back on his calves, allowing his eyes to spill over my fatigued body. Our bodies remained still until we caught our breath. He brought me a towel from my bathroom and helped me clean myself up. Once his warm cum is removed from my belly, I slipped underneath my blanket and watched as he got dressed. "Glad you could stop by," I said with an agreeable tone.

"Yeah?" he grinned. "Me too." He buttoned his jeans and gathered his shirt from the floor. "I enjoy my hikes with you," he said with a wink. He checked his watch and said, "I better be on my way. I'll see you around, Heidi."

I waved to him with my fingers, "Bye, Duncan."

Duncan left the same way he came, through the back door. We don't need anyone finding out the true nature of our relationship. I haven't even told Oliva about us because I know she would tell Ronny, who could break down and tell his parents. Who would then tell my parents and before you know it, Duncan and I would be forced to the altar. Neither of us want a serious relationship but we're happy to fulfill each other's desires when needed. And tonight, it was definitely needed.

I replayed my evening with Duncan. Thoughts of him ravishing my body carried me to sleep.

***

It's dusk and I'm back on Kingsman Trail.

I looked around to take in my surroundings. It appeared to be just me, the birds, and the trees. The one thing that wasn't here was the dirt path swarmed with thick tree roots that should be beneath my feet. In its place was a white, tiled floor covering the path in front of me. Behind me, the path was a brown smear, like it was out of focus. With my eyes, I followed the tiled floor down to where a dim light illuminates the middle of the path.

I decided to walk into the beam of light. Just as I get there, I'm suddenly surrounded by walls of baby products.

"What do you think about this, Aunty Heidi?"

Aunty who?

I turn my head in the direction of her voice. It's Olivia. She's holding up a tiny pink onesie that says, "Mommy's princess".

"Wouldn't this be so cute on the baby?" she asked as she turns to face me. Her belly was wide and round. She laid the onesie flat on the top of her belly as she pulls a tiny pair of ruffled pants off the nearby shelf. She unfolds the pants and held them over the middle of the onesie, pairing them together. "Isn't this just the cutest little outfit," she squealed.

My eyes widen and my mouth dropped. I impulsively reach out and place my hands on her belly. She's pregnant! I step back and take in the vision that is my older sister. She's beautiful pregnant. My heart instantly swells, and I gave her a tight hug.

"Oh my gosh, Heidi," she stumbles back as she braced me. "Is everything okay?"

My sister has always wanted to be a mom. Seeing her like this makes me hopeful that someday soon, she will be.

"Yeah." A smile beamed from my face, "I'm just so excited to be an aunt!"

"If you're excited, think of how excited Mom is right now." She chuckles and tossed the outfit in the back of the shopping cart and we continued down the aisle. "She's on cloud nine. This is all she wants for

us."

My smile fades. I'm glad at least one of us will be able to give her what she wanted. We stop walking once we reached the crib displays. Each crib was staged in front of a makeshift nursery wall. Each decorated with a different theme. I looked at the many choices my sister would have to choose from, and my sights were set on one in particular.

The nursery wall was decorated with white shiplap planks and a framed photo hung from it. It's a photo of a single purple flower.

I hear Olivia beside me, asking me something about the cribs, but I couldn't focus on her voice. I had already started to walk towards the photo.

Suddenly, I'm in the grey room again. The same one from last night's dream. And I wasn't alone. "Hello?" I called out to the stranger whose back was turned to me.

His head swivels to the left and I was met with a dark set of eyes hooded by furrowed brows. It was him, the dark eyed man. His expression softens when he sees me. His hands fell to his sides as he turns his body towards me. I notice now that he was standing in front of a closed door.

"Are you all right?" I asked as I took a step toward him. He didn't answer. I took another step, "Who are you?" Still, no response. I took another step, finally within arm's reach of him and I'm hit with an overwhelming feeling of fear. Like someone was watching me again.

Something isn't right. This feels dangerous.

A chill ran down my spine and I swallow hard. My eyes dart around the room, looking for an explanation. But there's nothing. I closed my eyes and took a deep breath, wanting to shake this feeling.

My mom's words echo in my mind – "It's just a dream."

I heard something else too. Beeping, I think. I opened my eyes. The dark-eyed man had turned to face the closed door, his back was to me once again. He's struggling against the door, it won't open.

The beeping sound was soft and rhythmic as it filled this tiny room, causing my heart to race.

My voice catches in my throat when I try to speak. We shouldn't be here. It doesn't feel safe. I want to reach out and touch him, to get his attention, but again, my arm doesn't comply.

I want to wake up. I need to wake up.

I look around again, trying to find a way out. Still, there's nothing.

The dark eyed man continued to face the door but he's motionless now. He's no longer struggling against it.

I swallowed another hard lump. I couldn't move at all. Tears pricked my eyes.

Wake up.

I felt the grip of someone, of something, wrap around me. I struggled to break free.

Wake up.

The rhythmic beeping sped up to match the pace of my panicked heart.

Wake up.

The grip tightened around me.

Wake up!

Chapter 5

Oliva was already at the store by the time I pulled into the parking lot. It was a little after 6:30 a.m. and the sun had started to peak its head out above the trees. Olivia was surprised to see me so early as I sluggishly entered the store.

"Good morning," I said blandly to her.

"Is it? You don't sound quite as chirpy this morning. Is everything okay?"

I tossed my purse on the counter and slumped into one of the rocking chairs. "Honestly, I'm not sure. I just had the scariest dream."

"Nightmares are the worst," she said sympathetically. "I'm sorry."

"No, this wasn't a nightmare. This was something different."

Olivia poured me a cup of coffee and handed it to me. "Here. Let's get some caffeine in you."

I blew the hot coffee before taking a sip. "Thank you."

"All right," she took a seat next to me. She propped her elbow on the arm of the chair and rested her chin on her fist, "tell me about this dream. If it wasn't a nightmare, what do you think it was?"

"I'm not sure. I've never experienced anything like it before. The dream started out fine but once I saw him…"

"Him," Olivia interrupted as her eyebrow arched. "Him who?"

"I don't know who. Some dark eyed man who randomly appeared in my dream the night before last. Then again last night."

"And that's strange?" she asked unsure. "I know when I dream, I don't always know the faces I see but I don't put much thought into it."

"There's something about this guy, though. Something that makes me feel like he's not some random character my mind made up." I blew on my coffee again, thinking about the last two dreams, before taking another sip. I looked at Olivia and said, "I think he's connected to John Doe."

Olivia gave me a disappointed look. "Heidi, you can't be serious." She sat straight in her rocking chair, looking ahead of her.

Turning to her, pleading with my hands, I said, "Olivia, I know you don't think any of this is real, but can I please tell you about my dream last night?"

She rocked silently for a moment. She didn't like fueling my dream theories. "Fine," she finally gave in. "Tell me about your dream."

"Thank you," I said softly. I stole a sip of coffee, recalling the details from my latest dream. "The first time I noticed him, he was staring at me from the parking lot." I pointed toward the door of the store. "I followed him and we wound up in this grey room. We didn't get the chance to speak because there was this awful feeling like I was being watched and I freaked out. I had to wake up to get out of there."

Oliva listened intently but didn't say a word.

"We were in the same grey room last night. He was trying to open a door. Really struggling to get it opened. I tried asking him questions to figure out what was going on, but he didn't answer. Which is weird, because I know he can hear me, but for some reason, he doesn't respond."

"Maybe because it's just a dream, Heidi." She said with a mordant tone.

I stood from the chair and huffed, "Never mind."

Olivia reached for my arm, "No, I'm sorry. Please sit back down and finish your story."

I looked at her for confirmation. She pointed to the empty chair for me to retake my seat. Reluctantly, I sat back down.

"So, he doesn't talk to you…" Olivia picked up where I left off.

"Yeah. But he responds by looking at me, so I know he can hear me. But before I could press him further last night, it felt like someone, or something had me."

"What do you mean, *had* you?"

"Like someone was holding me in a tight bear hug from behind. Someone freakishly strong. But there wasn't anyone else there. It was just the two of us. The grip around me was so tight, I couldn't move. My chest even felt tight. I felt paralyzed, unable to move my body, despite my desperation to do so." I took another sip of my coffee. "And what's even weirder, is that there was constant beeping around us. It started out calm and rhythmic, but the more scared I became, the faster the beeping rang."

"Like a heart monitor does?" She asked.

A heart monitor? I thought back to the rhythm. The more I thought about it, the more it fit. "Yeah. Like a heart monitor. But I didn't see one around us. So, I'm not sure where it came from."

"What do you think it means?"

I shook my head and stared off into the distance, "I have no idea. That's what scares me the most."

"That does sound terrifying."

I looked over at her, "Have you ever experienced anything like that before?"

"No, never. But I don't dream often, and if I do, it's nothing like the experiences you've described while dreaming."

"So, you believe me?"

Olivia sighed, "I believe that you believe it."

That was not what I wanted to hear. I don't know how to make her believe too. How can I convince her that these aren't just dreams?

"Is that all that happened?" she asked, pulling me from my thoughts.

"Oh!" I startled her with my outburst. "I can't believe I almost forgot the best part. You were pregnant," I squealed.

"Wait, me? I was pregnant?"

"Yes! And you were so cute with your round belly."

Olivia absentmindedly rubbed her flat stomach and smiled, "I can't wait to be pregnant. I want to be a mom so bad."

"Have you and Ronny ever talked about having kids?"

She leaned back in her rocking chair and looked ahead, "Yeah. He wants a family as much as I do. His hesitation is that he travels too much. And we want to get married first, but still, the fact that he travels too much is what's sort of holding him back from everything."

My mind wandered to what Duncan said the night before. He and Ronny were currently bidding for a local contract that would keep Ronny at home. "Would that stop you? If he has to continue to travel for work?"

She smiled and shook her head, "Not at all. I love Ronny and I know I want to spend the rest of my life with him. I want to raise a family with him. I miss him when he's gone but he's never gone for too long. And once we have kids, I'll have you, and Mom and Dad to help with the kids." Olivia grinned, "Could you imagine, mini versions of Ronny and I, hopefully with his strawberry blonde hair, running around in here."

I laughed at the thought of little feet running around this tiny little store, making a complete mess of things. "Our days definitely wouldn't be boring then." I yawned big and took another sip of my coffee. The caffeine hadn't kicked in yet. "It might be a two cup morning for me," I said, gesturing to the cup of coffee in my hand. "I wasn't able to go back to sleep after that dream last night."

"Want to play some tic tac toe or M.A.S.H. to get your mind off of it?" Olivia asked.

"Sure. The winner of three games gets to choose the channel we watch today." We relocated behind the counter and took a seat on the backless stools.

"There are only five channels to choose from. What could you possibly want to watch?" She pulled out a pad of paper and a pencil and started scratching lines to form the tic-tac-toe boards.

"There's supposed to be an episode of Judge Kimble that comes on where they're fighting for custody of a goldfish. I'm curious about how the visitation plays out."

Olivia laughed, "A goldfish huh? That does seem interesting."

After I beat her in the three rounds of tic-tac-toe, Oliva went over the inventory from the night before to prepare for an order and I turned on Judge Kimble. Today's episode was about a couple who had split after five years of being together. They didn't get into why they were no longer together, but they both wanted the goldfish. Apparently, the couple won it at a fair during their first date and neither wanted to part with it. The judge ultimately ruled that the goldfish would reside with the woman and the ex-boyfriend could come visit them every other weekend.

Olivia and I talked about that for a while before spending a few hours making small talk over Mom and Dad, Ronny and Duncan, and the bird that flew into the store yesterday.

After toying with the idea of telling her or not, I eventually broke down and told Oliva about Duncan meeting the woman in Easton City. "Want to hear something funny?" I asked without giving her a chance to respond. We were back on the stools behind the counter working on a couple of crossword puzzles. "The woman Esther saw Duncan with was a contract broker. So, all that fussing that Mom did was for nothing."

"That's right!" she said almost like she had an epiphany. "Ronny did tell me they were trying to get more work closer to home. I completely forgot Duncan was going to meet with her while he was on the delivery to Philadelphia."

I stared at her blankly, "You mean you had knowledge about the event that sent Mom into a tizzy yesterday, and didn't speak up?"

She looked at me apologetically, "I'm so sorry! I completely forgot all about it." She gently tapped the palm of her hand to her forehead. "Wait, how do you know who she is?"

"Duncan told me. He stopped by yesterday as I was closing up and asked if I wanted to walk Kingsman Trail with him."

"Oh, what else did the two of you talk about?" she asked teasingly.

"We talked about the store. The lumber yard. Our parents. The usual generic small talk you make with a friend." I said defensively and shot her a look. "You know, I already get enough of this from Mom, I don't need it from you too."

"I'm sorry, you're right," she said before shrugging her shoulder and flashing me an approving grin. "I can't lie, it would be amazing if the two of you settled down together." Leaving me speechless, she shuffled back to the office to grab a new pen before coming back out and saying, "It's not *that* weird since Duncan is adopted."

That is the least of my worries.

"I have too much going on in life right now to be worry about sharing the same set of in-laws with you."

"Yeah, yeah. I hear you."

Involuntarily, another yawn stretched my mouth wide. "Hey, I'm actually pretty tired. Mind if I take a quick nap? I'm too scared to head home to sleep. I don't want to be alone just in case I feel that terrifying stillness again."

Her eyebrow arched at the word "stillness", but she didn't comment on it. "No, of course not. It's not like we have a busy day ahead of us."

"Thanks." Making my way to where the rocking chairs sat, I carried one of them into the back office. "I'm just going to kick my feet up in here, so no one sees me."

"We won't be able to see you, but I'm sure we'll hear you," she teased.

"I do not snore! That was just an excuse you used to get your own room when we were kids."

"We'll see," she said with a chuckle.

I took a seat and propped my feet up on the desk. Stretching my arm over the arm of the chair, I used the tips of my fingers to nudge the door closed. I should be sight unseen for any tourists that might stop in. I relaxed my arms on the armrests, leaned my head back and rested it against the back of the chair, and closed my eyes. I started to gently rock myself so I could drift off to sleep.

***

I was outside, on a beach. It's peaceful. The sun was shining. I could hear the forceful sound of water behind me. Waves were crashing against the shoreline. Seagulls sound as they flew overhead. The sand felt soft and warm under my bare feet.

Down the shoreline, I saw someone standing at the edge of the pier. They're the only other person on the beach with me. I walked in that direction. Before I could reach them I was somewhere else entirely, standing on a bridge.

I looked around to examine the change in my surroundings. This bridge looked familiar. I took a few more steps before realizing water rushed underneath. I looked over the sides at the river below me. The current was powerful. Something catches my eye in the middle of the river. It's a backpack. It floats quickly down the river and under the bridge. I turn around to watch where it floated to, but I got distracted when I saw a pair of boots sitting on the right side of the bank.

A backpack and now a pair of boots. Where is your owner?

I raised my eye line to scan up and down both sides of the banks. Nothing stood out from this perspective. I walked to the end of the bridge, now standing on the bank on the other side of the river. Scanning the banks again, I didn't see anyone.

The boots were sitting further down the bank, close to the water. I carefully walked down to where the boots sat and inspected them. They're covered in mud. Whoever wore these had a much larger foot than my size sevens. Deciding to leave the boots there, I walked upstream along the bank to investigate my surroundings, hoping to find where these boots and backpack came from.

I've walked far enough to where the bridge was no longer in sight when I think I've heard something. I stood still, trying to tune out the sound of the rushing river beside me.

"Help," someone yelled. "Help! Someone, please help me!"

"Where are you," I yelled back. I listened for a

*moment with no response. "Where are you," I yelled
again. "I'm trying to find you!" I start walking again,
in the direction I think the voice called from. Yelling
into the woods, hoping for a response, my strides
quicken, evolving into a run. I need to find the owner
of those boots.*

"I'm here," someone yelled again.

*My eyes dart to the left, just along the tree line.
"Please! I'm here!"*

*"There," I whispered to myself as my eyes focus
in on where I'm sure the voice came from. I took off
in that direction, ducking and dodging tree branches,
rocks, and roots along my way. "Call to me," I yell
again. I hope I'm getting closer to him.*

"Here! I'm here."

*I stopped, feeling eyes on me. I turn to look and
scan the area around me. I almost missed him, but I
was certain it's him. There, on the opposite side of the
bank, stood the dark eyed man.*

Is that who's been yelling? Does he need help?

"Please, anyone!" I heard from behind me.

Okay, it's not the dark eyed man calling for help.

*I glanced behind me, then back to the man across
the river. As much as I want to chance the current to
get to him, I shouldn't. I needed to find the owner of
those boots. I had a feeling they were in real trouble.*

*I turned and ran in the direction the last call for
help came from. "I'm coming for you!" I yelled into
the trees. Finally, I saw a man sitting on the ground
with his back leaned up against a tree. "I see you!"
After a few more strides, I'm kneeling beside him. I
look over him, assessing his condition. His clothes
were ripped in various places. Blood escapes the cuts*

and scrapes that marked his body. His ankle looked injured too. His eyes were closed.

Oh no, am I too late?

I moved my hand over his heart to check for any sign of life. Relief washed over me when I feel it's still beating. I place my hands on either side of his head to steady it from tilting. His hair was wet, his skin muddy and scrapped. "Hello," I said gently. "Can you hear me?"

His eyes fluttered open in response.

"Hey there," I said with a smile. "I'm Heidi. Can you hear me?"

He nodded slightly.

"What's your name?" I asked.

"Michael," he coughed out.

"Hi, Michael. Are you able to tell me what happened here?"

His voice sounds hoarse, and he spoke slowly, but he was able to respond. "I stopped to capture a few pictures of the birds I heard overhead during my hike. I was walking backwards, looking up at the trees through my camera lens, not paying attention. I took one step too far and I slipped and fell into the river. Before I could comprehend what happened, I was being forced downstream." Michael's words were interrupted by a few coughs. "I was finally able to grab hold of some roots that were growing out of the side of the riverbank. I used them to pull myself out of the water and onto the bank. That's when I felt a pain in my ankle. I tried to ignore it and stand anyway but I fell back to the ground. Thankfully, I was able to crawl and pull myself to this tree. I've been waiting for someone to find me. And now you have."

"Y-Yeah. That's right, I've found you," I said hesitantly. "Michael, did you have a backpack with you by chance?" He nodded. "We're you also wearing boots?" He nods again as his eyes closed. "I need to go find more help. I'll be back."

But is this even real?

I stood and wiped the mud from my knees. Not sure where else to go, I decided to follow the river back to the bridge. I looked around, trying to locate the rushing water again. Once I found the river, I walk down through the trees and walked alongside it.

I need to wake up.

Chapter 6

My eyes opened. I sighed an involuntary sigh of relief. It was loud enough for Oliva to hear me because she called back to me and asked, "You all right in there?"

I blinked a few times to wake my eyes up before I stood to stretch out my back. "Yeah," I groaned. "I'm all right." I carefully poked my head through the threshold of the office to check for any customers. Realizing the store was in its usual state – empty – I brought the rocking chair back to its place beside the counter. "Did anyone come in while I was snoozing?"

"Just Mom and Ronny."

"Did either of them see me?" I asked apprehensively.

She chuckled, "No. Your secret is safe with me."

"Did Mom ask where I was?" I leaned against the counter in front of where she was sitting behind it.

"Yeah, I told her you were busy in the office. She didn't walk back there to check thankfully." I blew out a small breath of relief, about to thank her for covering for me, when she asked, "were you dreaming? You kept muttering incoherent syllables."

"Yeah. It was another strange one. I was at a beach, then on a bridge over a river. The railings of the bridge looked familiar to me." I walked over to the coolers to grab a bottle of water. "But before I could remember why, I saw a backpack float down the river."

Olivia's eyes widened as she said, "I don't like where this is going."

I twisted my water open and walked back over to the counter where Olivia is sitting. "Yeah, I didn't either. I eventually saw some boots and then heard someone yelling for help. On my way to find who was calling out, I saw the man with dark eyes." I took a sip of my water.

"Was he the one calling for help?" she asked.

"No," I shook my head. "For just a moment I thought about going to him. But I heard someone call for help again and decided to figure out who it was. Which I did. He said his name was Michael. He fell into the river while trying to take pictures of birds. Hurt his ankle pretty bad."

"Taking pictures of birds?" she asked.

"I think that's what I remember him saying."

Olivia peered curiously at me. "There's a group of bird watchers in town this week. Apparently, there's a hawk's nest near one of the trails up the mountain. Mr. Tim mentioned it when he dropped off mail the other morning." She stepped out from around the counter and went to the back of the store. "I think he even left a flyer for it up on the board back here." She scanned the board before pulling a flyer from the cork and bringing it to me.

I sat my water down on the counter and leaned against it as I turned the flyer to face me to look over its contents. The flyer had a picture of what I'm assuming was the bird they're here to see. Below the picture are details for a convention of sorts over at the Antlers Lodge. "Well, that's a little odd. Don't you think?"

"Maybe you saw the flyer but pushed it from your memory? Or maybe you saw a similar story on the news?" Olivia had always been the logical sister, especially when it came to me and my dreams. She tried not to encourage me to look too deep into their meaning. My dream about John Doe from the field of purple flowers for example, I still hadn't found anything about him. The longer I went without information about him, the more inclined I was to think she and my parents were right. That these were just dreams and not true events that are happening.

"Yeah, maybe," I shrugged in defeat, before getting lost in a flurry of thoughts of what these latest dreams might mean.

A little after two p.m. and the bell above the door jingled, letting us know we finally had a customer. Olivia and I paused the game of M.A.S.H. we are playing; something we played as kids and still played often to help pass the time here at the store. We both turned to greet the customer as he entered the store and shut the door behind him. I greeted the middle-aged stranger with a cheery smile.

"Welcome in!" Olivia greeted our second customer of the day. "Is there anything we can help you with?"

The gentleman reached out his hand to show us what he was holding. "Uh, yes actually." He turned, what I recognized now as a photo of someone, toward us. "Have either of you seen this man today?"

I reached my hand toward the picture, "May I?" The man allowed me to take it and examine it closer. Oliva looked over my shoulder to take a closer peek too.

Oliva said with sympathy, "No, he hasn't been in here today. Sorry."

My absent agreement with Olivia's response had them both looking curiously at me. I shook my head because it didn't make sense, but this man looked familiar. "Could this man have been in here on a different day?" I asked.

The gentleman shook his head no. "I'm afraid not. He only just got to town late last night. He left earlier this morning, said he wanted to see the sights before we went out to search for the hawk's nest. A group of us are staying over at the Antlers Lodge. We heard there's a hawk's nest located up the mountain. We're hoping to capture a few photos."

My gut began to swirl with fear and urgency. I knew why that bridge looked familiar now. Handing the photo back to the gentleman, I looked under the counter for a map of the trails in the area. As I open and laid the map on the countertop I asked Oliva, "Do you remember where Battell Trailhead is?"

Oliva shot me a questioning look before she bent down to look closer at the map. We used our pointer fingers to help us scan the map for the trailhead. "Here it is," Oliva said. She pointed to a place on the map.

I followed my eyes along the line marked as the trail, looking to where it intersects with water. I grabbed a pen from the cup next to the register, mine was under the map, and drew a circle around the intersection. I looked at the gentleman and said, "This is going to sound strange, but maybe take a look here." I pointed to the circle I drew on the map.

Oliva looked at me confused. I shrugged my

shoulders and looked back at her just as confused.

He took a closer look at the map. "What makes you say that? You some kind of psychic or something?" I could tell his question was intended to be a joke, but I could hear the worry behind his words.

"No, sir. I just have a gut feeling. There's a wooden bridge that crosses over this river and it offers an incredible view of the surrounding trees. If there was ever a good place to start, it'd be there." I said to him, feeling guilty because it's only a hunch. I'd hate to be wrong, and they lose precious time to find their friend. "I can come with you. I could help you look for him." I turned to Oliva, looking for her approval.

She nodded, "I'll call emergency services to have them send an EMT to that location just in case he needs medical attention."

"Thank you, yes, that would be helpful," the gentleman replied.

I tied my sweater around my waist then I folded up the map to bring with us. Olivia was already on the phone with emergency services as I walked around the counter to the door. Pulling the door wide open for the gentleman and me to hurry through, Olivia asked, "What's his name?" She gestured toward the photo he still held in his hand.

"Michael," he replied, not knowing he had evoked a shared look of disbelief between my sister and me. The door closed behind us.

As we hurried to the parking lot, I introduced myself. "I'm Heidi by the way."

"William," he responded.

"Nice to meet you, William. I'm sorry we're meeting under these circumstances." I gave a sympathetic look.

"Me too," he said. "Do you mind riding with me? I need to let the others in the group know so they can come with us and help us search. We're staying at the Antlers Lodge. Everyone is waiting in the lobby for an update."

"Not at all, the more eyes we have, the greater our chances are of finding Michael."

William started the car, and we pulled onto the road in a hurry. The Antlers Lodge was only a few miles East of the store, but we still needed to hurry.

"Michael is my brother-in-law," William said. "My sister will be awfully upset if I don't return him in the same condition he came in. A group of us go birdwatching every year, each year in a different location. This is the tenth annual trip we've taken. Most of us were in our late thirties when we picked this hobby up, but as we started to become empty nesters, we began to travel more to see a wider variety of birds."

I smiled. "That sounds like it could be an adventurous pass time," I said as I looked down the road ahead of us. I noticed that my dad's blue pickup truck was parked over at Mr. Ed's. "Oh! My dad is just across the street here. When we get to the Antlers, I'm going to run over there and let him know what's going on. Emergency services are probably already on their way, but my dad could walk these trails with his eyes closed. He'll be a great help in our search."

"That would be wonderful if he wouldn't mind

helping us," William said as he put the car in park, finally reaching the Antlers Lodge.

"He'd be happy to help." I opened my door to step out, "I'll be right back. My dad and I will meet you in the lobby." I darted off across the street, knocking quickly before heading right on into Mr. Ed's shop. He and dad were packing some supplies into a backpack.

Dad looked up and saw me and said, "Hey, sweetheart. You're just the girl I was thinking of. Do you think you can accompany Mr. Ed and I on a hike? There's a group of bird watchers over at the Antlers who need help finding one of their friends. I don't have all the details but one of the members came in asking if anyone matching his description came through here. They haven't seen him for a few hours."

"That's exactly why I'm here. I was going to ask you the same thing. One of the members, William, came into the store and showed Oliva and I a photo. Asked if we had seen him in today."

Dad and Mr. Ed paused their packing. Mr. Ed said, "Oh good, you've seen him then? I'll give emergency services a call back and cancel the request."

I shook my head. They both looked confused. "We haven't seen him today, but I have a gut feeling our search should start at the intersection of Battell Trail and the Johnson River."

"That bridge would offer a great vantage point of the trees there. That's a great hunch, Heidi," my dad said proudly.

"Thanks, Dad. Olivia called emergency services

too and told them where we'd be looking. I assume we'll be hearing the helicopter soon, but we should hurry. William is waiting with the rest of the group in the lobby of the Antlers."

Dad and Mr. Ed grabbed their backpacks and headed towards the door. Mr. Ed yelled to the back office, "We'll be back soon, dear. Going to look for a lost bird watcher. Love you."

"Stay safe, love you too," Mrs. Margie yelled back.

My dad headed for his truck and told me they'd meet me in the parking lot of Antlers. I ran across the street, heading into the lobby of the lodge and spotted William. "William," I said as I approached him. "Is everyone ready? My dad is out in the parking lot, ready to lead us to the trail head. It's a short drive from here."

"Yes, we're ready."

Three cars, full of passengers, followed my dad, Mr. Ed, and I over to the trail head. After arriving, we hiked, as quickly as a group of middled aged men and women could, to the bridge I saw in my dream. Halfway through our two-and-a-half-mile hike, we finally heard the helicopters overhead. The group of bird watchers, turned search and rescue, gave applause. My dad turned to the group and said, "Yes, the helicopters are a sign of hope, but we must stay vigilant. If your friend is in the area that we think he's in, there are dense trees that could hinder the pilots' view."

Silence fell over the group; a reminder that there could be a grim outcome to this search. I thought back to my dream and the condition I found Michael in. I'm unsure of all his injuries, but a shiver ran through me thinking a grim reality might not be far from true. Still, we trekked forward with determined strides.

Finally, the bridge was ahead of us. William and a few others in the group rushed ahead, eager to see if there was any sign of Michael. My nerves were rumbling in my stomach, I was anxious to find him too. More anxious as to what it might mean if we did find him. I stood in the middle of the bridge, like I did in my dream, and looked over the sides. Unlike my dream, there was no backpack floating down the river and no boots on the bank. Members of our search party had begun calling out Michael's name without a reply. I closed my eyes for a moment and tried to think back to what else I saw in my dream, searching for clues.

Roots!

I opened my eyes and turned to spot my dad in the group of people. "Dad!" I called.

He saw me and walked my way. "What is it? Did you see something?"

"Not yet, but isn't there a tree that grows a little too close to the bank of this river? One where the roots extend beyond the soil and into the river itself?"

He began to nod his head, "There is. It's about a quarter mile upstream off the North bank. Why?"

"Just thinking what if he fell in somewhere along the bank. Maybe he could have held on to those roots and pulled himself back to shore."

"Alright," my dad said to the rest of the group, "we're going to split up in groups of four. Two groups will take the North bank, the other two will take South. A group on either side will head downstream and the other will head upstream. Be sure to spread out into the tree line to cover more ground. Be sure to keep your partners in your eye line." Dad handed out maps, compasses, and radios to each group. "We'll use these radios to signal to each other. Try not to make big movements that could distract emergency services above, we don't want to draw attention away from Michael."

And with that, the groups split and headed in their assigned direction. My dad, Mr. Ed, William, and myself took the North bank heading up stream. This is the side I found Michael on in my dream, he said he pulled himself up with some roots that were growing out of the bank. We walked with urgency, and it didn't take long before we saw the tree that's too close to the bank with protruding roots. I slowed my steps and cast my gaze higher up the elevation. I called out, "Michael!" I paused just a moment to wait for a response. "Michael, can you hear me?" I called again. Just then we heard a thud a little further up in the tree line.

We raced through the trees, careful not to trip and hurt ourselves, until we saw a black backpack. William ran to it. His voice cracked, "This is Michael's." He blinked back tears. He continued to look around for him. "There! He's there!" William took off running ahead of us.

Our eyes finally saw what William saw; a pair of legs outstretched behind a thick tree truck. Boots still on his feet. By the time we caught up with William, my dad had already radioed the helicopter above and asked for them to send down a crew. He then radioed the other groups and updated them. "We've found Michael. Emergency services are sending a crew down now to assess his injuries and will take him to the hospital. William will go with him, everyone else, lets meet back at the bridge."

Chapter 7

There was a knock at my door. I finished towel drying my hair and secured my robe tightly around my waist to hide my tee shirt and lack of pajama pants. I'm not really in the mood for company after the day I've had. My thoughts were becoming jumbled with logic and absurdity, of how I could have possibly known where to find Michael. It still hasn't fully sunk in yet that I helped rescue him today. A second knock sounded from my front door.

"It's open," I called out as I walked toward my living room from the hallway.

The door opened, revealing Mom, then Dad, and finally, Oliva crossing the threshold into my living room. They were each holding an item. Mom had what looked, and smelled, like my favorite pot pie casserole. Dad had a couple pints of different flavored ice cream. Oliva, my dear sister, brought the most essential element to remedy any rough day, a bottle of red wine.

Mom spoke first. "I heard about what happened today, sweetheart. Your dad told me all about it when he got home this evening. I just knew I needed to bring you your favorite dinner to help get your mind off the events of today. Your dad and sister, however, had a different idea of what you might need," she said, referring to the ice cream and wine they brought.

I followed them to the kitchen. Dad placed the ice cream in the freezer, Olivia set the bottle down and searched for the wine opener, and Mom placed the casserole on top of the counter. I gave them each a hug and thanked them for stopping by. While I would have preferred to be left to my thoughts tonight, I'll admit it was nice having my family stop by and check on me. "You all didn't have to do this, but I will say that I appreciate it. Today has been anything but usual." I grab plates for each of us and Olivia grabbed us each a glass. Mom grabbed a serving spoon and began to serve the casserole.

We ate in silence for a few minutes before Dad spoke up. "So, Heidi, I have to ask. How'd you know where to look today?"

I cast a look at Olivia, eyeing her to please not say anything. "I already told you, Dad, it was just a hunch. I figured since they were here to look at birds, and that trail leads you pretty high up the side of the mountain, that bridge would give them a great view for some amazing pictures. Even if they didn't find the nest they were looking for, there's beautiful scenery in the area."

"It was a pretty spot-on hunch," Mom sounded as she loaded her fork with another bite.

"Well, we've all spent a lot of time on these trails at some point in time. I remember hiking that very trail with classmates in high school. I couldn't remember where the tree was located but that's where Dad comes in. He's spent more time on these trails than probably any other resident has."

I hope that will squash their questions about how I really know where Michael was. I'm not ready to confront the realization myself.

"That is true," Mom said to Dad with a chuckle.

"You would live outdoors if it wouldn't scare the tourists away. All the times you've gone camping and hike the same trails, you'll never tire of nature's beauty."

"I'll never tire of *your* beauty," he quipped.

Mom playfully slapped his knee and giggled, "Oh, stop it."

We all laughed because we know Mom loved a good compliment. We continued our meal with pleasant small talk.

After supper, Oliva and I walked our parents to the door for hugs and told them goodnight. We shut the door behind them and immediately headed for more wine. After pouring ourselves a hefty refill, we plopped comfortably on the couch.

"Why didn't you want to tell Mom and Dad how you really knew where Michael was?" Oliva asked me.

I sighed and rubbed my head, "I don't know. I think because Mom is already on my case about spending too much time in my head. If I were to tell her, it would have just turned into another argument."

She nodded, "Yeah, that's a good point. But I really do think they'd be understanding. Excited even."

I took a sip of my wine and narrowed my eyes at her, waiting for her to admit she's crazy to think there'd ever be a world where they'd be understanding, much less excited. "And is that what you are now? Understanding and excited?" Olivia has had her fair share of skepticism about my dreams. Not that I fully understand them myself, but she hasn't been as open-minded as I'd like.

"That's fair." She sipped her wine. "But to answer your question, yes. There's no other explanation for how you knew what you knew today. I'm a believer. And maybe Mom and Dad would come around too."

"Dad? Sure. But Mom? I don't think so. Which is why we will keep this to ourselves."

She sat, staring down at the floor, lost in thought. "Why do you think you had that dream? Did Michael recognize you when you all found him? Did anyone else in the bird watchers group question why you knew where he was?"

"Okay, slow down Seabiscuit. One question at a time," I chuckled.

"I'm sorry, this is all just kind of blowing my mind. I know your mind must be racing too."

I nodded in agreement, "It is. I'm not sure why, or even how, this happened. No one in the group questioned me or Dad. They were happy to place their confidence in us once they understood we knew the lay of the land." I took another sip of wine before continuing. "As for Michael, I didn't actually speak to him once we found him. He was unconscious and William confirmed his identity. From there, emergency services air lifted him to the hospital over in Easton City. I do hope he makes a speedy recovery and is able to continue with the rest of the trip."

Before Olivia could respond, she was interrupted by a knock at the door. We looked at each other, confused. I know I'm not expecting anyone, and Ronny is out of town for the next few days. It's pretty late in the evening so whoever it was, it must be important.

I opened the door to see no one other than Duncan

standing there, holding a bottle of wine. Shocked to see him, at my front door no less, I greeted him. "Oh hi, Duncan." Whispering through my smile, I said to him, "I was not expecting to see you. Here. At the *front door*." He knew if he's going to make a house call, to come to the *back door*. I slid my hand into my robe's pocket.

Oh shit. I completely forgot I'm wrapped in my bathrobe because I'm too lazy to slide into a pair of shorts.

I turned my gaze to Oliva who's perched on my couch, looking curiously back at us.

"My apologies, I didn't realize you had company already. I heard about what happened today and wanted to check in on you." He handed the bottle of wine to me. "I'll get going. You two have a great night."

"Oh, no worries, I was just leaving." Oliva said quickly. "Come on in. Heidi would love the company. It's been quite an eventful day, after all."

I shot her a pointed look, to which she just smiled cunningly in response.

"If you're sure you're up for company, Heidi," Duncan said.

"Sure." I hooked my thumb over my shoulder towards my glass of wine on the coffee table. "You'll have to catch up."

Duncan nodded awkwardly at Olivia then looked apologetically at me. He crossed the threshold and walked toward the kitchen to grab a glass. Oliva made her way to me at the front door. She squeezed my arm and teased, "just friends, huh?"

"Good night, Oliva," I said as I swatted her hand

off my arm before Duncan saw. Olivia didn't know the extent of Duncan and I's friendship and I wasn't ready to give up those details yet.

I watched her as she walked down to her house. She flicked her porch light twice to let me know she made it inside. We only lived a few doors down from each other, but we weren't close enough to actually see one another from our front porches. I shut the door and turned to see Duncan sitting where Oliva was sitting moments earlier.

"I'm sorry, I didn't think anyone would be here this late," Duncan said apologetically. "There wasn't a car in your driveway."

"It's really alright. Olivia and my parents stopped over earlier with dinner and ice cream. They wanted to check in on me too." I took a seat next to him on the couch. "As you can tell by how I'm dressed, I wasn't prepared for company."

He flashed his best panty dropping smile. "Oh, I don't know. You look prepared for me." He looked me up and down, then said, "And by prepared, I mean easily undressable."

Dammit! How does he always manage to make me feel flush?

I tucked my barely damp hair behind my ear, stalling, while I thank of a way to respond to that. I smiled coyly, "I'm just glad my parents left before you arrived. Had my mom seen you show up here, with a bottle of wine, she would have launched into FBI mode, asking all sorts of invasive questions."

"I don't think I could withstand the force your mom would apply to get answers," he said jokingly.

"None of us would. Which is part of why I can't

tell Oliva. I can tell she knows something is going on between us, but she doesn't know the full extent."

"I wouldn't want Ronny to know either. It would only be a matter of time before he let it slip to our parents."

I nodded in agreement, trying to hide the small sting I felt when he said that. Which doesn't make any sense because neither of us wanted this to evolve into anything more than what it was.

"Don't get me wrong, I could do a hell of a lot worse than Heidi Miller." Duncan took a drink of wine and spoke through a handsome smile, "I mean, you're the kind of woman a guy could write home about, you know?" He brought his eyes to mine for a moment before letting them fall to the ground, "But with all these unresolved emotions and questions about my birth parents, it wouldn't be fair to love someone else when I can't love myself."

I couldn't help but smile. That's probably the most personal thing I've ever heard him say about himself. My heart ached to think that he might not love himself. Even though he didn't owe me one, his explanation made me feel warm inside. "I understand. And for the record, I could do a hell of a lot worse than Duncan Johnson."

We sipped through a few glasses of wine as I caught him up on the events of the day before resorting to small talk. He was a good listener and asked thoughtful questions throughout our conversation, but I kept getting distracted by his kissable lips. Before I knew it, my legs were spread, resting my left leg over his lap.

His gaze spilled over me, stopping at the knot in

the sash that was holding my robe closed. He swallowed hard, moving his hands over the knot, working it until it finally opened, revealing my tee shirt and white cotton panties. I stared up at him, waiting for his next move. Anticipation tingled behind my lips. I desperately wanted him to kiss me. I leaned back on my hands slightly, revealing my hard nipples beneath my tee shirt, and shifted my hips a little closer to his lap.

In one swift motion, he wrapped his right arm around my hips and pulled me on top as he slid himself underneath me. His lips crashed into mine, hungry for a rapture. Grinding myself against his lap, I felt his cock grow hard, making me even more wet.

He abruptly pulled his lips from mine. He took my face into his hands and looked me in my eyes. "I'm going to regret this, but, you've had a big day and we've gone through two bottles of wine. Maybe we should pick this up another time."

Embarrassed, I climbed off his lab and sat next to him on the couch. "Yeah, you're right. Another night." Quickly, I closed my robe back up and walked towards the door.

He stayed seated on the couch. "Heidi, really, this isn't anything more than me trying not to take advantage of you, especially after the day you've had. I want you to be of sound mind when we're together. I don't want to hurt you."

"Mhm," I nodded, looking at my feet with my hand on the doorknob. "I understand. Thank you for your concern. I'll see you later for that raincheck." I opened the door and gestured for him to leave.

He sighed and looked at me apologetically. "I'm

sorry, Heidi." He walked over to me and planted a single kiss on my cheek. "Goodnight." Duncan walked down the steps toward his truck. He took one last look back at me before he got in and drove away.

Chapter 8

I'm on a beach. Waves crashing around my feet. The sun warmed my skin. The wind blew my long hair around my face. I gather the ends of my hair and twirl the entire strand into a single binding. Down the shoreline, I see someone.

Is this De Ja Vue?

I walked along the edge of the water towards the figure. I haven't seen his face yet, but I know it's my dark eyed mystery man. I can feel his presence. I yell out to him, not expecting a response, "Hey!"

He turned and faced me. "Hey."

Oh. My. Gosh.

"So, you can hear me? And you can see me?" I asked excitedly. Suddenly, we're standing face to face. The wind pushed through his dark hair. I could see his features much more clearly. His eyes, dark and soulful. His lips, full. His smooth, strong jawline, adorned with a small dimple on his chin.

He nods. He raises his hand to my face. "It seems that I can touch you too." His tone was smooth and seductive.

I felt his thumb stroke my cheek as he leaned in for a kiss. The moment our lips touch, pleasure explodes between my thighs. We linger with our lips locked until my body stopped vibrating from the delicious sensation of his touch. Our lips released and I looked up at him almost breathless. "I didn't know that I had been craving your touch."

I've had wet dreams before, but nothing like this. It's like I'm especially sensitive to his touch. Or maybe I'm still scorned from Duncan's rejection.

He grins a tantalizing smile at me and pressed his forehead against mine. "And I've been craving your sweet release," he said too confidently.

And just like that, a second wave of pleasure was released from me. My knees wobbled and he wrapped his arm behind my back to support me from crumbling.

He smiles at me. He's proud of his accomplishment, causing me to orgasm so effortlessly. "I have to go."

"What?" I asked confused. "What do you mean you have to go?"

Is this really happening right now? He can't be serious.

"I'm looking for someone." He gives my cheek one last stroke before he began to walk away.

Frustrated, I decide to follow him. It felt like there's miles between us now. I pick up the pace until I notice we're in the grey room again. The rhythmic beeping had returned. "Where is that coming from?"

Surprised to see that I had followed him, he said, "You shouldn't be here."

"You don't get to seek me out, make me cum all over myself, then tell me you've got to go." I looked around the room, noticing nothing had changed from the last time I was here. "What is this place anyway?"

His hand is on the doorknob of the single door behind him. "It's nowhere. And like I said, I've got to go." He tried to turn the knob on the door with no luck.

"*Do you need help with that?*" *I asked, taking a step closer to him.*

"*No,*" *he yelled.*

My eyes widen with fear. The beeping echoes violently around us. I feel the stillness start to creep in. It's happening again. I need to wake up.

Wake up!

I didn't want to be here. I started to panic. I looked around for anything that could help me wake up. Still, there's nothing. "*Help me, please!*" *I plead to my dark eyed stranger.*

He looked unsure. Like he's questioning whether to help me or not. He looks at me, looks behind him at the door, then back to me weighing his decision.

Wake up! I need to wake up!

His forehead wrinkled with worry. He rushed towards me, throwing me over his shoulder, and running with me until we're back to the beach. "*You really shouldn't be here,*" *he said.*

Wake up. Wake up. Wake up!

My eyes shot open, and I felt my leg jut out from beneath my blanket. My heart was racing as I replayed the events of my dream.

What the hell was that?

Was he controlling what I was feeling?

Is he the stillness I feel?

These were all questions I added to the previous day's wonderment. The sun was already out in full force, meaning it was well into morning. I got up, needing to get ready to head to the store.

Oh, my sheets.

Since they were wet with evidence of sexual

desire for a stranger, one that I probably made up, I balled my bed sheets up and tossed them in the hamper. I dressed my mattress with clean sheets and a fresh blanket from the linen closet before I headed out the door.

I took my bike into the store this morning with the intention of clearing my head. So far, all I can do is replay the dream over and over. I couldn't force my mind to stop reliving the paralyzing terror I felt. By the time I arrived at the store, I felt heavy with anxiety. The bell jingled, mocking my mood, as I entered the store.

"Hi, sweetheart," my mother chirped from behind the counter.

Oh man, here we go.

"Morning, Mom."

"Why are you getting in so late? It's almost eleven."

"I overslept. I had a bad dream that I couldn't wake up from," I said as I passed her and dropped my sweater and purse on the office desk. I mentally braced for impact as I exited the office.

"I knew you were going to have troubling dreams after the day you had yesterday. You've always been sensitive to them. And you wonder why I worry when you say you're spending your time searching for a murder you *witnessed*. You can barely handle a lost hiker; you look like a ball of stress."

I take a deep breath as I took up post behind the counter with her, "I'm not stressed by what happened yesterday, Mom," I said frustrated. "And as a matter of fact, yesterday was the first time I've felt anything other than numbing boredom in a long time. I hate that it came at the expense of someone getting lost and hurt, but it's the truth." Not that that will make much sense to her since I hadn't told her that I dreamed about finding Michael. But she made a comment about me making up dreams to make me feel like I have purpose. Well yesterday, my dream allowed me to have purpose, and I loved it.

She shifted her weight to her left leg and placed her hand on her right hip, "Then what's troubling you so badly that you're late for work this morning?"

I shook my head and tossed my hands in concession, "Just forget it, Mom, I'm fine."

The bell above the door jingled, letting us know that Oliva had returned. She shot me a look that told me she sensed the tension between Mom and me.

"Olivia," my mom said, "doesn't your sister look stressed?"

I rolled my eyes and waited for Oliva's response.

"Oh no, I'm not getting involved in whatever this is," Oliva said.

Annoyed, Mom said, "One day, you both will understand the fear and worry that stems from being a mother."

"Yeah, maybe one day Mom, but that day isn't today. It doesn't matter though, I'm fine. You have nothing to worry about. I apologize for being late to the nothingness that happens here each and every day. It won't happen again," I said, immediately regretting my sharp tone. I knew in my heart she was truly worried about me, but damn, she could be overbearing. I'm sure she'll send dad over later to talk about it.

"You're right, it's not today. Because all you care

about is getting lost in whatever adventure, murder, or job your little brain conjures up! Spending all that time in your head, worried about what your dreams are *telling* you. What your dreams are really telling you is that your life is a mess." With that, Mom grabbed her purse and stormed out of the store.

"Ugh! Why does she have to push so hard?" I exclaimed in frustration.

"It's all based on perspective. Mom sees it as wanting to protect you. You see it as she doesn't take you seriously. Maybe you're both right. Or maybe you're both wrong."

"Huh?" I asked confused. "What does that even mean, Oliva?"

She shrugged her shoulders, "I don't know? I just really don't want to pick sides here. I'm your sister and I love you but Mom's right, you look like hell. What happened last night? You looked fine when I left."

Her siding with Mom hurt more than I expected. I could feel tears sting my eyes as I tried to blink them away. "I had another dream. One where I felt stuck. And the man with dark eyes was there too. On my bike ride over this morning, I kept replaying my dream, how scared I was and how he's present anytime I get that feeling. I'm scared to sleep tonight, what if it happens again?" Tears were rolling down my cheeks now.

Oliva pulled me in for a hug and squeezed me tight.

I took a deep breath to calm myself down and hugged her back. I didn't tell her enough, but she truly was my best friend and I often forgot how much

I leaned on her.

"I'll tell you what, how about I spend the night with you tonight. I can keep you company and wake you up if it seems like you're dreaming."

I thought about her offer for just a moment before I remembered my dirty sheets. Or more about *why* they're dirty. I would be completely embarrassed if that happened while she was there. On the other hand, I'm too scared to sleep alone. I decided that I would give Duncan a call a little later to see if I could get that rain check another way. "No, that's alright. But I would love it if you could come keep me company for a little bit after I get off."

"You got it. Want me to bring dinner?" Olivia asked.

"That'd be great, thank you," I said as the bell above the door jingled again.

"Good afternoon, ladies," William said as he entered the store. I noticed he was wearing the same clothes from yesterday.

"William, how are you? How's Michael?" I asked.

"That's why I'm here actually. Michael wanted me to ask if you would come to visit and speak with him in the hospital. Thankfully, he'll make a full recovery, but the other birdwatchers and I are checking out of the lodge tomorrow and he won't be released from the hospital by then."

"Sure." I had some things I want to speak with him about too. Mostly, to try and get an idea of how I could have dreamed about him. "I would love to visit with him if he's up for company."

"Great! Let me leave you his room information."

William patted the sides of his jacket, looking for a pen and scrap of paper to quickly write on. He found a receipt to scribble Michael's room number on the back of.

William handed me the receipt. "Thank you," I said.

"No, thank you." His eyes turned glassy. "We may have not found him in time if it weren't for all your help." Before I could respond, he sniffled softly, nodded us a good day, and made his way out the door.

Olivia had already sat down and made herself comfortable in one of the rocking chairs at the end of the counter. "Drive safe," she said without me even having to ask if she'd cover for me. I suspect she knew I had questions for Michael. "Don't worry, I can handle all the activity happening here," she said sarcastically.

"Thank you so much! I'll owe you one." And out the door I went.

Chapter 9

I entered the lobby of the hospital and asked the woman behind the desk if she could direct me to room 405.

"Take this hall," she pointed to the hall to the right of me. "When you get about halfway down, you'll come to a vending machine. It only takes credit or debit and A5 doesn't work. You're going to pass that and take the first set of double doors on your left. Once you're through those doors, take elevator four or five up to the fourth floor. I'd suggest elevator five. Elevator four usually has a weird smell. After that, take your first right, then your next left and you'll come to a nurse's station. Tell them the room number of the patient and they'll buzz you through the blue set of doors."

I blinked at her dumfounded. If she thought I remembered anything after "vending machine" she was overestimating her ability to give directions. Thankfully, a member of the bird watchers' group was walking down that same hallway and recognized me. "Heidi?" She asked me. "I'm Margret. We didn't have an opportunity to introduce ourselves yesterday. Are you here to visit Michael?"

"Oh, hi. Yes, I am."

"Great! He'll be happy to see you. Let me walk you up. I was on my way out but it's easy to get turned around in here."

I could believe it, "Thanks, I would really

appreciate it."

Margret walked me to the nurse's station and wished me a good rest of my day. The nurses buzzed me through the set of blue doors. "Room 405 is going to be the first room you come to on your left-hand side."

"Great, thank you," I said politely, thankful there wasn't another maze to walk through. I knocked on the door for room 405.

"Come in." The voice called from inside.

I saw a now clean, but banged up man, sitting in a hospital bed. His leg, from calf to toe, was in a cast. "Michael?" I asked as I approached him. "I'm Heidi. It's nice to meet you."

"It's nice to meet you too." Michael gestured to the chair next to his bed. "Would you like to take a seat?"

"Yes, thank you." I took a seat.

"I just wanted to have the opportunity to thank you in person. William says you were the one who suggested where to look during the search."

"I appreciate that, but you don't have to thank me. I'm just glad my hunch paid off and you're safe," I said with a friendly smile. "But can I ask what happened out there?"

"Everyone has been asking me that all day," he chuckled.

"I'm sorry. You don't have to share if you don't want to."

"No, that's alright. It's normal for people to be curious." He shifted in his hospital bed. "I didn't plan to go off on my own. I was out exploring Battell Trail – it was so beautiful – and once I got to the bridge, I stopped to take a water break. Towards the end of the bridge, I saw a bird I hadn't seen before. I tried to snap a quick picture, but before its photo could be captured, it flew away. I decided to follow it into the tree line along the river. I finally saw it perched high in some branches above. I had my camera pointed up towards the branches, holding the shutter button to capture as many images as possible. I was walking backwards to get a better shot and lost my footing when I stepped into a damp patch of the bank, causing me to fall into the river. My backpack and camera strap kept getting caught in the rocks along the edge and the current was forcing me down stream. Thankfully, I was pushed into some roots that were sticking out of the bank and into the river. They were strong enough for me to pull myself back up the side of the riverbank. But when I tried to stand up, I felt a pain in my ankle that almost made me pass out. I ultimately army crawled for as far as I could before becoming too exhausted. Then I woke up in a helicopter with my brother-in-law, William."

Struggling to come to terms with what I was hearing, I knew I needed to push those thoughts to the side for now, I could confront them later. "That's terrifying. I couldn't imagine the thoughts that may have been running through your mind. I'm sorry to hear about your camera too."

"Yeah. Everyone says that your life flashes before your eyes when you're facing such a situation where survival isn't certain. But that wasn't my experience. I fought the feeling of fear and immediately began to try and figure out a way to survive. I wasn't ready to see my life's greatest hits one last time, as if I'm admitting defeat and saying goodbye. Even when I was resting against that tree, waiting to be rescued, I was still hopeful. As for my camera, it was found. One of the members found it tangled up in some downed branches near the waters edge. The camera will have to be replaced, but I'm hoping the memory card can be salvaged."

His words resonate with me. He pushed through the fear and found a way out. It makes me think back to my dream from last night. "Thank you for sharing that with me. I'm glad you're safe and recovering from your injuries. William said everyone is checking out of the lodge tomorrow. I'm sorry you're not able to finish out the trip. I do hope you'll be back once you're on the mend."

"I won't go chasing birds alone next time," he laughed.

"That sounds like a wise choice." I said lightheartedly. A quick knock rapped on the door of Michael's room. The nurse was here to bring him his medication. I stood from my seat, "We'll I'll leave you to it. Have a good rest of your day," I said as I reached out to shake his hand.

He reached up to shake my hand back. He gave me a knowing look. "Thanks again for your help, have a safe trip back to Mount Hopewell."

I smiled politely and nodded thank you.

"Are you sure we haven't met before?" Michaels asked before I could reach the door.

"I'm positive. Why do you ask?"

I'm curious if we somehow shared the same dream.

"I'm just having the strangest sense of De Ja Vue

is all. Thanks again for visiting, drive safely."

"Thank you," I said. Leaving his hospital room, I made my way back through the labyrinth.

On my way down to the lobby, I took elevator four, and the lady at the welcome desk was right, it did smell funky in there. The poster that hung in the elevator caught my eye. A poster for Keller Institute, with the tag line "Dream therapy; Overcome anxieties, fears, and addiction." Below that, a phone number was printed. I took out my cell and saved the number with a mental note to look up this institute once I got home.

On my drive home, I replayed the events of the past forty-eight hours. Talking aloud to myself, I asked myself the questions that had been taking up space in my mind.

"How could I have had a dream about someone I didn't know? His name, his injuries, how he fell and how he saved himself from the river all matched the account he truly experienced. If Michael was real, if I was able to communicate with him and learn the facts of where he was, could that be why Mom had that *gut feeling* about me researching the murder I thought I witnessed in my dream? Did she somehow remember the conversation from my dream? Could that be why Michael felt as if we've met before?"

My thoughts swirled around these questions for a bit, looking for a logical explanation that could make all this make sense. Among my search for reason, another question formed in my mind. One I wasn't prepared for; could my dark eyed mystery man be more than a figment conjured up by my dreams?

I was about 30 minutes from home when I

remember that I needed to call Duncan to see if he wouldn't mind spending the night with me tonight. I selected his name in my contacts list and pressed call.

He answered on the first ring. "Heidi," he cleared his throat, "how are you?" Duncan's husky voice emitted from the speaker of my phone.

"I'm on my way home from the hospital…"

"The hospital? Is everything okay? What happened?" he interrupted with worry in his tone.

"Yes, I'm fine. I was visiting Michael, the man we found yesterday."

"Oh wow. How is he?"

"All things considering, he's doing alright. But hey, the reason I'm calling is to see if you have any plans tonight?"

He hesitated for just a moment, "Er, not at all. Why do you ask?"

"I have an odd favor to ask. Could you spend the night with me tonight? I've been having some terrible dreams and I'm anxious about going to bed alone tonight. You could sleep on the couch though; I don't want you to feel like you're taking advantage of me." That last comment took me by surprise. I must still be hurt by him putting the brakes on what would have been some amazing sex last night.

There was a hint of hurt in his tone too. "Sure, Heidi, I'd be happy to help."

"Really? You're sure you don't mind?"

"I really don't mind. When I was a kid, I would have night terrors constantly, but I remember how scared I was and how real they felt. It's like I dreamed them only yesterday." He assured me.

"I really appreciate it, Duncan. Olivia is coming

over for dinner this evening. You can come by after. I'll give you a call once she leaves."

"Sounds like a plan," he agreed.

"Great, see you then." And I ended the call.

Chapter 10

Olivia entered through the front door as I was finishing putting away clean laundry. I didn't go back to the store once I returned from the hospital. Thankful that I could come home early, I went ahead and cleaned my sheets and put them away before Olivia arrived. All traces of my blissful release have been erased.

"I brought groceries. I was thinking we could have breakfast for supper. Pancakes, French toast, or waffles?" She asked, as if there was any answer than, "all of the above," we said together and let out a symphony of laughs.

Breakfast food has always been our comfort food. We always cook entirely too much but it's worth having options when you're in a sullen mood. "I'll start on the pancakes and waffles if you get the French toast started." I pulled out and preheated my waffle iron and griddle.

Oliva begins to crack the eggs for the French toast. "So, I've been dying to ask you all day, what brought Duncan to your doorstep so late at night last night?"

I knew she'd bring that up eventually. "Duncan came by last night?" I asked aloof, "hmm, I think I would have remembered such a thing."

"Uh huh," she said as she arched her eyebrow at me. "So, there's no reason at all, that a handsome, hardworking man, just randomly shows up at your front door? To the home of the woman who says she's not interested in any romantic workings of a relationship."

I poured batter onto the hot waffle iron, purposely delaying my response to her question. I stroke my chin with my thumb and pointer finger, "Now that you mention it, yes, I do believe he came by last night." Olivia looked at me, fishing for me to give up the rest of the details. I gave in. "He came by to check on me. He had heard about Michael and just wanted to make sure I was alright. It's not a crime for one friend to check in on the wellbeing of another is it?" I asked playfully.

Flipping the first batch of French toast she said, "Not at all. But spill the details. What did you talk about? He brought a bottle of wine, did the two of you have a *nice* time?"

"We did."

It would have been an amazing time if he hadn't stopped me from riding his dick.

I pushed the thought out of my head as I pulled the pancakes off the griddle and placed them onto the plate. "He didn't stay long but we mostly talked about the chaos of yesterday," I said as I admired my stack of pancakes. The first waffle was ready too. I added it to the plate of pancakes. They smelled so delicious, I couldn't wait to sit down and eat them.

"Then you two sure went through a lot of wine quickly, both bottles are in the trash."

Shit. Big sister detective skills at work again.

I gave her a look that said I'm ready to confess. I helped set the table and we sat while we waited for the second waffle to finish cooking. "Fine. He was here for a while, but we only talked."

She's still not buying it.

"Mostly." I added, without going into full detail of his rejection last night. "He may have given me a kiss on my cheek when he left last night." That should be enough to hold her off from any more questions. Neither Duncan nor I were ready to let our siblings in on the secret.

Olivia's jaw dropped, her eyes widened, and then she let out a squeal of excitement.

"Relax. It's not like we're running away in the night to start a life of holy matrimony," I reminded her.

"I know, but this is exciting! Even if it's because nothing noteworthy ever happens around here. But mostly because, he's *totally* smitten with you. And he's a good man, I know he'll treat you right. No matter the boundaries of your relationship."

I stood to pull the last waffle from the iron and brought it to Olivia. "I wouldn't say he's smitten. There aren't many options for either of us to choose from around here, but you're right, he is a good man." We began to dig into our breakfast spread when I reminded her, "Olivia, you can't tell anyone. Please, not even Ronny."

She nodded in agreement.

We finished our supper while we gabbed about the latest episodes of our favorite tv shows. Once we were finished, I watched her walk back down to her house, waiting for the double flick of her porch light. I waited a few minutes before I called Duncan to let him know he could come over. Once I had, I got busy cleaning my kitchen.

About thirty minutes later, a knock came from my back door, and I knew it was him. I dried my hands on a dish towel and hung it over my oven's handle. "Hey," I said simply, as I opened the door to let him in.

"Hey," he said, almost shyly.

"You can set your stuff in the living room. I need to make the couch up for you." I headed to the linin closet in the hallway to grab a couple of blankets and pillows. They piled high in my arms, obstructing my view.

"Let me give you a hand with that." Duncan took the pillows from the top of the pile. "There, now you can see where you're walking."

"Thanks. I figured if I tripped over anything, the softness of the pillows would save me from any real injuries. Only my ego would take a hit, and I think I've embarrassed myself enough this week."

Duncan's expression fell poignantly.

"I'm sorry. That's not fair," I said sincerely. "I've been in my head a lot today. Trying to sort some things out." I sat the blankets down on the coffee table in front of the couch.

"Heidi, listen," he sat the pillows down next to the blankets and took a seat on the couch, "I'm really sorry about last night. My intention was not to hurt or upset you, but to prevent you from feeling any sense of regret. I could tell your mind weighed heavy and I didn't want you to think back and feel I had taken advantage of you."

"I know, Duncan, and I'm grateful for your thoughtfulness. Truly."

"Always." He took my hand. The gaze of his

beautiful green eyes lingered over me.

In my effort to change the subject, and get my mind off last night, I asked "Want to watch some tv?"

"Sure. I don't have any preference, so whatever you're into, I'm into."

I set the channel to some nature documentary about big cats before retrieving my laptop and setting down in the loveseat to do some research. I hadn't been successful in finding the identity of the John Doe who died in my dreams, so I decided to occupy my brain with something else that might be achievable. In the search engine, I looked up the Keller Institute. After a few seconds of loading, a list of search results appeared. I found what looked to be the link for the website and clicked on it. The About page displayed a brief bio about the institute and a photo of the doctor who runs it, Dr. Jamie Keller. She sported bright blue eyes, high cheekbones, medium length blonde hair, and a white lab coat.

She looks like she was born to be a doctor.

The institute bio told me the institute offered a nontraditional type of therapy, dream therapy. I gathered from the bio that the Keller Institute began as a rehab for people struggling with addiction. Dr. Keller discovered that she could help people overcome their vices through lucid dreaming. Since the institute's inception, she now offered therapy for people who want to heal from anxieties and fears.

"Do you need anything from the kitchen? I need to get some water," Duncan asked, interrupting my thoughts.

"Sure, some water sounds great. Thanks." My eyes never left the screen.

Duncan returned with a couple glasses of water, handing one of them to me. "What's that?" he asked as he nodded toward the screen of my laptop before returning to his seat on the couch.

I moved to sit next to him. I sat crisscross apple sauce and turned my screen towards Duncan. "This woman, Dr. Jamie Keller, was the doctor at the Keller Institute. She specializes in dream therapy to help her patients overcome, anxieties, fear, and addictions."

"Dream therapy?" he asked skeptically.

"Yeah!" I said emphatically. "The website says she uses lucid dreaming to aid in her patients' therapy."

He looked at me puzzled, "Wait, are you looking for therapy for yourself?"

"Yeah. Don't you think I could benefit from it? I mean, I called you for a sleep over because I'm too scared to sleep in my house alone."

"Yeah, but everyone has bad dreams sometimes. It can take a few days to shake the feeling, but eventually you move past it."

"These dreams aren't your run of the mill bad dreams, Duncan. These dreams are something else entirely."

"How so?" He asked genuinely.

I shut my laptop and sat it on the coffee table in front of me. "Lately, I've been having dreams that paralyze me. I'm aware that I'm dreaming, but I can't move. I struggle to wake up. All the while, it feels like someone, or something, is standing over me, lurking, just out of eye's view. I try like hell to just turn head, and look terror in its face, to confront it, so I can vanquish whatever it is that's got a hold of me."

Duncan leaned forward and took my hands, "That sounds terrifying."

"It is," I admitted to, not only Duncan, but myself. It wasn't so bad before, when I thought my dreams were *my* dreams, but now, after everything that had happened with Michael, this felt more real than ever.

"I'm glad you felt comfortable enough to ask for my help." He locked eyes with me, "It means a lot that you would trust me to keep you safe."

I *do* trust him, I realized. I felt safe with him. With this realization, the place between my thighs started to tingle. "I do trust you. You're a good man, Duncan." I lifted his hand to my lips and kissed his knuckles. "Good night, Duncan," I said before I excused myself to my room. I couldn't continue to sit out here without my mind being invaded with dirty thoughts of him.

Showered, shaved, and moisturized, I slid beneath the fresh sheets on my bed. I relaxed all my muscles and tried to calm my busy mind. I reminded myself that Duncan was here, and I was safe. Clinging tightly to that thought, I finally drifted off to sleep.

***

It's dark. The northern lights danced brightly above my head, illuminating my surroundings. They're beautiful.

In the distance, a group of people were huddled together. I take in the sights above me for a few more seconds before I decided to walk towards the group. They're all speaking somewhat frantically, like something is wrong.

In the center of the gathering, a young boy is sitting. He appeared to be crying. The crowd is forced apart by another boy, who looks to be a little bit older. The young boy seemed to be calmed by the presence of the older boy. He looked up and dried his tears. "Come on, Duncan, you can be my brother," the older boy says as he reached out his hand towards the young one.

I can see now; the young boy's eyes are green. The older boy must be Ronny. The two of them leave through the crowd. I have the urge to follow them, but I'm distracted by a band of white light out in the distance. It appeared to be shining behind something. A door maybe. The crowd that was just here was suddenly gone. As were the northern lights above me. All I saw now was the light peeking out from behind a door. I make my way to it and open it. There, on the floor, the dark eyed man was down on his hands and knees. His head hung low. He looked defeated. I kneel and place my hand on his back. In that moment, a ripple of terror rushed through me.

"You shouldn't be here," he said fearfully. The dark eyes of my mystery man finally meet mine.

I didn't know why I shouldn't be here, but the feeling inside of me told me he's right. I need to go. But I can't leave him like this. "Take my hand," I said as I reached out for him. He struggled to lift his hand to me but eventually I had a firm grip. I start to stand up, trying to pull him up too, when suddenly he was no longer here with me.

What the hell?

I looked around to be sure. He's gone. There's

nothing here except terror and the sound of rhythmic beeping. My nerves, growing thicker in my throat, making it difficult to breathe.

I need to wake up now.

I can't lift my feet. I continue to struggle against the fear until finally I'm back in my room. But I'm not safe yet. I could feel the terror. It had followed me back. I could feel it watching me. Stalking me. Creeping closer and closer. It's relentless in its yearning to take me in its forceful grip.

I call out for Duncan. But no sound escapes my lips. I try again.

And again.

And again.

Over and over until my throat feels hoarse from my silent screams.

A warm embrace from behind startled me. I turned to see the source of it and thankfully see Duncan. I let out a sigh of relief and realized I was finally awake.

"I'm sorry," Duncan said. "I heard you gasp so I came to check on you. Your breathing was jagged. I tried to wake you up. But nothing was working and all I could think to do next was to hug you. Was it another bad dream?"

"Yeah." I squeaked out. I took a moment to take in a few deep breaths. "You said you *tried* to wake me up?"

"A couple of different ways. I said your name, gently shook you, placed a cold washcloth on the back of your neck. But you were out."

I noticed the washcloth around my neck once he mentioned it. "Well, thank you. Do you think you could sleep in here with me the rest of the night?" It was probably a bad idea, but I was too scared to sleep alone.

"Sure. Let me go grab the blankets and I can sleep on the floor."

I shook my head. "What I really mean is, could you stay here and hold me?"

Something unrecognizable flashed in his eyes. "Of course," he said softly. Duncan extended his right arm for me to lay my head on. He wrapped me with his other arm and pulled me close to his body.

The warmth of his body and security of his muscular arm wrapped tightly around me relaxed me. I closed my eyes and focused on the movements from his chest, expanding and contracting from his breaths, against my back. Finally, a peaceful sleep overcame me.

Chapter 11

Duncan was still asleep beside me when I woke up this morning. Images of young Duncan flooded my mind. He looked so afraid and lonely until, who I can only assume was Ronny appeared. It was hard to imagine Duncan so small and fragile. Duncan was homeschooled until he reached middle school, which was when I met him, so I didn't really know him as a young child.

I decided to leave him a note before I left this morning. It read "I can't thank you enough for your help last night. Please let me know how I can repay you. Help yourself to anything in the kitchen, but please be discreet and leave through the back door. I'll talk to you later. – Heidi."

I brought my laptop in with me this morning. Tim didn't drop mail off on Sundays, and Oliva won't be here until noon, so I had plenty of time to read more about the Keller Institute. I was curious if my recent fear of dreams could be treated with more dreaming. It felt implausible, but this institute was the closest place in a 100-mile radius so it's my only option for the time being. According to the website, the Keller Institute was opened seven days a week. I pulled out my phone and checked its signal strength. Three bars, that should be enough. I dialed the number and listened to the rings until a perky voice on the other end answered.

"Keller Institute, how may I direct your call?"

The voice chirped.

"Hi there!" I matched her tone. "I'm calling to get more information on your treatment options and programs."

"Of course, may I ask what you're seeking counseling or therapy for?"

"My fear of dreaming," I replied. There was a slight hesitation before she responded.

"Would you mind holding for a moment?"

"Sure?"

Did I just break this poor woman? She's probably thinking the same thing as me, how do you fix my dreams with dreams?

I listened to the jaunty hold music for a few minutes before another voice came on the line.

"Good morning. My name is Dr. Jamie Keller. Who do I have the pleaser of speaking with?"

Surprised to be speaking to Dr. Keller, I replied "Good morning to you too. I'm Heidi. Heidi Miller."

"Hi Heidi. Annie tells me you're seeking treatment for your fear of… dreams. Is that correct?"

"Yes, that's correct."

"Just so you're familiar, I specialize in dream therapy. Meaning the main course of treatment is delivered via dreaming. Is that something you'd be willing to explore even though you're experiencing an anxiety related to dreaming," Dr. Keller asked.

"It is. I haven't always been afraid. This fear is newly developed and I'm hoping to get help before it gets worse."

I heard clacking on Dr. Keller's side of the phone. "I have an opening tomorrow morning, at 10:15, if that works for you. If not, my next availability is

Friday afternoon."

Tomorrow is so soon. I honestly hadn't thought it'd move this quickly.

"I could be there tomorrow morning. How long does the appointment usually last?"

"The appointment usually lasts about an hour. We use this time to get a better understanding of why you're seeking treatment."

"Okay, great. I'll be there."

"Wonderful. I'll see you then, Heidi," Dr. Keller said.

"Great, see you then." I disconnected the line and stared at the phone in my hand. With feelings of nervousness and excitement for my appointment tomorrow, I busied myself with small tasks around the store until customers began to roll in.

Sundays were our busy days. Everyone usually comes in to stock up on the necessities to get them through the week. Today was also the first Sunday of the month, which was when residents who made handmade goods came to check on the inventory of their products. After Mrs. Trudy's homemade goodies, our next popular items were the handmade wind chimes Agnes and Jud made. Their grandkids help craft them when they're in town visiting.

Mr. and Mrs. Johnson are the first customers of the morning. Knowing their son was probably still asleep in my bed, I tried to act normal. "Morning Mr. and Mrs. Johnson. How's your Sunday treating you so far?"

"Morning, Heidi," Mrs. Johnson said. "Our Sunday is going well. Thank you for asking. We're here to get a few things to make some chicken noodle soup. Duncan isn't feeling well so I thought I'd better get a pot going first thing this morning."

Duncan's not feeling well? He seemed fine to me when I left him this morning.

"Oh, poor thing. What's wrong?" I asked curiously.

"He was supposed to meet a nice girl we set him up with. The nurse at our doctor's office over in Easton City is so sweet and educated…"

"And beautiful," Mr. Johnson added.

"Yes. She's also very beautiful. But above that, she's very sweet." Mrs. Johnson said, shooing her husband away. "But he called yesterday to let us know he'd have to cancel since he wasn't feeling well. I'm hoping this soup will fix him right up."

I smiled politely. "I'm sure it will. A mama's cooking always does the trick." Mrs. Johnson smiled and followed her husband to collect their groceries.

Why did he cancel?

I hoped he hadn't canceled for me, that was a lot of pressure. I didn't want to be responsible for preventing him from dating. It was one more thing I had to add to my already growing list of worries and concerns.

The next several hours passed fairly quickly with customers coming and going all morning. Oliva and Dad enter the store with a couple of sandwiches around noon. "Hiya, sweetheart," Dad called out. "Mom made us a couple of roast beef sandwiches for lunch today. She'll be by in a few to eat with us." Dad set down the sandwiches and gave me a hug. He looked around the store and noticed the aisles are looking skimp. "Today has been busy indeed. I'll give you two a hand with inventory tonight."

Olivia and I both said, "Thanks, Dad." Then, "Jinks. Double jinks!" We started to laugh. Here we were, two grown ass women, still jinxing each other whenever they said the same thing at the same time.

By the time the last customer checked out, Mom entered, sending the bell above the door to ring out furiously. "Sorry it took me longer than expected, I was chatting with Martha Thomas outside. Is everyone ready to eat?"

"I'm always ready," Dad said as he pretended to adjust the waist band of his jeans to accommodate a full stomach.

"Let's have lunch outside, the weather is nice, and I've seen just about everyone from town already today so we shouldn't have any other customers for a while," I suggested.

There was a grassy lot next to the store that we used for holiday barbeques, or arts markets during peak tourist seasons. Spaced throughout, we had a couple of picnic tables where we could sit and eat our lunch. We each took a seat, Oliva, and I on one side, Mom, and Dad on the other. Mom, sitting across from me said, "How'd you sleep last night, Heidi. Any more bothersome dreams?"

"I slept like a rock." I lied. "Made it to work on time and everything."

"Good. I was up worried about you all night."

I hid my eye roll; I didn't want to get into this today with her. I knew she did things out of love but sometimes it came across as hostility and it irked my nerves. "I appreciate it Mom, but I'm fine. I'm a big girl." I took a bite of my sandwich and chewed it slowly, hoping she wouldn't want me to talk with my mouth full and not ask another question. A tactic I've used before to keep her from asking me more questions that I didn't want to answer.

"I know you are, but you'll always be my baby." She took a bite of her sandwich and swallowed. "Oliva, when is Ronny getting back into town?"

"He should be back some time tomorrow. Probably tomorrow evening if he sleeps in," Oliva said.

"Any word if they're going to get that contract over in Easton City?" Dad asked.

Typical Mount Hopewell gossip. Everyone knew about the contract, but no one could put together that the woman he was "seeing" was the contract broker for said contract.

"No word yet." Olivia wiped her mouth with the napkin Mom packed. "They only had the meeting earlier last week. Ronny said he's expecting to hear something by the end of this week. I hope they get it though. It would be nice to have him home more."

"I know it would be, honey," Mom said sympathetically as she reached over to pat Olivia's hand.

"Heidi," Dad said, "Anything new going on with you?"

"Well, I've been meaning to talk to you and Mom again about redoing the floors in the store." I made something up. If I sat here quietly, Mom would pester me. If I told the truth about what I was really up to, Mom would pester me. It was a lose-lose situation. "They're so old and warped. Someone could get hurt if they're not careful. I also wanted to get your opinions on expanding our customer base. What if we offered products online?" These were ideas I've always had for the store. But change was a touchy topic for my Mom, especially when it came to the store. It was hard enough to get her to agree to upgrading our register.

"You mean, people could buy things from our store, on the internet?" Dad asked skeptically.

Mom followed that up with her own question, "Is that something we even need to do?"

"No, it's not something we need to do, but it's something that could bring value to the store and to the residents. Selling their items online to a broader group of people could help put money back into our town, into our school even."

My parents mulled the thought over. "Hmm? That could be something indeed," My dad finally said.

Mom just nodded. It was her way of not yet admitting defeat. "The floors are fine though. Those floors are the original floors your grandparents built. There's history in those floors."

It's the same spiel she gives every time I ask about the floors.

"Oh, that reminds me," Mom said. "I spoke to Annette Johnson this morning. She said Duncan wasn't feeling well. You might want to go over and check on him sometime today," She said looking at me.

"Me?" I asked. Mom nodded in response. "Why me?" I was starting to feel paranoid that people might know Duncan and I were more than friends.

"Because you're his *friend* aren't you. It'd be nice to check in on him."

I hated the way she says friend. She said it like it was a joke. "Mom, is this because Mrs. Johnson may have also told you they set him up on a date with the nurse from their doctor's office?" I felt Oliva's gaze hit the side of my face. She was going to ask me all about this the moment our parents were out of ear shot.

"Of course, it is," she said as if I should have known better. "You two are meant to be together. Mark my words."

"They're marked," I replied sarcastically.

Dad crumpled up the sandwich wrapping and his napkin. "Well, I think our lunch break is about over, dear," He said to mom, "We should be letting the girls get back to work."

Mom looked around at the remnants of everyone else's lunch and realized we were all pretty much finished. "I guess you're right." She folded the wrapping back over her half-eaten sandwich. "We'll get out of you girl's hair."

"Lunch was delicious, Mom, thank you," Olivia said.

"Yes, Mom. Thank you," I followed up.

We threw our trash away and walked Mom and Dad back to the car. "I'll be back this evening to help with inventory," Dad reminded us.

We waved as they backed out of the parking lot and drove away.

"So, Gerald and Annette set Duncan up on a blind date, huh?" Oliva inquired before our parents' car was out of sight.

"That's what they said when they came into the store this morning. Mrs. Johnson came to pick up some ingredients to make him chicken noodle soup. He told them he wasn't feeling well and that's why he canceled the date."

"Yeah, I'm sure that's why," she said doubtfully. Suggesting that I was the reason he didn't go on the date.

She must have heard his truck go by last night. Or maybe Duncan slept in, and she saw his truck in the yard this morning.

I refused to tattle on myself and would continue to keep this a secret until Duncan and I couldn't anymore.

"Listen, enough of that," I said trying to distract her from figuring out why Duncan really canceled his date. "I need a favor."

She turned to head back inside the store, "Of course you do. What's up?"

I updated her on my dream last night, carefully leaving Duncan out. Then I told her about the Keller Institute and that I had made an appointment for tomorrow morning. She seemed to understand why I'd seek out treatment and didn't mind covering for me.

We took a seat in the rocking chairs and started up a new game of M.A.S.H. to help the time pass. The results from our last round of M.A.S.H were for me. I would live in a mansion, here in Mount Hopewell, with seven kids. My job would be a travel agent, I would drive a private jet, and I would be married to… Duncan.

Even the stupid game thought we were supposed to be together.

Chapter 12

When I returned home from work yesterday, I found the note Duncan left for me on my pillow. It said not to hesitate to call him if I needed him in the middle of the night. Thankfully, I didn't. My dreams were surprisingly peaceful last night. No sign of the dark eyed man or the dreadful feeling of stillness. I almost canceled my appointment this morning, thinking it wasn't needed. But, to be on the safe side, I decided to keep it and showed up to the appointment.

The clock on the wall in the waiting room of the Keller Institute read 9:50 a.m. I finished up my new patient paperwork and returned it to the woman sitting behind the desk at the front of the room. She then handed me a brochure with pricing. This first visit, as the receptionist explained, was a consultation to make sure I was a candidate for dream therapy. If I were to choose to complete therapy, the initial treatment would cost me upwards of five grand. Which I could pull from my savings, but it would hurt. It took me a long time to save that kind of money and it killed me knowing I would probably have to spend it on this. I was saving it for a trip, once I could talk Olivia into going somewhere with me. Provided that I wouldn't have a bad dream that scared the idea out of me for the second time.

Another ten minutes passed before I was called back into an airly styled room. I took a seat on the light, indigo colored tufted sofa, occupied with a couple of white throw pillows. There were gold leaf accented side tables next to the sofa that held a box of tissues, a glass pitcher of cucumber water, and a single glass cup. On the small table behind the couch sat an oil diffuser that filled the room with a soft lavender scent. There was a matching high back, tufted chair across from the couch for the doctor to sit. The room had large windows that let in natural sunlight behind the decorative sheer curtains. On the walls, there were stunning photos of different types of foliage framed in black.

A soft knock sounded from the door. My attention pulled from the photos to the tall blonde woman that entered the room. I stood as she walked over to me and extended her hand for a handshake. "Good morning. I am Dr. Jamie Keller. You must be Heidi Miller."

I shook her hand. She looked exactly like her picture on the website. "Yes, hi. It's nice to meet you, Dr. Keller."

"Likewise." She gestured for me to sit as she walked around the couch to her chair. She opened up her padfolio to a blank sheet of paper. "Now, before we start, I want to ask if you have any questions for me before we begin."

I shook my head. "Not right now, anyway."

"Okay great. We'll get started then. Feel free to ask any questions, anytime during our session." She clicked her pen to prepare it for note taking. "What brings you in today, Heidi? When we spoke yesterday, you said you had a fear of dreaming, but could you elaborate on that a bit more?"

"Yeah." I readjusted my posture on the couch. "I generally really enjoy my dreams. Always have for as far back as I can remember. But these last few days, I have been experiencing a paralyzing fear. And I mean that literally. I can't move my body. I'm aware that I'm dreaming and try to wake up, but that terror I feel doesn't leave me until I'm able to move again. It feels as if someone, or something, is watching me. Has a hold on me."

Dr. Keller scribbled something on her notepad. "And this only just begun happening?"

"Yes. Last week it started."

"Is there anything that has happened, recently, in life that is causing you stress or frustration?"

I can think of five things off the top of my head. "Sure. But those frustrations aren't new."

"Like what? What are some of the stresses currently weighing on you right now?" She asked.

"For starters, my dreams. My parents and my sister think I spend way too much time in my head. Too much time trying to understand the meaning of my dreams. Or changing my life around something I dream about."

"Could you give me an example?" Dr. Keller inquired.

"My sister and I run the General Store back home in Mount Hopewell. My grandparents built and ran it until they retired and passed it down to my mom. Now that my parents are retiring, it's being passed to my sister and I. Part of me loves the fact that I'm a part of the store's legacy, but the other part of me wants to be given the opportunity to see what I can do on my own. Occasionally, I have dreamed of having an amazing, important career. A career that makes me feel like the work I'm doing is valuable. The most recent example of that would be when I wanted to go to school to become a zoologist. I was completely invested in taking that path until I had a bad dream."

"What happened in your dream?"

"A whale went on a rampage, attacking fishermen and beachgoers." I fiddled my thumbs a bit. "I saw a news story about something similar. That was all it took for it to infect my literal dreams and make me change my mind about becoming a zoologist." I paused and took a moment to replay the words I was saying. "Saying it all out loud, I feel a little embarrassed."

"You don't have to feel embarrassed here." Her tone was so comforting and safe. I really did feel like I could open up about everything. "You also mentioned you spend a lot of time trying to find meaning in your dreams. What do you mean by that?"

I looked at her, weighing the decision to tell her about the murder or not. Ultimately, I decided to tell her.

I'm here for help, and I believe she can help me. "I witnessed a murder."

Dr. Keller's eyes shot up from her pad to my face. "A murder? Did you call the police?"

"I couldn't. This happened in my dreams."

Her posture relaxed a bit, "And what makes you so sure this was a murder, and not something you may have seen on tv affecting your dream."

"The look in his defeated, blue eyes. The feeling of hopelessness I felt when he asked for my help, and I didn't. Couldn't. That was the first time I had ever experienced something that shook me too my core like that. I spent weeks trying to find him and any sign of existence. I looked for obituaries, I looked for news stories, I looked through social media, everywhere. I have yet to find anything though."

"Are there any other details you could tell me about this dream?"

"We were in a field of purple flowers. And he kept grabbing his chest and gasping for air..." I shuddered at the memory. I didn't want to talk about it anymore.

She must have been able to tell that I needed to move on from the subject. She wrote something on her pad and changed the subject. "What else is causing you stress right now?"

"Marriage. My mom is on me about getting married. I think she thinks that I can't be happy or live a full life without getting married. And not getting married to just anyone. But getting married to someone from home who wants to stay and raise a family. She has it in her head that I should marry my sister's boyfriend's brother." Dr. Keller raised an eyebrow out of concern. "They're adopted brothers," I chuckled, realizing how odd that must sound to a stranger. "It's weird, but not looked down upon in a chromosomally type of way," I reassured her. She nodded a comprehending nod.

"So, this guy, you sister's boyfriend's *adopted* brother, why is your mom convinced you should marry him?"

"Mount Hopewell is a small, rural town. Most kids we grew up with all moved away for college. They don't return unless it's just for a visit. Some kids from around there usually leave and don't return ever again. But Duncan, that's his name, I believe wants to stay in Mount Hopewell. He and his brother own and operate a lumber transportation business. They grew up there with no plans to move away. On top of that, Duncan is truly a good man and honestly, any woman would be lucky to spend her life with him."

"Do I detect a bit of sentiment in your tone?"

Damn, she's perceptive. "Honestly, I'm not sure. There's a definite attraction between us, but that might be all there is. Besides, I want to experience life outside of our small town. I don't think he does. I wouldn't want someone to hold me back from my dreams and I wouldn't want to hold anyone back from theirs.

She paused, as if she was recalling a memory, "That's very compassionate of you. To recognize that he might not want to follow you in your journey, or you in his. Being cognizant enough to know that about yourself before you commit to someone will serve you positively once you decide if you want to settle down or not."

"Thank you for that," I said gratefully.

Looking down at her note pad, she said "Family. Check. Relationship troubles. Double check. These are the top two stressors that many of my patients' experience. So far, nothing is jumping out at me that could be the cause of your troubling dreams. What else takes up space in your mind?"

I took a deep breath, bracing myself for her reaction. *She will probably want to have me committed once she hears this.*

"This past Friday, a tourist who visited town with a bird watching group, got injured during a hike. He was alone and couldn't reach out to anyone for help. He was found, thankfully, but the reason we were able to find him was because I knew where he was." She looked at me confused, so I continued with my explanation. "Earlier that morning, I wound up taking a nap while at work. The night before was the first time I experienced paralysis and didn't get a good night's rest. But anyway, I got to work and wound up taking a nap. During my nap I had a dream about a man, he told me his name was Michael, who had fallen into a river while trying to take a picture of some bird in the tree overhead. He was able to pull himself out of the river by using protruding roots that stuck out from the riverbank. However, he was too banged up to get back to the trailhead and found a tree trunk to rest against instead." She was writing quickly in her notes, trying to keep up with me.

"Go on," she said.

"He didn't tell me the name of the trail he started down in my dream, but I was standing on a bridge that looked familiar to me. I also saw some boots on the right-hand side of the bank and a backpack floating down stream. Once I remembered what trail crossed that bridge, we were able to go up and search for him. We had search parties on both sides of the river, some going upstream, the others going downstream. We found him on the same side of the river where his boots were placed in my dream. But unlike my dream, Michael had his boots on when we found him. When I visited him in the hospital, he recounted the events just the same way he did in my dream. And if that's not enough to freak anyone out, he said he felt he had met me before, that he had a feeling of De Ja Vue."

"It's not uncommon for people not to remember all the details of their dreams." She sat her pen down and leaned forward slightly, "Would you be open to overnight treatment? You would stay here for as many days as needed but we'll start with the remainder of the week. We would monitor you while you're sleeping, monitor your brain activity while dreaming, if you consent."

I thought quietly for a moment before I gave her an answer. "Could I give you a call after I discuss it with my family?" I also needed to figure out if I want to spend essentially all my savings on this treatment.

"Yes, of course." She pulled out a business card from her padfolio and handed it to me. "My personal number is on the back of this. Give me a call once you've made your decision."

I took her business card and slid it into the front pocket of my purse. "So, you don't think I'm crazy?"

"Not in the slightest."

We said our goodbyes and she walked me back to the waiting room. "Please, don't hesitate to call once you've made your decision," Dr. Keller reminded me. I continued to head for the front entrance. Before I could make it to the door, she called out, "Heidi, I think I could help you make great progress here."

Chapter 13

I got back to the store around two p.m. and Oliva was behind the counter starting a fresh pot of coffee. "Coffee this late in the day?" I asked.

"Hey!" Olivia chirped. "Yeah. Today has dragged on. I need some help to keep my eyes opened. How was the appointment?"

"It went well. The doctor suggested that I come back and stay overnight for treatment."

"What does that mean?"

"She wants to monitor me while I'm sleeping, to capture my brain activity while I'm dreaming. But I told her I'd need to talk to my family about it first." I walked over and grab some water and a snack from the aisle.

"What are your thoughts about all of this?" Oliva asked me.

"I think I want to do it," I said somewhat confidently. "I told her about my dream with Michael and she didn't look at me or talk to me like I was some mountain dwelling lunatic. I think she could actually help me."

Oliva took a seat in the rocking chair and motioned for me to come sit beside her. "How are you going to bring this all up to Mom and Dad?"

I took a seat, opened my Combos, and set my water on the floor beside me. "I haven't the slightest clue. Mom is going to lose it."

She nodded, "Mhm. You got that right."

"Maybe if I talk to Dad alone, he can help me sway Mom."

"I don't know, Heidi. It's a big ask to get Dad to take a stance opposite to Mom."

"Well," I popped a cheese filled pretzel in my mouth, "help me think of a lie then."

"You can't lie! They will find out and things will be so much worse for you."

We rocked in silence for a bit, wondering how to approach my parents with the news. "I guess I could always fake my death," I said jokingly.

"Ha!" Olivia let out a quick laugh. "Yeah, that'll do the trick."

"I guess before I think about asking them, I need to ask your opinion. Are you okay with me not being around for the next few days? Dr. Keller said to start, I'd spend the remainder of the week under observation. I'm thinking I should be back by next Monday at the latest."

"It's going to suck not having you around, but I understand why you would want to do it. And I support your decision."

"Thanks, Olivia. I really don't know what I'd do without you."

"I don't know what you'd do without me either," she joked.

The bell jingled above the door, causing us to both look towards it. It was Mr. Johnson.

"Hi Gerald," Olivia stood to greet her future father-in-law, "Anything we could help you with today?"

"Hi, girls," he gave Olivia a brief hug. "No thanks. I came to grab the mail." He rushed past us to the P.O Boxes. After pulling the mail from his box, he shuffled through it. He paused. He pulled a single envelope from the pile before tucking the remaining parcels under his arm. He stared at the single envelope in his hand.

"Is everything alright, Mr. Johnson?" I asked.

"Y-yes. Just received some mail I've been waiting for. I need to get home to Annette. You two have a nice evening." Mr. Johnson keep the cluster of envelopes tucked under his arm as he exited the store in a hurry.

"I wonder what that was all about?" Olivia asked with worry.

"Yeah, I'm not sure. I hope everything is alright," I said.

"Me too."

We went back to rocking in our chairs. "I think I'll just invite Mom and Dad over for supper tonight and talk to them. You don't have to come unless you really want to, but I know Ronny is supposed to be home tonight."

"Thanks. Yeah, he should be home sometime to tonight."

"Have the two of you talked anymore about the wedding? Any date or theme picked yet?"

"No date yet. We're not in any hurry right now. His biggest thing is that he wants to have more work closer to home."

"That's understandable," I said.

"I could care less about where he works, but I know it's important to him. We know we want to start a family as soon as possible, but he's struggling with the idea that he might have to leave us from time to time to continue his deliveries. We've talked about him hiring a secondary driver specifically for trips that take longer than three days. If this contract doesn't pan out, we might have to revisit the discussion."

"What about Duncan, couldn't he drive from time to time?"

"He could, but Ronny trusts him with the day-to-day running's of the business. If he stepped away to drive, someone else would have to manage the days that he is away."

"Ah," I said. "That's a good point." A brilliant thought evolved in my mind. I looked at Olivia, wide eyed, "What if *I* was the second driver?"

She pursed her lips at me and shook her head.

"I'm serious! Don't you think I could drive?"

"I know you could get your CDL and learn to drive. That's not why I wouldn't want you to do it."

"Then why?" I cocked my head to the side and looked at her, waiting for her to answer.

"Because, there would be times you would have to pull off into a rest area and sleep for the night. I would be nervous for you to be alone in a parking lot, predominately full of men."

Oh. I uncocked my head and sat forward again, crossing my arms. "Fine," I said, causing Olivia to chuckle at me. Changing the subject, I asked, "They expect to hear back later this week about the contract, right?"

"Yeah. Duncan said he felt good about the meeting. They're the closest lumber yard, but smaller than the other contractors that are also bidding for the work."

"Okay, well, smaller isn't always a bad thing."

"Exactly. They're smaller, but they have more connections with the surrounding areas. We're holding out hope."

"Me too. You and Ronny deserve the life you envision for your future."

"Thanks, Heidi, so do you. Call Mom and Dad, invite them for supper. But if I were you, I'd start thinking about how you're going to bring it up."

She was right. I needed to approach the subject gently. I really wanted to follow through with this therapy to see if it would help me. But, that all hinged on how my parents reacted. If they couldn't support my decision, I'm not sure I'll be able to follow through with it. The burden of cost is also weighing heavy in my mind. It's going to take me forever to save that money up again. And if I didn't call them now and invite them to supper, I might chicken out about it. I walked over to the phone behind the counter and dialed my parents' number.

"Hello," My mom said on the other end of the phone.

"Hey Mom."

"Hi, Heidi. Is everything alright, sweetheart?"

"Yeah. I was just calling to see if you and Dad wanted to come over for supper tonight. I have something I want to talk to you both about."

"How about you come over here, I'm making lasagna."

"Sure, that sounds great. What time will supper be ready?"

"It'll be ready by seven. Is your sister coming too?"

"I don't think so. Ronny should be home tonight, and I think they had plans to stay in."

"Alright. Tell her that there will be plenty for her and Ronny, Duncan too, if they decide to come."

"Will do, Mom. I'll see you later tonight."

"Bye-bye, love you."

"Love you too, bye." I placed the phone back on the receiver.

I called over to Olivia, "Mom said there'd be plenty for you and Ronny tonight if you decide to join us." She gave me a thumbs up but kept her attention in the word search she was working on. I guessed I'll really be fending for myself tonight. I hope Mom doesn't come too far off the rails.

Chapter 14

It was about twenty minutes past seven by the time I arrived for supper with my parents. Already not starting off on a good foot.

"Knock knock," I said, as I entered my childhood home. Smells of garlic and Italian herbs greeted my senses. "It smells really good in here, Mom," I called to her in the kitchen as I shut the door behind me. In the living room, Dad was sitting back in his brown recliner, flipping through the channels on the tv. "Hey, Dad. Anything good on?" I kicked off my shoes and hung up my jacket on the hooks beside the front door.

"Eh." He shrugged his shoulders. "There's always the news. But your mom asked me to turn this *depressing nonsense* off for dinner."

I chuckled at his impression of Mom. It's spot on. "I have to side with Mom on that one, Dad. The news can be pretty bleak. I don't know how you can watch it all the time and still maintain your happy go lucky disposition."

"It's just how the world works," Dad began to explain. "Things happen all the time all over the world, but that should never prevent me from living and loving to the fullest."

My dad's response made me smile. He and I have always been kindred spirits. I bent down and hugged his neck from behind and kissed the top of his balding head. "I'm going to go back and check to see if Mom needs any help."

"Hi, sweetheart," Mom called as I entered the kitchen. "it's so nice of you to join us." She glanced at her watch around her writs, "twenty minutes late, I might add." There it was. The first strike against me tonight. Hopefully it would be the last.

"I know Mom, I'm sorry." I poured myself a glass of water. "I got held up at the store a little later than normal and I wanted to head home to shower and change first." Opting for a pair of dark grey sweatpants and a plain white tee shirt, I wanted to be dressed comfortably while having this difficult conversation with my parents. That way, if I needed to make a quick escape back home, I could just crawl in the bed and be done with the day.

Mom turned and looked at me, up and down, assessing my choice of fashion for tonight's supper. "Oh," She said judgingly, "What a peculiar choice of wardrobe for this evening."

Strike two. I had to suppress an eye roll.

"Thanks, Mom," I said curtly. "Is there anything I can help you with?"

Mom removed her apron and washed her hands. She scanned the kitchen, looking for something for me to do. "You could go ahead and set the table. We'll be able to eat shortly."

"Sure thing, Mom." I made myself busy with setting the table with three place settings.

Mom stopped me and said, "You'll need a fourth."

"Oh, did Olivia change her mind?" I grabbed a fourth plate and glass and placed it on the table. "Ronny must be getting in later than originally planned."

"No, Olivia won't be joining us tonight." I must have had a bemused look on my face when Mom turned around. She said "Oh, did I forget to tell you? I invited Duncan to supper tonight too."

It took everything in me not to reply with a smart-ass comment, but I couldn't afford a third strike. She knew good and well she *forgot* on purpose. Now I understood why she was so critical of my sweatpants and tee shirt. And now I was regretting the decision too.

"It must have slipped your mind, Mom," I said through a clinched smile.

"I called Annette to check in on how Duncan was feeling. She said he seemed to be feeling much better. So, I gave him a call and invited him over tonight."

"Well, Mom, I was hoping to talk to you and Dad about something important tonight."

"Anything you say to us, can be said in front of Duncan too. He's your *friend* after all, isn't he?" There was that tone again. Sarcasm through and through. At least I knew where I got it from.

The sound of a knock came from the front door. I heard dad close the footrest on his recliner before getting up to open the door. "Duncan, it's so nice you're able to join us this evening." I heard my dad say from the living room. "Please, come in and make yourself at home. Supper will be ready shortly."

The door closed and Duncan replied, "Thank you sir. These are for Mrs. Miller."

"She'll like those very much. She and Heidi are back there in the kitchen."

Duncan appeared in the entry way of the kitchen

holding a bouquet of flowers wrapped in brown paper. "Good evening, Mrs. Miller. Thank you for inviting me for supper," he said as he handed the flowers to my mom. "Evening, Heidi," he said, managing to flash me a quick smile without my mom noticing. She was too charmed by the beautiful bouquet of flowers he brought. No doubt, those flowers were freshly picked from Mrs. Trudy's garden today.

"Well, I'll be. These are lovely!" she exclaimed as she placed the flowers in a vase of water. "How thoughtful of you, Duncan. Thank you." She admired the floral arrangement as she carried it out to the living room and placed it on the coffee table.

With my mom out of earshot, I turned to Duncan. "Why would you agree to supper with my parents?" I asked quietly as I stared up at him.

He looked confused. "I thought you knew I was coming. Your mom said it was your idea that I join you all tonight."

She had some nerve, that mother of mine. I let out a frustrated sigh, "Look at me. Look at how I'm dressed." I pulled at the sides of my baggy shirt and sweatpants. "Does it look like I knew you were coming?" His eyes fell to examine me closer. "And besides, even if I did want you to come to supper, why would you agree to it? And why wouldn't you text me to confirm?"

Mom adjusted the flowers in the vase a final time before asking, "alright everyone, who's hungry?" Mom made her way back to the kitchen, preventing Duncan from answering my question. I reset my facial expression to a neutral smile, erasing my irritation with how things were turning out this evening.

My dad hopped up quickly from his recliner. "I know I am!" He said, and he followed Mom into the kitchen.

We all made our way to the table. Mom sat across from Dad, which forced Duncan and I to sit across from one another at my parent's small square kitchen table. We ate in awkward silence for a few minutes before Dad asked Duncan how things had been going down at the lumber yard. "Ronny tells me that you all are bidding for more local jobs. Says you're the one who handles the negotiations."

"That's right, Mr. Miller…" Duncan started but was quickly interrupted by Mom.

"How wonderful, Duncan," Mom said unmoved. She was wanting to ask the question I knew she had been dying to ask since Duncan showed up this evening. "Tell us, are you dating anyone at the moment?"

I nearly choked at her bluntness; Dad rubbed his brows in frustration. "Mom!" I said embarrassed. "That's not really any of your business and is an incredibly rude thing to ask. I'm sure Duncan does not want to divulge his personal affairs to you, or anyone else for that matter."

"No, that's alright, Heidi," Duncan assured. "Honestly, it's a question I get asked a lot from the older women around town." Mom raised an eyebrow at the use of the term *older* women, but Duncan ignored her and continue. "People find it hard to believe that I'm not dating or haven't settled down yet. Which I understand. This is a small town and people either leave or start their lives here, and because I don't plan on leaving, people assume I want to lay down roots. So, I'll tell you, Mrs. Miller, what I tell them; one day I do plan on laying down roots. That *day* just so happens to be unknown. It's not fair for me to date women without the intention of marriage, so for now, I avoid it."

The honesty and charm in his voice had me hanging onto his every word. Hearing him speak so intimately was still a rare occurrence. Like a tiny window had been carved out of that wall he'd built around himself. It was refreshing and attractive as hell. I assumed it would be enough to pacify Mom and put an end to her incessant need for us to date, but it wasn't.

"All that matters is that I didn't hear *never*. There's hope for you two yet," she said cheerfully. "Now that the important matters are out of the way," Mom said as she turned her focus to me, "What was it that you'd like to talk to us about?"

That's what she finds important? Whether or not Duncan and I date? I don't think she's ever going to let this go.

Annoyed, I shot a look to Dad, hoping for assistance. He was too busy enjoying his lasagna to notice my eyes were like daggers on him. Everything in my bones yelled *Abort! Abandon mission!* But I had to face the eventual regret and dissatisfaction from my mom eventually. It was now or never. As I was getting ready tonight, I decided that I wanted this for me, regardless of how my parents felt about it. "I'm leaving," I finally said.

Mom's silverware clattered on her plate; Dad

finally looked up from his lasagna at me. Even Duncan's eyes grew wide with surprise.

"Tomorrow. For a week. Probably." Mom's expression was...anger? Hurt? I couldn't really tell. I looked over at Dad. He looked understanding. "It's only temporary, but I need to see a doctor. For therapy."

Now my dad looked confused. "Therapy? Is everything ok?" he asked in a sympathetic tone as he reached his hand for mine.

Before I got the chance to answer, Mom huffed and stormed out of the kitchen and down the hallway.

Strike three.

"I'll go check on her. Please don't go, yet." Dad sat his silverware down on the table and went after her.

I took a deep breath in and exhaled. Looking at Duncan, embarrassed, I said, "Sorry you had to see that."

He held his hand up and shook his head, "No. I'm sorry I inadvertently intruded on your plans."

That reminded me, "Why are you here again?"

"Your mom invited me, remember?"

"Yeah. But why did agree to come?" Lowering my voice, while pointing between the two of, I said "I thought we both agreed we'd keep this between us."

Duncan's eye lowered and his face hung, almost like he's been caught doing something he shouldn't have. "We did," he said, lifting his green eyes to mine. "But to be honest, I do see myself settling down with you, Heidi." He shrugged slightly, "I thought that maybe you felt the same way?"

"Settling down with you?" I searched his eyes for

answers, "Where is this even coming from, Duncan?" My mind was racing with so many thoughts.

"Not right now, of course," he reassured me. "But in the future. I know that neither one of us are in the right head space right now, but I'd like to think that maybe one day, we both would be ready."

Oh. In the future. I let my mind wander to a future where I could be Mrs. Duncan Johnson. Surprisingly, I smiled at the thought, it could be nice. Nice to have someone to come home too each day. Nice to be able to hold hands in public. Nice to look into his beautiful green eyes any time I wanted. Filling his dick inside me, any time we wanted. The warmth that started between my thighs quickly froze.

What if all of those things would have to be experienced here, in Mount Hopewell, without a chance for adventure?

I've known Duncan for a long time. We've been fucking for years, but we had never talked about developing our relationship beyond what it was now. If he was adamant about living here, would he open to stepping away occasionally to experience something different? What if he thought I spent too much time in my head, in my dreams, like my family did and started to resent me for it?

I took his hands in mine, "Duncan, I…" I heard my parents coming down the hall. I snatched my hands away from Duncan's and placed them in my lap.

"Heidi," Dad entered the kitchen with Mom, "your mother has something she'd like to say to you."

Mom slid her chair closer to mine and took a seat. "Sweetheart, I'm sorry for the way I reacted. As a mother, you do everything humanly possible to be there for your children. To love them, support them, to protect them, and to heal them when they're hurting. And to hear, out of the blue, that you need therapy, hurt me."

"Mom, I…"

"Let me finish." She placed her hand on my knee. "To know that you can't come to me about things that trouble you tells me that I'm failing you. Now, on top of that, I'm scared to lose you."

"Mom, I'm just going over to Easton City. I'll only be gone for a week. Olivia will cover for me at the store."

"It's not that. You'll be in the city for a week. You've spent your whole life here, dreaming of wild and exotic alternate lives. I'm scared that once you get a taste of city life, you won't be coming back. I'm worried you're going to like it better in the city and leave us behind and never look back." Tears began to roll down Mom's face.

I reached out and hugged her tightly. "Mom, this will always be home. If I do decide the city life is for me, it's not like I'll never come back." I was in awe of my mom's vulnerability. I've never seen this side of her before.

"There's just so much we'll miss out on if you're not here with us every day. It's a privilege to have my daughters still with me. But I love you and want you to be happy. There's no need to seek therapy." She squeezed my knee and smiled at me. "I'll do better at supporting you. I'm sorry I made you feel like you needed therapy because you think I'm such a terrible mother."

I narrowed my eyes at her. "It's not because I think you're a terrible mother. That's not at all why I'm seeking therapy."

Mom's eyebrows pulled together as she straightened up in her chair and put her hands on her hips, "Then what for?"

"I've been having some terrible dreams lately. And I need to figure out what's causing them so I can hopefully stop them."

She stood forcefully from her chair and adjusted her eyes from me to Dad. "Do you hear this, Arnold? She needs therapy… for her *dreams*. I told you not to encourage her. I knew something like this would happen." She rubbed her temples with her fingers before turning to me, completely ignoring the fact that Duncan was still sitting beside me. "They're just dreams, Heidi. There's nothing more to it than that. Your dreams are not special. You're just bored," she hissed.

I saw my dad shift his weight from one foot to the other out of the corner of my eye. "Maxine, that's enough. Our daughter is hurting. Regardless of the reason." He offered me an apologetic look.

"Oh please. She does this all the time. Makes impulsive decisions and puts all her energy into the outlandish thoughts she gets from those dreams. Mark my words, she's got this idea that she needs therapy, but she'll be back. She'll get there, have a *bad* dream, and come running home. Letting her dreams dictate yet another decision in her life."

I refused to continue to sit here and listen to her anymore. I slammed my fists on the table and shoved my chair behind me as I stood up. I gave my mom the dirtiest look I could muster before shoving behind Duncan and pushing past my dad standing in the doorway of the kitchen.

Pulling on my shoes and jacket quickly, I slammed the front door behind me as I left. I pulled my phone from my back pocket as I made my way to my car. In the passenger seat of my car sat my purse. I pulled Dr. Keller's business card from the front pocket and dialed the number listed. Her voice mail answered. "Dr. Keller, it's Heidi Miller. I'll be there in the morning."

Chapter 15

"Well, that could have gone better," I said aloud to myself as I closed my front door behind me and leaned against it. I can't believe Mom thought I needed therapy because I felt she was a terrible mother. She drove me nuts, but I've never thought that of her. Even more, I couldn't believe she said she'd be more supportive, then turned right around and acted the exact opposite. So much for seeing her vulnerable side.

I groaned as I finally peeled myself away from my door. I kicked my shoes haphazardly across the living room floor as I walked toward the hallway. The hard wood floors creaked beneath my feet, echoing how I felt inside – buckling from the pressures that surrounded me.

My home, like my dreams, had always served as a solace for me. I think it would be an adjustment for me to be anywhere else for the rest of the week. Even though it was only temporary, I worried that I would miss it.

I bought this house when I was just twenty-two years old. I wasn't ready to be a homeowner then but surviving under the same roof as my mom without Oliva proved to be difficult. This house was the first to go up for sale after Olivia moved out. It was two doors down from hers and I knew it was the perfect opportunity to get out. We knew we wanted to live close to each other and I didn't want to miss the opportunity. I was hoping that the house next door to her would eventually go up for sale, but it never did. And it still hasn't in the four years that I've lived here.

My home was nothing fancy, like I expected to see in the city, but it was all mine. It was small, like a lot of other homes in Mount Hopewell. Most homes around here only had two bedrooms. A few, like my parents' and Ronny's for example, had three bedrooms. The one thing all these houses had in common was a sizeable chunk of land. Each house sat on at least an acre, some had more.

Growing up, these yards were full of kids. Running around, playing tag, or hide and go seek. It was sad to see these yards mostly empty these last handful of years. We still had several kids around, but it wasn't anything like it was when I was a kid. It was one more reason that made me hesitant to settle down. If I decided to raise a family here, would there be neighborhood kids for them to play with?

I shook away my train of thought, I needed to get busy packing.

As I pulled my duffle bag down from the top of my closet and carried it to the bathroom with me, a ball of nerves began to unravel in my stomach. I replayed my mom's words over and over.

What if she's right? What if I get there and come running back home?

No. I couldn't think like that. I needed to do this for me. I needed to understand my dreams, and why this paralysis was happening to me.

After I brushed my teeth and washed my face, I packed my tooth paste and moisturizer into a small bag with my mascara. I packed the rest of my toiletries up and placed them in my duffle bag. I needed enough to last me the week. I wouldn't be coming home early.

Setting the duffle bag down on the foot of my bed and making my way back to my closet, I glanced at the minimal options I had to choose from.

What are you supposed to wear during a week of therapy? Jeans. Sweatpants? What if I want to wander out in the city, should I bring something nice?

I fingered my way through the selection of clothes hanging up, looking for anything that might be acceptable, but I found it lacking. Letting out a sigh, I decided on my usual style of jeans and tee shirts.

As I began to fill my duffel bag with my lousy choice of clothing, my thoughts wandered back to supper again, back to Duncan.

Why the hell did he think it was okay to show up to supper with my family? We have an understanding.

I heard a quick knock from my back door.

Speaking of Duncan.

I dragged my socked feet down the hallway, across the floor to my unlit kitchen to the back door. Duncan's tall figure shadowed against the door jam. "May I come in?" he asked. I stepped aside, allowing him just enough space to squeeze through. I let the door close heavily behind him.

Crossing my arms, partially annoyed with him I asked, "You didn't get enough drama for one night?" He swallowed hard and the muscles in his shoulders tightened under his long sleeve button down shirt.

"I'm sorry. It felt like we needed to finish our conversation."

"Why? What good would it do?" I wondered aloud as I walked back to my bedroom to finish packing. He followed behind.

"Because, Heidi, I want to be honest with you. About how I feel. I'm serious when I say I can see a future with you. And one day, not today, but some day once I've worked through my demons, I hope you'll feel the same."

I turned to him and looked up into his eyes. I was seeing a side of him tonight that I wasn't sure even existed anymore. It was hard to resist him. "Is that why you canceled your date with the nurse?"

He ran his hand through the hair on the back of his head, his biceps flexed under his sleeve. "You know about that, huh?"

"Yeah. Your parents came by the store needing groceries for chicken noodle soup. They said you told them you weren't feeling well and had to cancel your date. But we both know you were here, in my bed." Warmth started to coil in my belly thinking how good it felt to be wrapped in his embrace. "Why would you cancel on her just to sleep on my couch? It's not like I would have been hurt if you told me that you had other plans. I heard she's educated *and* beautiful. Sounds like you missed out on a good one," I teased.

"Because, it's *you* that I care about." He placed his hands on my hips and pulled me closer to him. "Tell me you don't feel the same way I do."

My heart raced as butterflies fluttered around in my belly. I cared about him, but I was scared, so I lied. "I'm not sure that I can." Duncan and I have known each other since we were eleven years old. We've always been friends. But there's a difference in knowing someone and knowing someone intimately. There was a time where I had big feelings for Duncan, and thought he had feelings for me, but sometime after high school, his walls went right back up. And now, I didn't want to complicate our relationship. Right now, there were no strings attached. It was easy and didn't hurt.

He leaned down and greeted my mouth with his. His lips soft and warm, locked with mine. Before I allowed myself to get lost in the draw of his mouth, I stopped him. "Duncan, how can you say that? How can you feel that way? We don't really know each other outside of the bedroom. Outside of our childhood." Guilt flashed behind his eyes at the mention of our childhood. He tried to interject but I was on a roll and couldn't stop. "What if my mom is right? What if I love the city and don't come back? After tonight, I'd say there's a strong possibility of that happening."

His voice low and breathy, he said, "Then I'll wait for you."

The honesty and vulnerability at the end of his words sent ripples of wanting through my body. I reached up and wrapped my arms around his neck. Duncan held his arms under my butt and lifted me to wrap my legs around him. Our lips met again, quick and ravenous. Duncan pushed my duffle bag off the end of my bed before taking a seat with me still clung around his waist. Wasting no time, I began to unbutton his shirt, drinking in the vision underneath. I pushed his shirt down over his broad shoulders and he shook his arms free of its sleeves. With my hands on his chest, taught with muscles, I ran my hands through his thin tufts of chest hair. I lowered my hands over his abs, following his happy trail to the buckle of his belt. His chest was heaving, and I could smell the sweet scent of arousal on his neck as I left a trail of kisses. Slowly, I undid his belt buckle, then the button on his jeans, exposing the smooth elastic waist band of his boxers.

Tugging at the hem of my shirt, Duncan pulled it up over my head and tossed it on the floor. His hands made their way up my back, to the clasp of my bra, and effortlessly undoes it. The straps fell low on my arms, exposing my breast. My nipples firmed with anticipation. He pulled my bra off and tossed it before taking each of my breast in his strong hands. Rolling my nipples between his finger and thumbs. I felt his eyes wander down my body as I leaned my head back in indulgence. He turned us over and laid me on the middle of the bed. He took a hold of the waist band of my sweatpants and panties and pulled them down over my feet. He took his time to look over my bare body, wet and ready for him.

"Are you going to make love to me?" I said teasingly, provoking him to remove the rest of his clothes and finally freeing his erection.

He flashed me a devilish grin and spread my legs with his knees. Teasing my folds with the tip of his cock, he leaned down to my ear and growled, "No. I'm going to fuck you."

Filling my insides, Duncan thrusted his dick deeply between my thighs, causing me to gasp. My back arched involuntarily, and he slid his arm under my back, pulling my hips closer to his. He leaned back as he held my hips in place. He slid out of me, allowing me to feel each of his inches before he slammed back into me. Over and over again. Grunting with each thrust.

I started to grind against him each time his pelvis met mine. Duncan's strokes got faster, bringing me closer to climax. I looked up to his eyes, his expression was primal. The pleasure building inside of me finally sent vibrations from my center, allowing me to lose myself in a blissful release. Duncan fucked me for a few more strokes before he guided his warm load all over my belly. He rolled and laid beside me, calming his breaths, before he fetched a towel to wipe his cum off me.

We settled underneath my blanket and laid side by side in silence. Focused on settling my pounding heart, I drifted off to sleep.

***

I'm in the store, Olivia is in the back speaking with a customer. The bell above the door jingles and Duncan comes through it.

"Hey, babe," he said as he leaned over the counter and plants a tender kiss on my lips.

"Hi!" I said gleefully.

"I brought us some lunch; thought you could step away for a bit."

I yelled back to Olivia that I'd be back in a bit. She waved us on.

Duncan and I take a quick walk to the stream in the woods behind the store. We took a seat at the top of the bank and he passed me a wrapped B.L.T. "The contractor stopped by the office today. He gave us the green light to drive out to the property to take a look at the house." Duncan took a bite of his own sandwich.

"Really! I can't wait to see the progress they've made. Did he say we were still on track to move in in six weeks?"

"He did. He also said he needs our paint samples for the bedrooms. I couldn't remember what shade of blue you were wanting for the nursery. What was it again? Skye blue? Baby blue? I really can't remember."

Nursery?

I laughed at his attempt to recall the correct shade of blue I had picked for our baby boy's nursery. "Maya blue, babe." We continued discussing plans for the house, and how we planned to decorate it, while we finished our lunch. We stood to walk back to the store when I noticed him watching us, the dark eyed man. Duncan continued to walk ahead but I was transfixed by the gaze cast upon me from the dark eyes. He seemed sad. I walk towards him, butterflies and arousal started to grow between my thighs. I closed my eyes to focus on this feeling. I could feel it grow stronger the closer I got to him. I opened my eyes. We're on the beach and it's just the two of us now. The cool water rushed over our feet.

"You left me," I said to him. "Why?"

"I didn't mean to." He takes my hands in his and rubbed his thumbs over the tops of them. "I found you tonight because I wanted to tell you that I'm sorry. And to tell you goodbye."

"Goodbye? So, you do exist outside of my dreams?"

"Please don't follow me or try and find me."

"Find you? I don't even know you. Please," I plead, "Tell me what's going on."

He runs his hand through my hair and leans down to take me in a kiss. Pleasure erupts from my center, and I can't help but to lean into him, meeting his kisses with my own. But when I opened my eyes, it's Duncan's face that I see.

Chapter 16

Five a.m. came and the alarm from my phone rang out, letting me know it was now or never. Looking over the screen, I noticed I had a voicemail. I played it out loud on my phone's speaker, "Hi Heidi. It's Dr. Keller. We'll have your room ready when you arrive. See you soon."

"So that's Dr. Keller, huh?" Duncan's voice startled me.

I completely forgot he was still here. I turned over to look at him. His head rested gently on his pillow and his eyes were still closed. For some reason, the sight made me smile and thoughts of my dream came flooding back to me. It's going to be hard to pull myself out of this bed and away from him.

His eyes finally opened, and he looked up at me. "Hey, is everything alright? You look upset." He placed his hand on the side of my face, softly stroking his thumb along my cheek bone.

I allowed myself to sink into his touch for just a moment, still reliving the scenes from my dream. Before seeing the dark eyed man, I wasn't troubled by the depiction I witnessed during my slumber. Duncan and I, starting a family. "I'm okay. I just have a lot on my mind, and I'm worried that I'm getting cold feet."

"This will be good for you, Heidi. Not only will you get help for your sudden dream anxiety, but you'll also get to experience a place outside of here. Even if it just for a week," Duncan reassured me. "Do you have time for breakfast? Maybe I could whip you up something before you go?"

"I appreciate the offer, but I really should get going." I begrudgingly slid out of bed and tidied up a little, picking clothes up off the floor from last night and tossing them into the hamper. I picked my spilled duffle bag off the floor and set it on the foot of the bed. Careful not to hit Duncan's feet, I began looking for my toiletries bag. I forgot that I'd need it again this morning before I actually left for Easton City. It wasn't in there. I kneeled to check under my bed. Where was that damn bag? I needed to shower.

"Heidi." Duncan called my name, disrupting my search. From my hands and knees, I peeked over my bed at him. He's leaned up against the headboard, one arm behind his head, his dick becoming erect, "If you're looking for your toiletry bag, it's over there." Nodding his head in the direction of my closet.

I turned and saw the black and purple accented bag lying on the floor near my closet. It must have slid out when Duncan pushed my duffle bag off my bed last night. "Yep," I said, standing to my feet before walking over to grab it. "I didn't think I'd need to wash the dried remnants of cum off of me this morning. Not that I mind," I smiled, "but I need to shower and get ready."

"Mind if I join you? Send you away on a proper goodbye," he said as he eyed my naked body up and down.

The husky tone of his voice sent heat between my thighs. "I would enjoy that very much." I turned to make my way to the bathroom, turning the shower on for the two of us. He came up behind me and grabbed both my breasts, pulling me into his body. He leaned down and kissed my neck. His throbbing erection was pressed hard against my lower back. I reached my hand under the water to test the temperature, it was perfect. My inner thighs were slick with arousal, and I was eager to feel him inside me.

The heat of the water stung my skin in all the best ways as we stepped inside, turning my skin pink. Duncan's hands traveled down my body, traveling toward my mound. Inching closer and closer, a breath escaped my throat, desperate to feel his touch there. Right before he reached it, I heard my name being called from the living room.

Duncan froze and my eyes widened. We paused to still ourselves, trying to listen over the sound of water rushing from the shower head.

"Heidi?" We heard someone call again.

"Shit, it's Olivia." I started to panic. "Fuck fuck fuck. Where'd you park your truck?"

"Down at the trail head. Did you leave your door unlocked?"

"No. But we have keys to each other's houses." He looked curiously at me. "Don't you and Ronny have each other's house key?"

He shrugged, "Are we supposed to?"

"Oh! We don't have time for this, Duncan," I said, playfully hitting him in the chest. "Stay here." I said quietly to him. I stepped out of the shower and wrapped a towel around me. Still dripping wet, I carefully made my way across my bedroom floor. Rounding the corner to the hallway, Olivia and I frightened each other, damn near running into one another. I placed my hand on my chest, "Oh my gosh!

Olivia, you scared the hell out of me," I said laughing now. "What are you doing here?"

"I just wanted to come by and see you before you left. Mom told me what happened last night."

"No, I mean, what are you doing here. In this hallway?"

"Well, I knocked for a few minutes, but you didn't answer. I got worried and decided to use my key."

"Oh, yeah, sorry. I was in the shower."

"I can see that," she said walking towards my bedroom still, forcing me to walk backwards. "I figured you could use some help packing and we could talk about what happened at Mom and Dad's last night."

Unable to stop her, Olivia suspiciously eyed the state of my room once she reached it. My sheets were a disaster, my duffle bag still disheveled, and my shower was still running.

Noticing that I'm dripping water everywhere, she asked "You couldn't have dried off a little before running out here?"

"Yeah, no. You're right. What was I thinking?" I said, trying to brush her off and ger her out of here. "I was going to call you last night. But it was late, and I know Ronny just got back. I didn't want to spoil your evening with the drama of my life."

Olivia narrowed her eyes at me, "Uh huh." Continuing to cast her gauze wall to wall, analyzing every detail. She eventually stopped at the bathroom door that I left ajar. "You need to turn your water off before you run out of hot water. Wouldn't want Duncan getting cold in there would you?"

Dammit.

"Duncan?" I looked around, "Where?" I said in a lousy attempt to try and sidestep this whole thing.

"Duncan," she called toward the bathroom, "Go ahead and turn that water off. You know you don't have much longer before it turns cold on you."

I squeezed my eyes shut when the water shut off. "How'd you know?"

Oliva pointed to the pile of blankets on my bed. "A. You don't sleep wild enough for your sheets to look like that, even when you have bad dreams. B. If you *did* have a bad dream that made you move erratically in your sleep, you would've told me about it by now. And C. I see the sleeve of what looks like a man's shirt poking out right there." She shifted her finger slightly to point to a different area of the bed.

I looked to where she was pointing. Sure enough, wedged in-between my mattress and foot board, crumpled in with the throw blanket I keep at the foot of my bed, was Duncan's shirt. "O-okay. Well. How'd you know it was Duncan?" I asked crossing my arms at her with all the attitude of a child who just got caught red handed.

"Heidi, I see how the two of you try so hard to avoid each other's gaze whenever anyone is around. The secret glances you two shoot each other when you can't hold it in anymore. It's so painfully obvious to everyone, except to yourselves, that you have feelings for one another. What I don't know is why you felt you couldn't tell me about it."

Oliva sounded hurt. I hated that I had disappointed her. My eyes began to sting with tears.

Duncan opened the bathroom door, towel

wrapped around his waist, "It's not all her fault, Olivia."

Olivia turned to face him just long enough to realize he was half naked. She looked off in the distance beside him. I assumed it was an awkward situation for her. "Regardless of if she's partially at fault or not, I'm her sister." She said now looking at me, "We tell each other everything. Why couldn't you trust me with this?"

"Because I asked her not to." Duncan interjected again, trying to shield me from my sister's wrath.

"You know what, I don't have time for this. Good luck with therapy, Heidi." Olivia stormed out. I could hear the front door slam behind her as she exited the house.

Rubbing my forehead, I said, "We've fucked up now, Duncan."

He took a seat on my bed and turned me to face him. "I'm sorry." He tried to take my hands, but I pulled them away.

"I think it's best that you go." I walked back towards the bathroom to turn my shower back on. I didn't get to finish it earlier and I desperately need one now. "Your shirt is balled up between the foot board and I think I threw your jeans in the hamper. Please be gone by the time I'm out." I slammed the bathroom door behind me.

Standing under the warm spray of my shower head, I struggled to clear my thoughts. They were going in too many directions.

I hated that I had hurt my sister. She was truly my best friend. We didn't keep secrets from each other. I knew I would be hurt if I were in her shoes, so I understood her reaction. When you grew up in a town like ours, you learned to appreciate those who stuck around. Families that came through here, looking for residency, usually didn't stay longer than a year or two. And kids who lived here permanently were ready to leave the first chance they could. And sure, when old friends came to visit, it was a wonderful time, but it was temporary. They would soon return home, to their busy and eventful lives, and forget about this place until it was time for their next visit.

And Duncan. If I was being honest, I could see myself settling down with him too. Especially after these last few days. Seeing the vulnerable side of him made my chest swell. It reminded me of when we were younger. But how would I know if it was because I cared for him, or if it was because there's literally no one else worth a damn around here. And I could say the same for him too. How would I know he truly cared for me when he didn't have many options around here either?

How could I even be thinking about Duncan when my dreams had been plagued with this dark eyed man? Why was he always there? Was he a figment of my desires or was he real, like Michael?

If Michael was real, that means the dark eyed man could be too. And if the dark eyed man could be real then, so could the man who died in a field of purple flowers.

And what about the stillness? Could the stillness be real too?

The icy shock of the cold water halted my dizzying thoughts. I quickly rinsed my hair and turned off the water. I grabbed a fresh towel, since the first one I used was still soaked, and wrapped it around me. I steadied myself before I opened the door, wondering if Duncan had left or not.

Did I want him to leave?

Yes.

Right?

But what if he was still there? Still sitting on my bed. What would that mean? I contemplated the thought for a few minutes before opening the bathroom door, revealing that I was alone now. Duncan's towel hung from the foot board of my bed. A tinge of longing had been left in my chest seeing my empty bed. I rubbed my face with my hands, trying to rid my mind of these thoughts. "I've got places to be today, I need to pull myself together."

Retrieving my duffle bag, which was still a mess, I took a quick inventory to make sure I had everything packed. I carried it out to load it, then myself, into the car.

I'll call Dad from the road to let him know I was leaving.

But first, I needed to text Olivia.

Heidi: I'm sorry that I didn't tell you sooner. I promise I'll tell you everything when I get back. Love ya.

Chapter 17

Entering the lobby of the Keller Institute, I was greeted by the cheery, brunet receptionist. "Good morning and welcome to Keller Institute. Do you have an appointment?"

Gosh, I would hope so. Otherwise, this big duffle bag I've got slung over my shoulder looks really suspicious.

"Hi, yes. I'm here to...check in?" I wondered if that was the correct terminology. "My name is Heidi Miller."

The receptionist looked over the screen of her computer. "Ah, yes. Hi Miss Miller. Take a seat and someone will be out shortly to escort you to your room."

I took a seat on one of the lush mocha-colored couches and picked up a magazine from a near by end table and started to flip through it. The pages were filled with celebrity gossip and photos of celebrity weddings. Seeing women in their beautiful gowns at stunning venues made me think back to Duncan. Was life in Mount Hopewell so bad that I'd give up a man like him?

Maybe I should just go back home, I haven't had a bad dream in two nights.

"Heidi! I'm so glad you could make it." I looked up in the direction from which my name was being called and saw Dr. Keller walking towards me. I placed the magazine down and stood to greet her.

Meeting her outreached hand for a shake, she said, "Please, follow me, we have your room prepared for your stay."

Nerves started to weigh heavy in my stomach, "You know, I may have acted too rashly. I haven't experienced a bad dream in two nights. Maybe I don't really need therapy after all," I said suddenly second guessing my decision to come here.

"You're exactly where you need to be. You've already made the journey here, why don't you give it at least one night. You're free to leave at any time," Dr. Keller assured me.

After mulling it over, I nodded in agreement. "You're right." I reminded myself, this could be an opportunity to learn more about my dreams, not just heal me from the stillness.

"Great!" She said a little too enthusiastically if you'd ask me. "Follow me, I'll show you to your room." We started down a hallway with three offices, a set of doors labeled as the gym, a stairwell, and a single elevator. The walls were decorated with black framed photos. All with different subjects. "Rita, our administrative assistant will be by shortly to go over some paperwork with you and you're proposed treatment plan." Dr. Keller pressed the button indicated with a number two to take us to the second floor.

"My proposed treatment plan?" I asked as the elevator doors closed and began our journey up. I noticed there's also a B on the panel of buttons. Basement?

"Yes. Based on our preliminary session, I'm confident I know exactly what you'll need." We rode in silence for the next minute or two until the bell dinged, letting us know we were on the second floor. She motioned for me to follow her. "We're a small facility, and don't function like a normal institute or rehab. Most of my patients seek treatment for addiction but all of our patients are free to come and go throughout the day. We do have a curfew. Because we use dreams to help overcome these addictions and anxieties, or in your case a fear, and it's best to get to bed at a decent hour. Your sleep quality isn't optimal if you're overly tired from the day." We stopped at the end of an L shaped hallway, to a set of double doors. The sign above the door reads *Cafe.* "Here is where you'll come to get all your meals. You can eat here with other patients or take it back to your room. The hours are posted here," she pointed to the decal posted on the window of one of the Café doors. "In your room, you'll find the menu for the week. New menus are dropped off each Saturday for the following week."

We began to walk back towards the way we came. We stopped at the next room after the Cafe with a sign above the door labeled, *Nurse.* "We have a nurse on site twenty-four seven. Like I said, some patients are recovering or trying to overcome addictions and have to detox during therapy. But if you need over the counter medicines for any reason, here's where you'd want to come."

Turning left back down the main hallway, toward the elevators, we passed a series of rooms. Three rooms on one side of the hall, two rooms on the side with the elevators and stairwell. Each only labeled with a number, one through five. "These are our patient rooms. Each patient has a key to their respective room, but the staff also have copies in cases of emergencies." Dr. Keller pulled out a key ring with a single key and an oval key tag with the number four imprinted in it. "You'll be in room four, here at the end of the hallway. She unlocked and opened the door to the room and led me inside. I placed my duffle bag on the floor near the door.

The room was much cozier than I expected. There were more enlarged, black framed photos hanging on the walls around the room. Instead of various subjects, they were black and white photos of bodies of water. Beaches, rivers, and waterfalls, all breathtakingly beautiful. The center wall was accented with a matte silver damask wallpaper, the bed sat in the middle with cream-colored pillows and bed spread. Two warm brown throw pillows sat decoratively at the head of the bead. On either side of the bed were small, circular, faux gold leafed tables. There was a cream-colored armchair in the corner of the room, just outside the door to the adjoining bathroom. On the opposite wall of the bathroom, there was a small closet with a pocket door and a chest of drawers for putting our clothes away in. "This is lovely. Definitely not what I was expecting," I said to Dr. Keller.

"Thank you," she said proudly, "we get that a lot. Therapy, of any kind, can be daunting and we want to ensure our patients have a space where they can come relax and clear their heads if needed. Downstairs, we also have a small fitness room with some light workout equipment. From there, you can head to our outdoor area. It's not much, but it's private from the street's view, guarded by tall hedges. There are places to sit in the shade under the pergola or enjoy the sunshine if you'd prefer." She walked over to the chest of drawers where a welcome packet sat and picked it up. "In here, you'll find the hours for the café, nurse's office, and the fitness room. There's also a key card for you to reenter the building with if you're out after hours, just keep in mind of the curfew, which is nine p.m. That information is in here too." she said as she sat it back down. "I know this has been a lot of information. Do you have any questions about anything so far?"

Hmmm. "When does treatment start and how does it all work," I finally asked.

"Rita will process your intake paperwork and then you and I have an appointment scheduled for two p.m. This appointment is to get more details that we may not have been able to discuss during our initial appointment. After that, we'll talk you through the process of measuring your brainwaves with an electroencephalogram."

"An electo-what-now?" I asked confused and a little nervous.

Dr. Keller chuckled softly, "It's not as scary as it sounds. It's just a cap that we place around your head that holds electrodes attached to your scalp. We mostly use it to monitor your REM sleep cycles." I had another confused look on my face at the mention of REM. "We'll get into all of that the next time we speak. But I promise, it's not as scary as it all sounds. I'll see you in a bit." She exited to the hallway, shutting the door behind her.

I flipped through the packet left on top of the

chest of drawers and grab the key card knowing I would be needing it later. In all my twenty-six years, I have only come to Easton City for doctor's appointments or to visit the big box stores.

When my sister and I were kids, we'd come up here for school supplies and clothes if we didn't have them in stock at the store. In the past, as a young adult, I had still only come here for the big box stores. That was before I discovered online shopping.

None of my friends from school moved here either since it was pretty close to home. Outside of shopping for things I couldn't find back home, I've never ventured out here. Not even for leisure. But this time, I planned to take advantage of the city while I was here.

Grabbing my duffle bag from beside the door, I brought it over to the closet and began to hang up my clothes. I put my toiletries away before settling into the surprisingly plush mattress and pulling out my cell phone. Still no response from Olivia. I made a mental note to remind myself to check on her later tonight.

I heard a knock from the door.

A sweet faced, pleasantly plumped woman, who looked to be in her early fifties, entered after the knock. "Hi there! My name is Rita, I'm here to process your intake paperwork. We'll also go over your payment plan," she announced cheerily.

Payment plan. A brief wave of nausea hit my stomach. I swallowed it away as I continued to remind myself the money spent will be worth it. I sat up straight on my bed and swung my legs over the side. "Hi there, I'm Heidi." I said as I offered a subtle wave.

"Mind if I take a seat?" She gestured toward the chair in the corner of the room, I nodded my head in response. Rita did and she flipped open the front panel of her tablet's folio case. "This won't take too much of your time, I just need you to sign a few forms," she said as she tapped away on its screen. "A few forms for HIPAA, your contact information, Health History, etc." Once she was finished on her tablet, she brought it over to me. "Tap next to take you to each signature. For your contact and health information, just tap the fields to edit. Let me know if you have any questions as you go through the forms."

"So, everything that I answer on here, automatically is saved in your system?"

Rita looked confused but answered anyway, "Erm, yes?"

"Hmm," I nodded my head with a thought of how this could be something we could use at the store. "Interesting." I filed the thought away, to ask Mom and Dad once we were on better terms, then I got to work on completing those forms. "So…how long have you worked here?" I asked because I don't know how not to talk to strangers.

"Oh. Umm, since its inception. So, eleven years almost." Rita, answered.

"Oh, wow! You like it here, huh?" I continued to fill out the forms on the tablet.

She nodded and smiled warmly. "Dr. Keller does amazing work and it's a true pleasure seeing her patients happy. I don't have any medical or psychology background like she and the rest of her family, but this field of work has always interested me. And I enjoy being a part of it."

"The entire family are doctors?" I asked, amazed, continuing to fill out the last form.

"Not quite. Her husband gave up his medical research career to become a photographer. These are all his pictures you'll see hanging up all throughout the Institute." She gestured with her hand toward one of the framed photos on the wall. "But her son is a therapist. He also works here at the Institute."

"I wasn't aware this was a family practice." Made me think about my family and the store, maybe I was lucky to be able to work with my family. "That must be nice for Dr. Keller."

Rita shrugged her shoulders, "It is, but it has its moments. She and her son, Graham, don't always see eye to eye."

"I can relate," I said with a sympathetic nod. I handed her back the tablet. "All done."

She scrolled through and tapped a few things before she said, "Great. Any questions about any of the forms?" I shook my head no. "Alrighty then. Let's go over your payment plan. We don't charge you until your therapy is completed. You can pay in full, bimonthly, or monthly. Please indicate which schedule you prefer. The balance for your proposed plan is here." She pointed to the number at the bottom of the page which nearly made me faint. I quickly selected monthly, signed on the bottom line, and handed it back to her before my cold feet returned. "Thank you for your time and have a great rest of your day." And with that, she left and went on about her day.

I looked up at the photos and wondered if Mr.

Keller was a professional photographer, he must had seen some really beautiful places to have captured these.

Once I was done marveling at the photos, I returned my attention to my phone. I looked for something to do while I was waiting for my appointment with Dr. Keller. One of the first recommendations listed was a nail salon.

That could be interesting. I've never gotten my nails done before.

I grabbed my purse and made my journey to the lobby. On my way from the elevator, I viewed the framed photos adorning the walls with a different perspective. With more intent. To know that someone physically captured these stunning images, in person, made me a little envious. The photos were mostly of places, objects, and nature but never of people. The exception was a set of black and white photos hanging towards the middle of the hallway, one on either side of the hall. In one of the photos, you could see what looked like pyramids far off in the background, but a child's smiling face was taking up the majority of the frame. His light-colored hair was a mess with his eyes squeezed tight and a grin from ear to ear. His happiness was evident. In the other picture, the same pyramids, but this time, the boy's eyes were opened.

Something about them felt familiar, but I couldn't quite place it.

Chapter 18

Using my freshly manicured hand, I knocked on Dr. Keller's door. "Come in!" Her smiling voice rang from inside. She gestured for me to take a seat on the couch in front of her. She was writing a few things down in her folio as I settled into a comfortable seat. Once she was finished writing, she flipped to a fresh page and looked up at me, "Ah, you got a manicure I see," referencing my bright blue nail color.

"I did! It was the first time I'd ever gotten a manicure. In a nail salon anyway. I've painted my nails once or twice, but they never turned out this well."

"Yes, I find it best to leave it to the professionals. I was never any good at painting my own nails either," she said with a smile. "So, when we last spoke this morning, you seemed to have questions about the electroencephalogram."

"Yes," I said nervously.

Dr. Keller picked up a swim cap styled cap with tons of holes all over its surface. "We'll place this cap on your head, for you to wear while sleeping, and we'll attach little electrodes to your scalp through these openings," she said pointing to a few of the tiny holes. "We use a special type of glue that will keep the electrodes in place." My eyes got big at the mention of glue. "Don't worry, the glue won't ruin your hair, but you will want to wash it after the cap is removed."

"Does it hurt? All those electrodes on my scalp like that?"

"Not at all. The worst thing about this is that the cap may be uncomfortable while you sleep. But what we'll use this for is to determine if you're experiencing any REM sleep, or Rapid Eye Movement sleep cycles. And if you are, we'll need to measure how long you're in the REM sleep cycle. This will help us understand your sleep architecture. Studies show that you're able to experience the most vivid dreams while in your REM cycle." Dr. Keller placed the cap back down on her side table. "Any questions so far?" I shook my head. "Okay. Stop me if you have any. Tonight, is only to capture initial measurements of your sleep cycles. Depending on the results, we may have some sleep aids and techniques to help you prolong your REM cycles." She wrote something down on her note pad and asked, "How often would you say that you remember the dreams you have? Meaning, you can vividly retell the account of the dream or dreams you had the night before."

Pursing my lips in thought, "All the time actually. Each of my dreams feel real, like I'm physically there. They almost feel more like memories rather than dreams, in the sense that I'm aware of and can recall emotions or sensations I might be experiencing. But also, not like a memory at all. It feels like I can control what I do in my dreams, that I dictate the actions of my dream self. If that makes any sense at all."

Dr. Keller smiled and nodded, "It does." She took a quick note. "You told me about a dream you had, that allowed you to locate a hiker?"

"A bird watcher, who went hiking," I corrected. "But yes. It felt like I was there, on that bridge looking over into the river below me. The sound of rushing water was loud in my ear. I could even feel the warmth from the sun. When I saw that backpack and then those boots, I felt panicked that someone may be hurt."

"Is that dream the first dream you've experienced where you've been aware of your emotions and senses?"

"No. If I'm standing on a beach and the water rushes over my feet, I feel the icy touch it leaves behind. In a dream I recently had, my mom and I got into an argument. She was angry with me, and I felt frustrated."

"Why did you feel frustrated?"

"I decided to tell her about the murder I witnessed in my dream – the same one I told you about. But she was furious with me. I only told her because I wanted to get it off my chest, hoping it would alleviate my need for wanting to actually tell her. It wasn't a topic I could bring up with her in life, but I had hoped I could get what I needed from her in my dream. But that didn't happen."

"What did you need from her?"

"Support. Understanding. To feel heard. What I expected was rainbows and butterflies, but what I got was the same grumpy mother who is always disappointed with her youngest daughter. The next day when we saw each other, she accused me of not pursuing a relationship because I was too busy being stuck in my head about that *silly* dream."

"And was that the first dream you were able to Connect with someone while dreaming?"

Connect? What does she mean, connect?

"I'm sorry, I don't know what you mean by Connect."

"No need to apologize. Connecting is when you're able to communicate with someone's consciousness and for it to communicate back to you."

What in the hell is she talking about right now, Connecting with consciousness?

She must have pick up on my confused expression. She decided not to wait for my answer before asking me her next question. "Or how about the first time you were able to dictate your actions?"

Oh, I can answer this one.

"Being able to dictate my own actions is something I've always been able to do, even at a young age. That's how I learned how to ski as a kid. I dreamed that I was back at the top of the slope, listening to the instructor, and eventually I was skiing in my dream. I asked my parents the next day if we could go back so I could test out my new dream achieved skill, and I've been able to ski ever since." Dr. Keller continued to take note of my words.

"Have you ever had occurrences of not being able to dictate your own actions?"

"Outside of times I felt legitimately paralyzed?" She nodded in response. I thought about the times where I wanted to reach out and touch the dark eyed man but couldn't. "Yeah."

"Would you be comfortable sharing those experiences?"

"Um, sure." I readjusted my posture on the couch, "Recently, I've been having dreams of a guy that I'm sure I don't know, he doesn't look familiar to me. Last week, I saw him watching me. I decided to approach him, but when I did, he took off. I followed him. When we finally stopped, and I tried to approach him, I couldn't." I decided to stop sharing there. No need to divulge why I wanted to approach him or any of the delicious details of his touch.

"Did the two of you talk about anything?" she asked.

"No. Not then anyway. Only in my last two dreams with him have we talked. The last time I saw him, he said he was sorry and goodbye."

"What was he sorry for?"

"In one of the dreams, he looked like he needed help, so I went to him. He was resistant and told me I shouldn't be there, but I couldn't just leave him. He was on the ground, on all fours, head hanging in distress. I knelt to take his hand but once I did, he was gone. But as I tried to leave, I experienced the stillness and struggled to wake up."

"Does he make you nervous? This stranger."

"He didn't at first. But now I'm not sure." I started to pick at my freshly manicured nails. "I realize anytime that I follow him, we wind up in the same place. Rhythmic beeping tones sound from everywhere and nowhere. It's in that place, with that noise, where the stillness comes alive. It feels like there's another presence around me. Or maybe both of us. Watching, tightening its grip. If I don't wake up or if I can't get away from that feeling quick enough, the paralysis usually sets in shortly after I become aware of it."

Dr. Keller turned to a fresh page in her pad, "What does this place look like?"

"It's a boring, dimly lit, grey room. And a door. A single door. That apparently can't be opened."

"And how did you get there? Is it the same way every time?

"No. The first time, I followed him. This most recent time, I approached a picture of a purple flower.

"Do any of those details hold any meaning to you? The flower, the grey room, or how about the beeping sound?"

I shook my head, no. "None of those things hold meaning for me."

"What about the door that can't be opened. Seems strange that you couldn't open it if you wanted to."

"Well, I'm not the one trying to open the door. The dark eyed stranger is."

She gave me a questioning look, "Then how do you know it can't be opened

I thought about her question. She made a good point. I guess I didn't know if it could be opened or not. "I guess I don't. It just seems like he struggles when he tries to open it. But why do those things matter?"

"Just trying to determine if it's your dream or his?"

I arched an eyebrow out of curiosity.

"Connecting. You could be Connecting to him."

My heart began to thump furiously behind my chest. My thoughts from this morning began spiraling around in my mind again. "Are you saying that he could be… real?"

"He very well could be. There have been instances where individuals have shared dreams, or Connected, with another person. But a recurrence has never been documented before."

I started to feel dizzy. This was a lot to process. Earlier, it was just an unlikely hunch. Now, it was plausible.

"Currently, there's not enough research on those instances of Connections. We have yet to determine whose brain the dream is originating from and who's the visitor," she explained. "Would it be alright if I shared something personal with you?"

Surprised she felt the need to ask to share something, I nodded my head. Maybe it would help distract me from my intrusive thoughts. "Of course."

"This phenomenon, Connecting, is what first piqued my interest in the field of dream study. My son, who is also a therapist here at the institute, shared a dream with his cousin when he was about seven years old. My nephew, who was ten at the time, had fallen into a frozen pond near their home and was hospitalized for a few days, he thankfully made a healthy recovery. But my son woke up one morning, telling me he had a terrible dream about Nicky being cold, wet, and scared; that Nicky had fallen in the pond. He was insistent that I call my sister to check in on him. After realizing my son was able to tell us things he couldn't have known unless he had witnessed the events himself, I decided to shift my field of study. Throughout mine, and my colleagues' years of researching Connecting, we eventually discovered that our minds are still busy working while our bodies are sleeping. For example, you learned how to ski because you dreamed about it, right?"

I nod, trying to focus on her words.

"Right. You experienced a lucid dream, meaning you were aware that you were dreaming and had the ability to control your actions within your dream. As a result, your body remembered your brain's programming for skills required to ski successfully. We take that same principle and turn it into a mechanism for healing. For my patients who are striving to overcome addiction, we introduce a few techniques to put them in a lucid dream. From there, our goal is to trigger thoughts or events of pain and turmoil. To put them against their addiction and have them overcome and build strength against their urges. This way, they're able to practice being sober and turning down their vices, giving them more opportunities to be confident in their healing and their sobriety. For my patients that seek help to overcome anxieties or fears, we try and have them dream about whatever it is that weighs heavy on them and give them opportunities to confront it. To become stronger than their fear."

Sitting, just staring at her, somewhat amazed, I tried to process what she was telling me. People being taught to control what they dreamed about and being taught how to control their actions doesn't sound so crazy to me. But *Connecting*, or whatever it was called, is what I was struggling with. I thought the dream with my mom, and then again with Michael, could be flukes. And to be honest, that was what I was hoping they would be. That way, I could put the murder and the dark eyed man out of my mind and focus on what was causing my paralysis. I decided to keep an open mind and tried to understand a little bit better. I might as well get the most out of this opportunity. "But if I'm here to get over my fear of dreaming, how can you help me get to a dream state, if I'm scared to dream to begin with?"

"That's just it, you're not scared of dreaming, you're scared of feeling paralyzed, activating your fight-or-fight response." I thought on her words for a moment, realizing she was right. I did love to dream, but the feeling I got when the stillness overpowered me, I was terrified. "After understanding your sleep architecture, I will discuss some techniques that would best benefit you in achieving success."

Considering everything she just said, a question came to mind. "So, if I'm understanding you correctly, lucid dreaming isn't uncommon for people to experience." She nodded in agreement. "But sharing dreams, or Connecting isn't common?"

"Correct. Lucid dreaming is more common in a greater population of people, but it doesn't necessarily mean that lucid dreaming is experienced often within that population. Connecting is a rare occurrence across an already small population. And even so, recurrence has never been documented if it's ever been experienced by anyone. But that could change with you."

"Come again?"

"I believe you have experienced a recurrence of Connecting. Your first occurrence would have been the dream you shared with your mom. The second with the bird watcher. Not to mention, these dreams you have of this man, this could be another instance of recurrence. It would be a major breakthrough for dream studies."

The thought is overwhelming. My mind started to drift off to several questions again when a knock sounded from the door.

"Ah, that must be Graham," Dr. Keller said as she checked the time on her wristwatch. "I've asked my son to stop by towards the end of our session so I can introduce him. He will be assisting in your treatment." She looked towards the door and called, "Come in."

I hear the door open from behind me. Still in my seat on the couch, I turned towards the door, expecting to be greeted by a blond hair, blue eyed man of average height. Instead, a tall, dark-haired man entered. The white collared dress shirt he was wearing practically glowed against his warm skin.

He gave his mom a subtle smile and nod hello.

I was becoming lightheaded.

He then turned his attention to me. The smile he wore had morphed into a mask, trying to conceal a revelation.

I was unsure at first glance, but now I was certain.

The look in his eyes was unmistakable. The man that entered the room was the dark eyed stranger who plagued my dreams.

Chapter 19

Slamming the door of room number four behind me in a hurry, I was finally alone with my thoughts. I paced the floor of my temporary room here at Keller Institute, replaying the most awkward of introductions ever. Dr. Keller's son was the dark eyed man from my dreams. How could that be?

Three. There have now been three examples to prove that my dreams are more than just a *dream*. They were something more.

This can't be a fluke, or just a coincidence. Because, if that's true. Then maybe, just maybe, so is the murder of the man in the field of flowers.

Oh wait. The flower.

Dr. Keller asked if I had any association to the flower I saw before going to the grey room with the dark eyed man – whose name was apparently Graham?

"Focus, Heidi," I said aloud to myself.

I took a deep breath and thought back to the flower. With the exception of my dream about the murder, I didn't have a connection to flowers.

Are the two dreams somehow related?

Continuing to pace the floor, I weighed the possibility of my last question.

It seemed unlikely that they could be related. The other elements of my dream with *Graham* – the grey room, the beeping, and supposed locked door – didn't connect to me in any way. The flower must be a coincidence.

But why did it lead me to him? Graham.

I had to immediately excuse myself once I realized who he was. I left no time to register his reaction to seeing me. I thought I saw a glimmer of recognition but didn't stick around to be sure.

Feeling physically ill, I told Dr. Keller that I needed to excuse myself to my room. I had to get the hell out of there as fast as possible. I would check in with her later.

Pressing the palms of my hands to my pounding head, I wished Olivia was here. She'd know how to calm me down and help me distance myself from overwhelming thoughts. All of this was a lot. Even for me, and I was used to being consumed by my thoughts.

I checked my phone again to see if she had texted me back yet, but still nothing. I paced over to the chest of drawers and sat my phone on top. I guessed I would have to calm my thoughts down without the sisterly advice I was used to receiving.

I took a few more deep breaths, trying to calm not only these rushing questions, but the nausea brewing in my belly. Once I felt a little more relaxed, I tried and sort through and assess my questions again.

Okay, lets start with the first question: Graham – Since it's apparent that he's real, how did he wind up in my dreams? Does that mean Dr. Keller is right, Connecting is real?

A soft tapping interrupted my internal questioning. "I'm alright Dr, Keller, but I'm not feeling very well right now. I'll check in with you in a little bit," I called to the door.

"It's not Dr. Keller." A familiar male's voice responded. With my heart pounding and the nausea returned, I stopped pacing and faced the door. "It's Graham. May I come in?"

I took a deep breath in and exhaled slowly through my mouth, steading my nerves. I walked to the door and opened it slightly. His face was even more handsome in person. His soulful brown eyes looked down to meet mine. The urge to reach up and touch his smooth jawline was powerful, but I resisted.

"Hi." It was all I could manage to get out, my voice breaking from nerves. I held the door open wide enough to allow him inside, but he didn't move. We stood, just staring at each other. His eyes scanned rapidly over my face in disbelief. His chest seemed still, as if he was holding his breath. It appeared he was just as thrown off guard as I was.

"May I…" He moved a fist over his mouth and cleared his throat before swallowing hard, "may I come in?"

I nodded.

He took the chair, and I awkwardly took a seat at the foot of the bed facing him. My heart was beating so loud that I could hear it in my ears. My stomach was twisting. Mostly from nerves but something new had been introduced – a craving. He ran his hand through his dark brown hair, and I could tell he was nervous too.

My phone rang, forcing my attention to where it sat. I entertained the thought of not answering it, but what if it was Olivia? I didn't want to miss her call. Looking apologetically at Graham, I said, "I'm sorry. I need to see who that is." I walked over to the chest of drawers. Olivia's name flashed across the screen. I turned back to him, "I'm sorry, I have to take this," tapping the green circle on the screen. "Hello," I answered as I faced away from Graham.

"Hi."

"Hi." I said holding my breath, waiting for her to unleash on me.

"I'm sorry…" we both said at the same time before we started to laugh at each other.

"No. I'm sorry," I said. "You're right, I should have told you everything. And I almost did the night you asked me about it. But Duncan and I agreed to keep it between us. I didn't want anyone catching wind about us. And I was trying to honor his wishes too."

"No, Heidi, you're completely right. That's between you and Duncan. I'll admit, it feels weird that you were able to keep something that big to yourself, but I understand why. Duncan is a good man. I know he has internal struggles and prefers to keep things about himself more private."

"Yeah. But hey, now that you know, I can give you all the details," I said with a giggle. "But, Olivia," I reminded, "please don't tell Ronny."

"I won't, but you'll have to back me up if he finds out that I've known, and he gets upset with me like I got upset with you for not telling me."

"Deal!" A smile spread across my face, happy to know she had forgiven me. I hated fighting with her.

"So, how's it going so far," Olivia asked.

"Umm, it's going." I'd like to unload all of my thoughts from the last time I saw her. Tell her all about my day so far here. And I really want to talk to her about my most recent feelings towards my *relationship* with Dunch, but Graham is still in here with me. "but hey, I actually do need to call you back, if that's okay. I am so sorry."

"No need to apologize. I understand. Give me a call tomorrow, okay?"

"I will. Love ya!"

"Love you too!" And we hung up.

I turned around to face Graham again. "Sorry about that. That was my sister. We had a bit of a fight this morning."

"About Ronny?" he asked sadly.

"What? No. Ronny is my sister's boyfriend. Or fiancé. She doesn't have a ring yet but they're planning on getting married."

"And what about Duncan?"

My eyes fell from his gauze. What about Duncan? I asked myself. He was just in my bed this morning before I left home and now, here I am with Graham trying to ignore the sensual craving between us. "It's a little complicated," I finally said.

"You care for him." He sounded wounded. "I could tell when I saw you two last night."

My eyes darted back up to him with slight embarrassment, remembering now that he was there in the dream I, or Duncan, had. Duncan and I were a family, with a baby on the way and a house being built. I'd be lying if I said the thought didn't make me feel warm inside. "Like I said, it's complicated." Wanting to change the topic, I asked, "why were you there last night?"

Graham stood and took a few long intentional strides towards me. He took my hands in his,

"Because, I needed to move on from you. I couldn't do that without telling you goodbye."

His touch felt intoxicating, but I was too confused and annoyed to get lost in it. "What does that even mean? You've popped up in my dreams… or I popped up in yours…" I tried to recall Dr. Keller's explanation, "it's all very confusing." Shaking the thought away, I refocused, "You've seen me a couple times and you're already so smitten that you have to *move on*? It really makes no sense."

He shook his head, "Not a few times, Heidi. For months." Reflexively, Graham's hands quickly pulsed around mine. "Just about every night I have seen you, but I wasn't sure if you could see me. It felt like I was just outside your view. At first, I wasn't aware that we were Connecting. But for months, I have tried to reach you. Talk to you." He moved one hand to my lower back, the other to my cheek and stroked it with his thumb, "*touch* you." He pulled me in, "I can't explain it, but you captivate me in ways that I've never been." He stared deeply into my eyes. "I had to say goodbye because you were a distraction."

I removed myself from his embrace and gave him a suspicious side eye, "*I* distract *you*. You sought me out remember?"

Graham looked apologetically at me, "I only meant that I have a job to do. To help people. Not only am I a therapist during the day, but I also have other… obligations at night. But I haven't been able to focus since I've found you. When I see you," he reached for my hand again, "I lose all track of my objectives. You consume my thoughts. You become my only priority."

A notification from his watch caused it to chime, causing him to glance at it and sigh. "I'm sorry," he said, "I have to go."

I shrugged, becoming exhausted and over stimulated with my thoughts. "Fine. I think I could benefit from a nap anyway. Today has been a lot."

"Okay." He squeezed my hand. "Please make sure you eat something soon though. And again, before you go to bed tonight. I'll be back tonight with my mother, I mean, Dr. Keller, and we'll set you up on the EEG." He offered an apologetic smile and left.

My shoulders felt heavy as I walked to the center of the room and laid my exhausted body on the bed. Pulling one of the accent pillows close to my chest, I curled my body tightly around it, trying to process these last few hours. As usual, my thoughts went on and on, leaving me to deal with an array of questions and feelings I was not ready to confront. The most unexpected feeling was guilt. Guilt about feeling attraction towards Graham. It was different when I thought he was a figment of my dreams, but now that I knew he was real, so was my attraction. It seemed to be reciprocated too, which made me feel even worse. I wasn't lying to Graham when I said it was complicated between Duncan and me. And because of our apparent ability to Connect, he was privy to it.

***

A knock on my door woke me from my nap, but I didn't get up. If I ignored it, maybe whoever it was would go away and I could go back to sleep.

A second, more persistent knock, told me it must

be important. I sat on the side of the bed to stretch before answering the door.

"Did I wake you?" Graham stood in the hallway, holding a muffin. "I wasn't sure if you had eaten yet or not, but I thought I'd bring you a snack. It's chocolate chip."

I hadn't eaten yet, I realize, and I'm starving. I smiled up at him as he handed me the muffin. I stood back and allowed him to enter. "Thank you." I closed the door behind him. "I haven't had a chance to eat yet and this looks delicious." I pinch the top of the muffin off with my fingers and carefully placed the moist bit in my mouth. I closed my eyes and reveled in the rich chocolate as I swallowed the sweet bite.

Graham watched me intently as I licked the chocolate remnants off the tip of my thumb. His eyes flickered with covetousness and his jaw tightened. Instantly, I became intoxicated at the sight of him. Overwhelmed at how badly I wanted him, I searched for understanding of what brought these feelings on so strongly.

Did I find him captivating too?

I stared up at him with doe eyes. "Is everything alright?" I pick a chocolate morsel from my muffin and sucked it from between my fingers. Still, his eyes stayed locked on my lips. I picked one more morsel and brought it to my lips.

"Please, stop."

I part my lips slightly.

"Heidi," he warned.

My name sounded sinful coming from his lips. I want him to say it again. I tease the morsel with my tongue as I held his gaze with my own.

He closed the gap between us, causing me to drop my muffin but not the morsel. "Heidi," he growled and held out his hand for me to hand over the morsel that was causing him so much temptation.

I rolled my eyes and held the morsel towards him, still between my thumb and pointer finger, forcing him to pluck it from my grasp.

He did.

I smiled coyly up at him as I lick the chocolate from my fingers before turning my attention to his. Before he has a chance to walk away, I suck the melted morsel from his fingers. "Mmmm," I hummed. I slowly slid his fingers between my lips and licked and swirled my tongue between and around them.

Graham grabbed my hip with his free hand and pulled me to him. "I'm trying to behave, but I can't ignore what you do to me. If you keep on the way you are, I might just have to take you right where you stand."

I released my lips from around his fingers and look up at him. Impulsively I say "Take me, then."

In one swift motion, he tangled his hands in my hair pulling me into a deep, longing kiss. He selfishly released me from his embrace before assuring me. "In due time."

My jaw went slack..

"I've touched you. I've kissed you. But now, I want to taste you."

My knees weakened and my breath quickened.

Holy hell. What has come over me. I'm acting like a fiend. Oh wait.

Am I dreaming?

Graham unbuttoned my jeans, kneeled in front of

me, and pulled them down to my ankles. Holding the back of my thigh, he looked up at me, removing my shoes, then pulling my jeans over my feet.

I must be. Graham had to leave. It seemed important.

With his lips at my belly, he began to kiss me softly, teasing me over my panties right to the top of my mound. His hands traveled up my sides, under my shirt, towards my breast, causing my skin to pebble with thrill.

He can't be dreaming too, can he? Not in the middle of the day. And at work, no less.

With his lips still against my panties, and his hand tugging at the band of my bra, he said, "Take this off."

This must be my dream. And if it's only my dream, I guess there's no harm in indulging myself.

I reached up behind my back, under my shirt, and unhooked my bra. I pull it out through the sleeve of my shirt and toss it on the floor. Immediately, his hands cup each breast, rubbing his thumbs over my nipples.

My hands found a place in his hair, working hard to steady myself. Ripples of gratification tear through my body. My breathing turned into panting, "Please," I said, "please let me feel you."

He replied only with a seductive smile, which only teased me more.

I snatched off my shirt, leaving my top half exposed. I'm hoping this will entice him to give in and put me out of my misery. I felt my panties growing more damp in anticipation of him.

Finally, he releases my breasts and pulls down my

panties, leaving me completely naked and wanting. A sensual "mm" sound leaves his lips as he took me in with his eyes. Running his hands from my ankles, up my calves, then thighs, he stopped at my ass and gave each of my full cheeks a squeeze before coming to his feet again. He leaned down to my ear and said, "Sit down on the chair. And spread your legs for me."

I do just as he says. I spread my legs wide, feeling my lips open, spilling my lust onto the chair. "Like this?"

He licked his lips and looked at me greedily, his cock was hard beneath his slacks, "Exactly like that." He knelt back down in front of me, placing his hands on top of my thighs and his thumbs in my bikini line. He starts slowly, using his thumbs to rub the outsides of my lips, up and down.

My eyes close and my head rested against the back of the chair, becoming consumed by the deliciousness of his touch. My breathing became more rapid as he slid his thumb from my wet center up to my clit, skillfully circling it before jerking his thumb back down to my center and back up again.

Getting closer to my climax, he threw my legs over his shoulders, grabbed my ass, and pulled me to the edge of the chair, finally getting his taste of me. His tongue replaced his thumb, but it followed the same strokes.

I covered my mouth with my hand to muffle my moans. I'm so close. His tongue moves with purpose, sliding in and out of me, over and over again before it travels upward to find its final target - my clit. He flicked his tongue vigorously across it. My hands found their way back to his hair. "I'm so close," I whined. Pleasure built. My toes curled. His tongue didn't let up, and finally, my orgasm spilled into his mouth as I let out a gratifying moan. My body twitched from the vibrations that my orgasm left behind. Graham widened his tongue and licked my slit from bottom to top, ensuring he got every drop of my satisfaction.

He looked up at me, eyes dark with arousal, pleased with the outcome of my release. He wiped his mouth with his hand, "you tasted better than I thought you would." He pushed me back in the chair and placed my feet back on the floor before standing back to his feet.

I noticed his penis was bulging against the zipper of his pants. "I can help you with that if you want," I said while my gaze stayed fixed on it, hoping he'll whip it out and fuck me.

"You will. Just not now," he replied with a wink.

I'm getting hot all over again. I begin to fan myself. He gathered my clothes and handed them to me, "Why don't you get dressed, so we can have a proper introduction," he teased. "I'm Graham, by the way," he said with a chuckle.

Sliding on my tee shirt and panties, I remembered that we were never properly introduced. I couldn't help but giggle too. "Nice to meet you, Graham. I'm Heidi."

His eyes traveled down my body and back up again. With a seductive grin, he said, "Hi, Heidi."

Chapter 20

I had a couple of hours before Graham and Dr. Keller came by tonight to set me up on the EEG. To kill some time, I decided to take a stroll through the city. The institute was only a few blocks from a waterfront park I saw in my search earlier today. Some fresh air and a walk would help take my mind off the dream from earlier.

Making sure to grab my key card and my coat, I made my way down to the lobby. Passing all the same pictures as earlier, I stopped again at the photos of the little boy. I wondered if this was Graham. I decided that I would ask him the next time I saw him. His eyes though, in the picture, were more cheerful. Whereas today, it looked like he was carrying sadness behind them.

As I made my way toward the end of the hallway that led into the lobby, the receptionist entered with a man, who looked to be my age. She nods and smiled politely as she passed me on their way to Dr. Keller's office. I returned her polite smile with my own. The man following behind her kept his gaze fixed on the floor. The look on his face made my heart ache. He looked genuinely troubled. I hoped he would get the help he was looking for.

Making it outside, I pulled my coat tightly around me as a chilly breeze rolled in. It sent my long brown hair into even more of a tangled mess. Once the wind died down, I combed it out with my fingers the best I could. To keep it tamed, I twisted it into a single strand and pulled it over my left shoulder.

The streets here were noisy. Not loud, but busy. There were always cars on the road. I saw the occasional biker on the street too. They took up space on the road right along with the cars instead of riding on the sidewalks, where it was safer in my opinion. If all I had to protect me from a couple thousand pounds of impact was a helmet, I know I certainly wouldn't want to share the road with vehicles. But, drivers seemed to give bikers their space, which I'm sure they were grateful for.

Approaching the second block of my walk, I noticed there were a few shops up and down the street on either side. One of the buildings on the left side of the street caught my attention. It had a pink and white striped owning hanging over the door. The smells coming from that direction made me think it was a coffee shop. Or maybe a bakery. I decided to make my way to it and see what they had to offer.

The name painted on the window read Main Street Eatery. The door was propped open, which explains why I could smell the delicious aromas all the way from the cross walk at the end of the street. The inviting scents swirling around in the tiny shop made my stomach growl. I never made it to the café at the institute to eat. I approached the counter where a cute young girl, with blonde hair and black framed glasses greeted me.

"Hi there! Welcome to Main Street Eatery," her chipper voice rang out, "What can I get you today?"

"Hi," I smiled at her. I glanced at the coffee menu and immediately decided against it. I didn't want to be hopped up on caffeine and not be able to sleep tonight. The assortment of baked goods and sandwiches behind the glass case looked amazing. It was too hard to decide. "I know I'd like a bottle of water," I started to say as I looked over the delicious options behind the case. "I'd also like the ham and Swiss wrap, and..." Now for something sweet. Too bad there weren't any chocolate chip muffins. "Hmm. I can't decide. All the sweets look so good. What do you recommend?"

"Oh," she flicked her writs at me, "that's easy! Our red velvet slices are my favorite, and we usually sell out on the weekends."

"Then I'll have a slice of that too, please."

"Ok great!" She rang up my purchases. "That'll be $19.65." I winced at the amount. They didn't have prices listed on the items in the case, but I didn't think it would be almost twenty whole dollars for a quick bite to eat. It must taste real good if it costs that much. I handed her my debit card to swipe. She does and began to pack my things up in a pink paper bag.

"Are all these items homemade?" I asked her as she handed me back my card and bag.

She let out a laugh that implied that I've asked the most ridiculous questions. "No. We get these delivered from our supplier."

The look on my face fell. "A supplier?"

"Yeah. But someone there had to have made 'em, right? So, I guess it depends on what you mean by *homemade*."

In my opinion, homemade can only mean one thing. And it's not being made and delivered from a distributor. Not wanting to appear too brazen, I chuckled and replied, "I guess you're right. Thanks again." I turned and made my exit.

"Have a nice day," I heard her call from behind me.

"Thanks. You too."

Back outside the shop, walking towards crosswalk, I opened and took a couple sips of my water.

The park was just over on the next block. I could see people moving up and down along Lake Jericho. People were jogging, walking, or riding their bikes. Kids were running wild in the grassy field along the walkway. The closer I got, the more I saw how truly busy this little area of the park was.

Further down the walkway, there was a playground, filled with kids and parents grouped together on the benches surrounding it. On the opposite side, another grassy field was busy with dogs running off their leashes. They ran freely with other dogs or played fetch with bright colored frisbees. There were benches sporadically placed up and down the walkway along the lake. There, people sat and talked, or held hands, or even shared kisses.

Once I made my way to the park, I found a shaded spot under a tree where I could sit and enjoy my very late lunch. Happy with my seat, I took out my ham and Swiss wrap and took a bite. I listened to the sounds of conversations that rumbled around me. They mostly all sounded pleasant with laughter and high energy.

I panned my head up the bank of the lake, taking in the view of glimmering water and interactions from the park goers. It felt so strange seeing so many people in one area. The field next to the store didn't even get this crowded when the whole town came to celebrate the Fourth of July.

Taking another bite, I decided that this ham and Swiss wrap was uneatable. It was making me queasy. I wrapped it back up and placed it in the bag to throw it away once I got back to the institute. Still with time to kill, I decided to people watch. I wondered what their lives were like. I wondered what kinds of jobs they had, what their families were like. Were they married, dating, or in love with anyone? Thoughts like these continued to play out as I swung my vision in the opposite direction. I heard someone crying nearby. It sounded like it was coming from behind me.

Peeking around the tree to get a better look at what might be going on behind me, I saw a fairly tall man, dressed in a white long sleeve dress shirt and navy slacks. His hands gently held the shoulders of a beautiful young woman. Her hair was black, shiny and long. Dressed in a form fitting red dress and black heels, her petit body looked frail, and limp compared to the man standing in front of her. Her hands carefully wiped tears away from her eyes without messing up her make up. She looked up to him and shook her head saying what sounded like "Why?" I couldn't make out what he was saying since his back was turned towards me, but it looked like he's trying to console her. Once he finished speaking, she wrapped her arms around his waist and squeezed him tightly before turning and walking away from him.

He ran his hands through his almost black hair

and watched as she walked away. He turned in my direction but didn't notice me watching him. It was Graham. I turned back around quickly, leaning up against the trunk of the tree, hoping he didn't walk this way. I took a few deep breaths before peeking back behind me to see if he was still there.

He wasn't.

I scanned down the park to see if I could find him in the crowd. Finally, walking the same crosswalk I took to get here, I spotted him making his way towards the line of parked cars along the street. I watched him as he walked away. He doesn't look terribly upset but he wasn't skipping away either. I wondered who that woman was and why she was crying.

Oh. Is that his girlfriend?

It would make total sense for someone like him to have a girlfriend. Smart, successful, and handsome, how could he not be taken.

I immediately felt guilty about my dream. He was tongue deep in me and I enjoyed every second of it.

I wondered if that's why he had to leave earlier.

But, if he had a girlfriend, why was he so worried about my relationship with Duncan? He seemed hurt to have witnessed the dream about the two of us.

Graham disappeared behind one of the parked cars along the street and I turned back around to peer out over the water, feeling certain he wouldn't be making his way over here.

My thoughts wandered back to Duncan. How would he feel if he knew about my attraction to Graham? It's not like I've just been sleeping with Duncan all this time. We weren't exclusive, but it felt different this time. Duncan had shown a more vulnerable side of himself lately. It was refreshing and attractive.

When Oliva and Ronny first started to date, she invited both our families over for supper. Not for anything formal – our families have known each other for forever – but to get everyone used to the idea that instead of friends, we'd all be one family. It was an overall pleasant evening, until my mom started going on and on about when I was going to find myself a nice man. I was annoyed and may have had one too many glasses of wine to dull my mom's sting. Duncan noticed that I would benefit from some fresh air, and he asked if I'd like to step outside on the back porch with him for a bit.

At that point, I was more than happy not to be in the same room as my mom. Duncan provided the perfect excuse for us to be dismissed from the gathering and I quickly accepted. I couldn't be rude to our guest and decline his request, after all. Once we were outside, we just sat. Sat in silence for, well, I'm not sure for how long really. It felt like a long time, almost to the point where it felt too awkward to speak, so we didn't. Not until he finally did.

We started with small talk about the people in town and how sometimes they can have narrow minded views about things. Things like marriage, schooling, or the jobs we worked. After we ran out of things to talk about, I asked if we could go on a walk. I needed to sober up and sitting outside in silence for so long made me realize how drunk I really was. I led him down through the woods to the part of Kingsman trail that ran through Olivia and I's back yards.

Without realizing it, I started to walk in the direction of my house, and he followed behind. I began to rant about marriage and why I felt there were more important things in life. He listened so patiently and never interrupted so I just kept rambling on in my drunken state. I didn't remember all that I said but I remember eventually saying, "All I really need, is a good fuck every once in a while!" To which he replied, "I couldn't agree more."

It wasn't until that moment that I allowed myself to think of him in a lustful way again. We had been teenagers the last time that happened. But something in his voice that night sounded so primal and sexy, causing the skin around my nipples to pebble.

Once I noticed we were near my house, I asked if he wanted to come inside. I wasn't hiding my intentions when I asked either. I knew exactly what I wanted once we got inside if he'd agree. He looked down at me with those guarded green eyes of his and seemed to play the decision out in his head. I suddenly felt stupid for asking and said, "never mind," and turned to leave.

"Wait," he called to me, "are you sure?"

I was more than sure. The trail wasn't a short walk between mine and Olivia's house, and I was more than aware of what I was asking for. "Positive." I flashed him an assuring grin and we headed to my house.

It was a little awkward for me at first. Duncan had grown into a sexy man and there he was, totally naked in my bedroom. He wasn't thin and chiseled like the guys you'd see in magazines, but he was sturdy and muscular, like a fine ass lumberjack. He ran his large, calloused hands over my body and suddenly, it didn't feel awkward anymore. I was aroused by the simple act of his hands becoming familiar with my bare skin again. No one had ever made me feel that way before. And no one has since.

Throughout the years, I've occasionally seen him with a woman around town. Never the same woman twice and never anything serious. I knew none of his relationships were serious because if they had been, the whole town would have known about it – word traveled faster than lightning.

None of my relationships were serious either. None were ever worth putting much emotion into. But Duncan and I, we knew what our arrangement was, and we were happy with it. As long as neither of us were seeing anyone else, we were free to be with each other.

I had never felt guilty when sleeping with someone other than Duncan. And I'm sure he didn't feel guilty either. Yet, somehow the boundaries of our arrangement now felt as if they had shifted.

Which is probably why my attraction to Graham makes me feel guilty.

There was an unexplainable pull I felt towards Graham. One that made it difficult to push him from my thoughts.

However, my feelings have resurfaced toward Duncan. I'm not sure what those feelings mean, but they can't be ignored.

A ball came rolling towards my feet, distracting me from my thoughts. A little boy, maybe around the age of ten, came running towards it. "I'm so sorry!" he said.

I picked it up and handed it to him, "That's alright. Here you go."

"Thank you!" he said and ran back towards his family where they begin to kick the ball around again.

Standing to my feet, I dusted the butt of my pants off with my hand. I checked my watch, it was almost six p.m., and I still needed to get something to eat since that wrap twisted my stomach. Grabbing my water and the pink bakery bag containing the distributor made wrap and red velvet cake, I strolled down the walkways alongside the bank of the lake. I'll grab supper from the café once I get back to the institute. Then I'll give this red velvet cake a try.

But before I could think too far about what to eat for supper, my thoughts traveled back to Graham and the crying woman. She was stunning. Even more so compared to me. Her with her perfectly styled hair and expensive looking dress. Me with my wild wavy hair, jeans and a tee shirt. I wasn't sure what it was that he saw in me, but he'd be a fool to let a woman as beautiful as her go.

Chapter 21

Back at the Keller Institute, I made my way up to the café and got some supper. The menu wasn't extensive, but they had a few selections on the hot bar, and a few made to order items I could choose from too. One of today's specials on the hot bar was meatloaf. It looked like it might taste alright, so I ordered it with a side of steamed carrots, Brunswick stew, and a slice of corn bread.

"Will that be all for you today," one of the women, who's name tag read Erin, behind the counter asked me.

"Could I have a bottle of water too please?" I finished the bottle I purchased earlier on my walk back to the institute.

"Sure." The tone of her voice was as bland as the look of those steamed carrots.

"Thank you," I said, prompting her to pass me the bottle of water. She then passed me my plate for me to place on my tray. I slid my tray past Erin to the station of condiments. "So, have the two of you worked here long?" There were no other patients in here to talk with, and I didn't want to sit alone with my thoughts right now. I hoped making small talk with at least one of the women behind the counter would help distract me from the flurry of frustrating and confusing thoughts that filled my mind. I couldn't quite make out the name tag of the other employee. She was too busy standing in the corner with her arms partly crossed, scrolling through her phone.

"Eh," Erin began, "I've been here for about six months." She then pointed with her thumb behind her to the young woman standing in the corner. "Tara's been here for about four years though. She's a bit salty since her friend stopped working here. I was her replacement."

"I can hear you ya know," Tara said to Erin without looking up from her phone. "And I'm not *salty*, as you like to say. He did Amanda wrong and yet he walks around here like he has no clue about how bad he hurt her?"

Erin rolled her eyes as if she had heard this story one too many times. But I was curious and wanted to know more.

"What happened to her?" I asked scanning the kitchen behind them for other employees. The only other person in here was the man in the kitchen cooking. But it appeared he had headphones in and probably couldn't hear us anyway.

"It doesn't matter," Tara said sullenly. She stared down, through her phone, and shrugged her shoulders.

Erin shot me an annoyed look, like she thought Tara was being dramatic with her response.

When Tara still didn't speak after another moment, I decided to find a seat at one of the cold, white tables behind me.

As soon as I slid the chair out for me to sit, Tara ended her pause for dramatic effect. "Amanda and I started working here at the same time. We were both in college at the time and needed a fairly simple job that wouldn't take time from our classes. After working here for a while, she developed such a huge crush on Dr. Graham Keller. He's the other therapists here and Dr. Jamie Keller's son if you haven't already met him."

Oh, I'm familiar.

"Anyway, Amanda had such a crush on him, and he knew it. Her eyes would light up whenever he walked in here. One time, their hands touched when she passed him his plate and she wouldn't stop talking about it for like, 3 hours. It was ridiculous how much she liked him, but he never asked her out. Eventually, she got tired of waiting and hoping and instead, she decided to ask him out. Do you know what he said to her?" Tara held for another dramatic pause. "He told her that they couldn't date because they were colleagues and he preferred to keep things strictly professional between them."

The door to the café opened suddenly, causing Tara's lips to fall silent. I turned to see who had entered. It was Dr. Keller.

She nodded to me, then to Tara and Erin. "Hello ladies. Hope each of you are having a wonderful day," she said with her perfect smile as she walked to the counter. "Could I get a bottled water please?" Erin handed her a bottle. "Thank you," she said. She then turned to leave the café, "Have a good evening, ladies." She left just as quickly as she entered. You could tell she was a very busy woman.

Once the hall was clear, Tara continued her story. "Where was I," she wondered out loud. "Oh, I was at the part where Graham Keller turns out to be a total asshole."

"Okay, Tara," Erin said in Graham's defense.

"He's not a total asshole. He's a decent guy."

"Yeah," Tara scoffed, "Because you haven't been around long enough to see it. After he turned Amanda down because they were *colleagues*, she started to look for another job. At that time, she only had half a semester left until she graduated. She felt like she could manage a full-time job along with her remaining classes. Fast forward, she finds a new job, graduates college, and asks him out again. This time, he says yes."

My heart sank a little. Maybe the woman in the park today *was* Amanda. "What does Amanda look like? Does she have black hair?" I blurt out. My curiosity got the best of me. I hoped I didn't sound as panicked as I felt.

"She does." Tara shot me a curious look. "How'd you know that?"

Shit.

"Just a guess," I shrugged. "So, they start to date, yeah?"

Please don't ask me any more questions about how I know.

I took a bite of my meatloaf, hoping that she wouldn't want to wait for me to finish chewing before answering any more questions.

"Yeah, they started dating. And Amanda was happy. Like, really happy. Things seemed to be okay in the beginning, but about three months or so ago, she told me that she had a feeling he may be cheating on her. She asked for me to keep an eye out while I was here working."

"And tell her what you found," Erin said.

Tara's head had dropped again, "Nothing. I

haven't found any proof that he was cheating on her."

"Did she have proof?" I asked, trying not to sound too eager for information.

Tara shook her head. "She didn't. But a woman knows. You don't need proof." Tara walked towards the counter and leaned on it with her elbows. "He broke up with her two weeks ago. But they didn't stopped hooking up." Tara's phone buzzed in her hand, but she didn't seem to realize. "Amanda told me that during one of the nights he was sleeping over at her apartment, he was mumbling all night in his sleep. She couldn't make out every word he was saying, but the one thing she did hear was "I can touch you too." When she asked him about it the next morning, he said he didn't remember. Which is total bullshit. Dreams are his *job*, of course he remembers." Her eyebrow arched, "so why did he lie?" The phone in her hand buzzed a second time. Her attention finally fell to its screen and her eyes scanned back and forth feverishly. She sucked her teeth and gestured to her phone, "And now he's just told her they can't hook up anymore."

Fuck. I feel sick.

The words Amanda heard Graham speak in his sleep were to me. The first time he touched me. Meaning he was sleeping next to another woman while dreaming of me. Was I the reason he ended it with her? "Did he give any explanation?"

Ugh, why did I ask that?

"Apparently he said he needed to focus on work. Which doesn't make any sense to me. Based on what Amanda has told me about their time together, he has always been focused on work but would make time for their relationship. Which he should. She's incredibly smart, kind, and beautiful." She added. "But this is what really pisses me off, why would he keep sleeping with her, knowing good and well how she felt about him? He's leading her on to think she still has a chance to be in a relationship with him. All the while, he comes in here, walks around without a care in the world. I've heard him on the phone, making plans for dinners or dates and my friend is just back in her apartment, thinking she's still gets to be with this guy."

"How do you know he's talking to a woman romantically, and not someone for business, when he's making these *supposed* plans," Erin asked the same question I had.

"Because he sounds excited. And you don't say things like "I can't wait to undress you" to someone you work with."

"He's just walking down the hallway talking like that?" Erin asked a follow up question.

"Um, not exactly." Tara looked down at the end of her apron and began to pick at it. "I may have stood outside his office when he didn't have appointments to see if I could eavesdrop." Finally looking up at us, she said, "Which totally worked by the way." No longer looking ashamed, but proud she invaded someone's privacy for the sake of her friend.

Erin's hands slapped the sides of her thighs in exasperation, "Damn, Tara. The man has needs still. So, what if he's seeing more than one person at a time? They were broken up, weren't they?" she asked rhetorically. "You can't label a man a douche bag for being a man. If he broke up with her, even if they're still sleeping together, they're not exclusive. It might not be the best way to handle a breakup, but if they both understood they weren't exclusive with each other, no one is doing anything wrong."

"Whatever," Tara said. "You come back and talk to me when it's your best friend who's being hurt by a guy she cares for."

They both looked my direction, waiting for me to chime in a be the tie breaker. Who's to say he wasn't talking to Amanda when he said that? Was Graham an asshole, or just a man with *needs*? The jury was still out on that one, but I couldn't say that to them. If Tara caught wind of this apparent attraction between Graham and I, she would put me on her shit list along with Graham. I was going to be here for the rest of the week and couldn't afford to make any enemies. "To be honest, I don't think I have enough experience in the matter to weigh in on this one. I'm from a small town and things like this don't happen. Mostly because all the young people move away the second they're old enough to do so, taking any potential drama with them."

"Why didn't you," Erin asked.

I smiled and set my fork down on my plate. Realizing after all the bites I stole while Tara was talking, I was damn near finished. "Family obligations," I said. I wiped my mouth with my napkin before I continued to speak. "For starters, my parents didn't have the money to send me away to college. But mostly, I think part of me doesn't want to disappoint them. Well, my mom, more so than my dad." They both nodded their heads as if they could relate. "Being here, in therapy, is the first time I've been away from my family. In addition to seeking help, I'm using this experience to see if it's something I can do. Be away from them, I mean. My sister is my best friend and I love my parents dearly, but being from a small town, and *never leaving* that town are two very different things. I sometimes feel suffocated by the thought of living the rest of my life there."

"Do you have a boyfriend back home," Tara asked. "You didn't mention a boyfriend but you're too pretty to be single."

Her kind compliment made me smile. Complements from women always felt more genuine than complements from men. Although, I definitely didn't see myself as pretty, especially compared to the women I've seen here, I appreciated her for saying that I was. "Thanks, but no. I don't have a boyfriend back home. My mom wishes I did though," I said as I rolled my eyes. This made Tara and Erin laugh which made me laugh. Even though we were strangers, it felt nice to have girl talk since my sister wasn't here.

The door to the café opened again, causing our laughter to die down. We all looked to see who was entering this time. It was Graham.

I could feel the air in the room go out as he entered. I offered him a polite smile and a nod as he walked past my table to the counter where Erin and Tara were. Tara went back to scrolling through her phone and completely ignored him. Erin greeted him with, "What can I get you this evening, Dr. Graham?"

He took a moment to look over the hot bar before answering. "I'll take a bowl of the Brunswick stew and an unsweet tea, please."

"Did you want it for here or are you taking it back to your office?" Erin's expression remained neutral. I don't think she had a negative or positive opinion about Graham. I don't think she cared.

"I think I'll take it back to my office. Thanks."

I let out the silent breath I hadn't realized I had been holding, waiting for his answer.

Erin nodded. She fixed his order up and placed it in a brown paper bag before handing it to Graham. "Thank you. Have a good night, ladies." He turned and walked back towards the door, passing me once again. He stopped at my table and said, "Dr. Keller and I will be by in about an hour to prep you for the EEG." The tone of his voice remained even and professional, as if we didn't share a secret.

"I'll be there. I'm finishing up my supper and I'll be sure to be back in time." I could feel my voice start to shake but I pulled it together. I didn't want Tara and Erin to suspect anything.

"Great." He flashed me a smile that only I could see. It nearly made me melt. I had all these conflicting thoughts about him, and I still felt attracted to him. Had I been standing, I probably would have fell flat on the floor due to my weak knees. I felt heat rising to my cheeks. I hoped it wasn't noticeable as he walked away and was no longer shielding me from Tara and Erin's view.

Once he left the café and enough time had passed to assume he was safely away from the door, Tara mumbled, "jerk."

Erin couldn't help but smirk and let out a chuckle.

I don't think anything will convince Tara that he is a good guy. Not saying that he is or isn't, but all of this adds another layer of confusion to my already jumbled thoughts about him.

I stood to return my plate, silverware, and tray to the counter. "Thanks, ladies, for keeping me company. I'm going to go ahead and head back to my room to shower and get ready for whatever the hell I have coming with this EEG."

Chapter 22

Back in my room, I was freshly showered and resting in my bed. I picked up my phone and started to scroll through my eBook library trying to find what to read while I waited for Dr. Keller and Graham. I needed to distract my mind. I didn't want to appear overwhelmed in Graham's presence while Dr. Keller was around.

I also decided to try that slice of red velvet cake I got earlier today. It was horrible. Nothing compared to Mrs. Trudy's homemade baked goods. I don't know how anyone could enjoy such artificial flavors. It deserved to sit at the bottom of my trashcan.

I read a few chapters of a cozy mystery book before a knock rapped at my door. Quickly straightening my bed back up before walking to the door, I opened it to see Dr. Keller and Graham. "Hi, Heidi! How are you feeling? You left rather abruptly this afternoon."

"I'm feeling better. Thank you."

"I hope you don't mind us coming a little earlier than expected. May we come in?"

I stood aside and opened the door wider to allow them to enter. "Of course not. Come in." Dr. Keller entered first, followed by Graham with what looked like a computer on wheels in tow. He didn't miss the opportunity to lock his eyes with mine as he walked past me. The slight grin on his face carried our secret and it was almost too much to bear. They stopped in the center of the room and roll the computer, and all its equipment, to face me. I shut the door and approached them. Pointing at whatever the hell it was that I was looking at, I asked, "What is that?"

Dr. Keller and Graham smiled with amusement. "This is an EEG machine." She placed her hand on Graham's shoulder. "And this is my son, Dr. Graham Keller. I didn't have the opportunity to properly introduce the two of you earlier."

Graham extended his arm towards me for a handshake, which I met. "Hi, Heidi."

My eyes widened. That's exactly how he said it in my dream this afternoon. I wondered if he was a part of it after all. "Nice to meet you too," I said, trying not to hold his gauze for too long.

"He's a talented and skilled therapist here at Keller Institute," Dr. Keller said proudly before holding up a medium sized box and opening it towards me. "Our objective tonight is to gather some initial scans of your brain activity. As I mentioned earlier, this is the cap you'll have to wear. It may be uncomfortable at the beginning, but it shouldn't impact your quality of sleep." She closed the box and set it on the foot of my bed. "If, in the morning, you feel as if you didn't get a good night's sleep, let me know and we'll capture more scans."

Graham rolled the machine against the wall on the left side of my bed and started to plug it in and hook things up. I watched him intently.

"Do you have any questions or any concerns?" she asked. I quickly looked back to her and shook my head. "Okay, great. But, if you do, at any time during the night, I have written Graham's number on the back of his business card." She walked over and sat it and an index sized card down on the end table. "You already have my number so feel free to call either of us, or both of us, if you have any questions at all. I've also placed the nurse's info here for you too. Give them a call when you wake up and they'll come and remove the cap. Same in the evenings when you need to have the cap put back on."

Graham had finished plugging the machine in and turned his attention to me. Attention unbeknownst to Dr. Keller. "Sure. Thanks," I said, trying to ignore Graham's gaze.

"Unfortunately," Dr. Keller continued, "I have had an unexpected conflict arise this evening and I won't be here to set you up for the EEG. Graham will assist you in placing your cap on tonight. You're in competent hands. But again, please, do not hesitate to give me a call at any time tonight if you have any questions or concerns," Dr. Keller finished.

"Okay. Thank you, Dr. Keller."

"Of course. And with that, I'll have to be going now. Graham will take everything from here. I will check in with you tomorrow, Heidi."

She headed for the door and exits. If I'm being honest with myself, I'm glad Dr. Keller couldn't be here. I wasn't sure what it was about Graham, but I struggled to keep my composure around him. I could feel him staring at me and I was trying to look everywhere but at him.

With all the new information I've learned today, I shouldn't have been so eager to feel his physical touch. But here I was, basically speechless, desire brewing between my thighs, reliving the feeling of his fingers and tongue circling my clit in that delicious dream earlier today.

"Heidi," Graham pulled me from my daze.

"Yeah?" I answered, looking down at my manicured nails pensively.

"Can you look at me?" His voice was soft and wanting. He was standing so close that I could smell his cologne. I pretended to examine my nails for a few more seconds before finally giving in and meeting his soulful brown eyes. Without hesitation, he pulled me into him, burying his hands in my hair. "Can I kiss you?"

I didn't say yes, and I didn't say no. All I could do was close my eyes and part my lips. Feeling his soft lips lock with mine, my panties instantly became damp with eagerness. I pulled myself away from him. Graham looked confused and almost doleful. "Wait," I said, steading my breath. "I have questions."

"About…the EEG?" he asked with a curious smile.

That smile.

"No. Not about the EEG. I mean, I'm sure I will, but not right now. But I have questions about Amanda."

With an amused expression he asked, "What about her?" Somehow, he hadn't looked surprised that I knew about her.

"I don't want to be a homewrecker, Graham. I saw you two at the park earlier today." I walked over and took a seat on the edge of the bed. "She looked really upset."

Graham let out a soft sigh and took a seat next to me on the bed. "She was. Amanda and I only dated for a couple of months. We met here at work, she worked over in the café. She actually asked me out, but I turned her down. We were coworkers and I didn't want to act unprofessionally. Eventually though, she put in her notice. When she asked me out again, we were no longer coworkers and were able to date. But, we broke up recently." Graham looked over at me, "the moment I realized you were more than a nighttime illusion, I broke up with her."

Shit. I'm already a homewrecker.

"She must have known I was distracted. The night before we broke up, she asked me if I was cheating on her. And, while physically I wasn't, and would never, my thoughts were preoccupied by you."

My gut wrenched at the thought of being the reason for someone's hurt.

"It wouldn't have been fair to Amanda had I stayed with her. I can't explain it, but there's something about you that I gravitate towards. No matter how hard I have tried to dismiss your existence, I still sought you in my dreams." Graham tucked a strand of hair behind my ear.

"But you kept sleeping together," I stated plainly.

I could tell he was surprised this time by how he cleared his throat. "We did." He stood and strode back and forth across the floor. "She texted me the day after we broke up to apologize for how she acted and invited me over for dinner. Once I got there, things fell into a familiar groove. I didn't stop her when she leaned in for a kiss. One thing led to another and yes, we slept together. That night and on a few other occasions." He stopped to face me. "But we both understood and agreed that we were not back together." He closed the gap between us to kneel in front of me. His hands rested easily on my knees. His eyes lingered between my thighs before forcing his gaze onto my face. "I can't think about a relationship with Amanda when you occupy most of my thoughts. She asked to meet me in the park today, for lunch, but instead, I told her we had to stop seeing each other completely."

He might be one hell of a smooth talker, but I got the impression that he was telling me the truth. "I appreciate you being honest with me." I placed my hands on his. "And I'm sorry."

"Sorry for what?" he asked.

"Sorry for interrupting your relationship. If I would have known about her, I wouldn't have ever pursued you in my dreams. I hope you know that."

He smiled. "Yes, I know that. And I found you first, remember?"

Dammit, his smile made me weak in my knees. *Be strong, Heidi. Be strong.*

"But..." I started, causing Graham's smile to fade quickly. "It's not too late. You and Amanda can still be together."

"Heidi," his hands moved higher up my thighs. "I'm not going to be able to be with anyone knowing that you're out there."

Becoming frustrated, I stood up. How in the world could he throw a relationship away on account of some stranger he *met* in his dreams. "Graham, what do you think is going to happen here?" I said, pointing between the two of us.

He stood too and rubbed the back of his neck. "Well, I really hadn't gotten that far."

"Right, well let me remind you. I don't live here."
Now, gesturing to my hair and clothes, "I don't look
or dress like the women who live here. There's no
way, if we had met under ordinary circumstances, that
you'd even give me a second glance. My hair isn't
straight and shiny like Amanda's. I'm not thin, like
Amanda. And I certainly don't dress like Amanda."
Graham parted his mouth to begin to speak but I cut
him off quickly. "And besides, even if I did live here,
and looked more like the type of women I'm sure
you're accustomed to, I am not in any position to be
in any type of relationship. So, completely ending
things with Amanda was just dumb." I finished with a
huff.

He looked down at me and brushed my hair over
my shoulder. "You're right," he admitted. "Maybe
you don't look like the women I usually date. That's
not to say you're not beautiful and sexy as hell."

My cheeks started to warm.

"I couldn't resist searching for you. No woman
has ever made me feel the way you make me feel.
You're electric, Heidi Miller. The way you invade my
dreams and my thoughts. I'm attracted to you in a
way that goes beyond appearances. I'm not sure what
to do about it, but I know I don't want to stop it."

Volts of ecstasy shot down my core, straight
between my thighs. Unable to resist him anymore, I
reached up and wrapped my arms around his neck to
bring him in for a kiss. Our lips collided fast and hard
with fervor.

Graham's hands wasted no time undressing me
down to my bra and panties. He lifted me and sat me
on the middle of the bed. I watched impatiently as he

started to undress. His shirt came off and fell to the floor first, revealing his smooth, chiseled abs and a sharp V leading down to his groin. Next, he kicked off his shoes before removing his slacks. Seeing him in nothing but his tight boxers, I couldn't help but compare him to Duncan.

Duncan was definitely stockier and taller in build. He wore his soft fuzzy chest hair like a badge of honor instead of shaving it off. But still, Graham wasn't hard on the eyes.

Graham's brown eyes burned into mine as he leaned down and left a single kiss on my lips before kneeling on the bed in front of me. His dick was solid beneath the fabric barrier, begging for it to be touched. I reached out, wanting to slide my hand inside his waist band and wrap my hand around it.

Before I could slip my fingers inside the band, an unexpected wave of nausea stopped me. I pushed against Graham abruptly and rushed to the bathroom. Only able to reach the sink before I felt my throat filling, I bent over and heaved into it, leaving my stomach completely empty.

Graham rushed to meet me with a towel. "Heidi, are you okay?" The concern his voice carried made me feel worse. Amanda was the one he should be concerned with, not me.

I wiped my mouth with the towel and sat down on the bathroom floor, allowing the cold tile to shock the semi bare skin of my butt and thighs. I know Duncan and I have seen other people during these years we've been sleeping together, but we truly had an understanding of our arrangement. Duncan wasn't the type of man to sleep with me, or any woman, if he knew they had feelings for him, with no intention of a relationship. And so far, I hadn't done that to him. I couldn't deny my feelings for Duncan any longer. Especially knowing how he feels about me.

If I were to sleep with Graham, I'd be just as low as him. Sleeping with Amanda, knowing that it wouldn't progress back into a relationship, *is* kind of fucked up. I agreed with Tara. Because he knew how much Amanda cared about him, while allegedly still seeking attention from other woman, and me, made him a… what'd she called him, a douche bag? But that didn't mean I wasn't attracted to him. Because I was. And it was incredibly difficult not to be, but I definitely needed to slow down and not make any decisions I might later regret.

I sounded like Oliva, so logical. I was proud of myself, having such constructive thoughts without becoming overwhelmed.

But something was still bothering me. I looked at Graham, who was now sitting on the floor beside me. Ignoring the question he asked me, I had to know, "Do you ever nap on the job?"

He looked confused and then his face softened as he prepared to reply.

Another wave of nausea hit me. I stood quickly and leaned over the sink and heaved again, preventing him from answering me.

Why am I suddenly sick?
Am I nervous about the EEG?
Do I miss home?
Do I feel guilty about Amanda?
Do I feel guilty that I'm half naked with another man?

Graham's hand rubbed my back to sooth me. "I think we've had enough excitement for one night. Let's get you in the shower." After turning the shower on for me, he waited for it to warm up. I could hear the interruption of the stream as he checked the temperature periodically with his hand. With my head still hung over the sink and my arms tucked in tight beneath my chest, I heard his footsteps approaching. His still damp hands unhooked my bra causing the straps to fall slowly down my shoulders. Had my hands not been pressed against the cups of my bra, my tits would have been on full display.

"Graham," I said hoarsely. I was here for a reason, to figure out what the hell was paralyzing me in my dreams. Not to get fucked by the literal man of my dreams, no matter how badly I thought I wanted it. "We shouldn't."

Chapter 23

I'm at home in my bed. The shower is running.
I hear someone.
No, I hear more than one someone.

I sit up, confused, trying to figure out where the voices were coming from. They sounded distant, yet nearby. The curtains and blinds over my bedroom window were opened. The water from the shower shut off. "Duncan?" I called towards the bathroom.

"Good morning, sleepy head," he called back to me as he pokes his head from behind the door. "There's a pot of coffee on for you in the kitchen."

I got out of bed, wanting to join him in the shower. Instead, I found my feet searching for the source of the voices. Staring out my window, where I usually saw the wooded area that surrounded my house, I saw lush green grass occupied with people. Curious, I made my way to the back porch through the kitchen, ignoring the inviting scent of freshly brewed coffee, to explore. The full scene was now in view – the river front park in Easton City.

I walked down the steps of my back porch, past the crowds of smiles and laughter, to the shoreline, taking in the breeze and sunshine. Once I reached the walkway, I saw Amanda sitting cross legged on one of the benches. Her hair, long and black, flowed behind her as the breeze rushed towards her from the water. I watched her, wondering what she was thinking. Trying to decide if I wanted to approach her or not, silence suddenly fell around me.

Looking around, all the families that were just sprinkled throughout the park, were now gone. Except Amanda and now Graham, who were in the middle of it.

"Is he dreaming about her?" I whispered out loud to myself.

"No. This is her dream," the familiar voice responded, startling me.

I turned, confused at how Graham was suddenly standing behind me. Then I quickly turned my sights back to the scene starting to play out in the middle of the park. And then back to him standing behind me. "How are there two of you?"

Before he could answer, Amanda's voice drew my attention back to her and Graham.

Dream Graham, now on his knees, has his arms lifted up to Amanda, begging her not to leave him. That he loves her and will do anything for her as long as she'll have him. She practically scoffed at his plea, flipped her long, shiny hair away from her shoulder and said, "In your dreams."

More like, in her dreams, I thought.

She then turned and walked away from him, leaving Dream Graham wanting and groveling for her.

I didn't understand how there could be two of him. Turning back to the Graham next to me for an explanation, the scenery behind him had changed. We were in my backyard. My wooded backyard. No sign of lush green grass or Lake Jericho.

"That was Amanda's dream. Not mine. And not yours."

"How do you know?"

"For starters, there were two of me. I've never experienced that before." A suggestive grin grew on his lips. "And I wasn't thinking about Amanda when I fell asleep tonight."

Heat rose to my cheeks, knowing that he was referring to me. The thought caused butterflies to take flight in my belly. I pushed them down. I couldn't do this. Not with Graham. Not when things are so up in the air with Duncan right now.

"What made you look for her?" he asked.

"I didn't know I was. My dream started here, in my room with…" I trailed off, suddenly remembering that Duncan was here before I came outside.

"Duncan." Graham said, finishing my sentence. And not in the cutesy, upbeat way that's depicted in movies. His tone and expression were flat and sad.

Nodding, I tried to move quickly past the realization. "I didn't realize I was looking for her. I saw the park through my bedroom window, and when I came outside, I was there. With her, and the…two…of you?" Rubbing my eyes with my thumb and pointer finger, "I still don't understand any of this. But what were you doing there?"

"I was looking for you?"

"Why?"

"I wanted to check on you."

"Thanks. I'm fine." I tucked my hair behind my ear.

"Good. I'm glad."

We stood there, just staring at each other.

"Is this it? Is this your home?" Graham said, staring up at my home.

"Yeah, this is it." I toyed with the idea of inviting him in or not. He was my therapist. And I did have to work with him to try and figure out what's been going on in my dreams. I needed to understand.

I decided there was no harm in inviting him in. Unless Duncan was still here. I turned to walk up the steps to my back porch, opening the back door slowly before sticking my head inside. I listened carefully for any sign of him. I didn't hear any. I wiggled my nose a few times sniffing for the smell of coffee. Nothing. "Duncan," I called out. No reply. I turned to look down at Graham, who was still standing where I left him, just at the end of the steps. "Come on in," I called down to him.

"Take a seat." I said as he shut the door behind him. I pulled out a chair from my kitchen table and he did the same.

The kitchen table was a neutral place to hold a conversation with someone you're unexplainably attracted to, right?

"All of this Connecting stuff is new to me. Is it alright if I ask you some questions?" I asked.

"Anything."

"How did you show up at the park?"

"It was the first place my dream started in. I went to bed, thinking of you, and that's where I found myself."

I tapped my thumb on the top of my table. "And there were two of you. That means it wasn't your dream?"

"That is my assumption."

"So anytime, there's two of me, it means it's someone else's dream?"

"Not necessarily. You could Connect with someone and become interactive with their dream scenario. Meaning, you're imposing yourself on their unconscious energy. They just might not be dreaming about you."

I tried to apply that explanation to the dream I had about Duncan. The one where we started a family together. "Could two people have the same dream?"

His expression fell again. "You're wondering about your dream with Duncan, aren't you?"

I didn't want to lie. "Yes."

He sighed. "Okay." He hesitated but eventually said, "Theoretically, yes. Two, or even more, people could share the same dream. We think that could happen when the energies are in sync."

I forced the smile away from my lips. It felt cruel to boast the spark of joy that just flickered in my heart. Could Duncan and I be synced up so much so that we had the same dream? It would make sense. He said I'm the one he wants to settle down with one day. If we did share the same dream, I wonder how it made him feel.

"We haven't found a way to prove one way or another though. It's all just a theory."

"I understand." Needing to change the subject, I wanted to ask him about his own experience. "Your mom, I mean, Dr. Keller, said you had a Connection experience when you were younger. Could you tell me about it?"

"Yeah." Nodding, Graham began to recount the event. "My parents and I were supposed to go and visit my aunt, uncle, and my cousin, Nick one winter. But at the last minute, we weren't able to go.

Something came up for Mom at work and we had to cancel the trip. I was so upset. That night, I went to bed thinking about all the things my cousin and I had planned for our trip. Tubing, building snowmen, snowball fights, the works. When I eventually fell asleep, I was outside somewhere, and it was snowing. And cold. So damn cold. I remember playing in the snow anyway and deciding to throw a snowball at the nearby pond. I wanted to see if I could throw my snowball far enough and hit it. When I threw it, the snowball shattered as it landed on the pond. It was frozen. I went over to check it out and that's when I noticed the hole near the edge of the pond. I saw Nick under the ice. All I could do was scream for help. I screamed until I eventually woke up. It was still dark out, so I guessed it was still the middle of the night. I was completely freaked out. I had never had a nightmare like that before, where it seemed so real and vivid. But I was able to calm myself down and fall back asleep. I didn't have another bad dream for the rest of the night. When I woke up the next morning, I remembered and just had a feeling that we should check in on him. That's when my mom called my aunt, and she told us what happened. That Nick had fallen into a frozen pond trying to retrieve his ball."

Without thought, I reached over and grab his hands that were clasped together and resting on the table. "I couldn't imagine what that must have felt like for you. Especially at such a young age. I'm really sorry you had to experience that." And I meant it. I remember so many of my bad dreams that scared me into either Olivia's bed, or my parents' and they always left an awful feeling.

"Thanks." He unclasped his hands and placed one on top of mine, making a Graham and Heidi hand sandwich.

I pull my hand back into my lap, not wanting us to get lost in each other's touch, or send the wrong signals. He's persistent, that's for sure. And somehow, it's a part of his charm that made him hard to resist.

He cleared his throat and continued speaking. "After that, my mother threw herself into her work. More so than usual. It caused a real strain in our house since both of my parents were doctors. Well, my dad spent his career as a medical researcher technically. But because my mother showed no intention to slow down at work and share the load of parenthood, my dad quit his job and took up his hobby full time instead."

"Photography."

With an amused look he said, "You have a knack for knowing things, Heidi Miller."

I laughed. "Rita told me. We chatted a little when I was signing some forms. She said all the pictures in the institute were taken by him. He's very talented."

"Thank you. I think so too."

"So, the pictures, downstairs in the hallway, of the boy blocking what I'm sure is a stunning shot of the pyramids, is you?"

He looked as if he's remembering the moment when the photos were captured and laughed. "Yeah. That's me." Graham readjusted to a more relaxed position in his seat, "My dad did a wide range of photography. He did portraits, shot photos of nature, animals, buildings, anything you could think of. If it could be captured in a photo, I'm sure my dad shot it. At that time, he wanted to travel outside of the states to see something different. He decided on the pyramids of Egypt. It was about a half days trip to the actual pyramid from where we were staying in Cairo. During the whole trip, my dad took pictures of everything. I didn't particularly like to have my picture taken so I gave him a hard time anytime he pointed his lens at me. He got the shots he needed once we arrived and asked if I had any ideas of anything else he should capture while we were there. To which I responded, "Yeah! This!" He squeezed his eyes shut and grinned ear to ear, reenacting his pose in the photo from the hallway. "Then I gave him a normal smile to capture. Mom loved them both and was adamant they be hung in the institute."

"What a beautiful story."

Duncan has never shared anything so personal about his childhood with me before.

"It's one of my favorite stories of me and my dad. I miss him a lot."

Oh, I didn't know his dad had passed. "I'm so sorry. He sounds like he was a great man," *I said with a sympathetic smile. I don't know what I'd do without my dad.*

"Thanks. Thankfully, I have more than enough memories of him that allows me to keep him close. We traveled all over the world together after that. Each one a new adventure in my upbringing."

"What about your mom. Did she ever go with you?"

"No. Not a single time. Her work is her life. And while I sometimes admire that, I also struggle with

the fact that she was nonexistent until I became an adult. I got into psychology because I wanted to have something in common and be able to bond with her too. Turns out, I developed a real passion for it and decided to make it my career. Which I love and it's very important to me. But, when I have my own family, they will be priority."

Wanting to completely sidestep his last comment, I decided to ask about his travels. It sounds like he lived an exciting life. "You traveled a lot then?"

"We did. Mostly over the summers before I graduated high school. Once I got to college, we traveled at least once a year, sometimes more, depending on my class schedule. Thankfully, the university offered online classes and I was able to keep up with my classes while we traveled."

"Did you ever get the photography bug like your dad?"

"I tried. But it never caught on."

"So, what did you do while he was busy capturing photos?"

"We toured a lot of the cities we visited but in my spare time..." he trailed off like he was looking for the right words to say, "I made friends."

"Ah. Lady friends I assume." The thought of him being with beautiful, exotic women sent an unexpected jealous ping to my stomach.

Graham cleared his throat, "Yeah."

"Do you still travel?" I asked, wanting to change the subject.

"I do. Just not as much. Anytime I find the free time to go, I take it."

"That sounds nice. To be able to pick up and take

off without worry."

"You should come with me. We could go anywhere. Is there anyplace you want to visit, or revisit?"

"I've never been anywhere to be able to revisit it."

"Never?"

"Never. I tried to plan a trip with my sister, to anywhere, but she didn't want to go. It's too much on my parents for us to leave the store behind for too long. I do, however, get to dream of places that I read about or see in movies, and it feels like I'm actually there." I smiled big, "Those are my favorite dreams."

"So, Duncan has never taken you anywhere?"

It felt like he's trying to get more details about Duncan and I's relationship. But I don't even know what those details were at the moment. I've asked Duncan one time if he'd leave Mount Hopewell. He responded with distance and taller walls. "Like I've said. Our relationship is complicated." This wasn't a topic I wanted to talk about with Graham. Especially since I hadn't had time to sort thought all my thoughts.

Thankfully, Graham caught on. He could tell this was a touchy subject for me and moved on. "So, I never got a chance to read your file. What made you seek therapy?"

This I could talk about. "My dreams, ironically. I've had a few dreams that ended with me being completely paralyzed. I sometimes refer to it as the stillness. It's where I feel like I'm being watched by someone or something and they've got a hold on me. Literally. Like giant hands are wrapped around me,

holding me tight. Not allowing me to move or even
speak." Graham's eyes widen. "But it seems to
always happen in the same place. The same place I
always follow you to."

"So, it's not just me."

My alarm rang loudly from my cell phone. My
eyes flew open in response. "Ugh," I groaned in
protest. "Dammit. I forgot to turn you off," I said to
my phone as I rolled over and silenced the alarm.

I rubbed my face with my hands, recalling my
dream, "What did Graham mean by "it's not just
him?"

Chapter 24

I spent most of my morning in the gym at the institute. After the EEG cap was finally removed by the nurse, my thoughts began to spin again, trying to process the events of what happened in my dream.

I somehow *found* Amanda.

There were two Grahams.

I was then somehow back in my own dream. With Graham.

At least, I'm pretty sure that was Graham.

The thought of calling Graham had crossed my mind this morning. I needed to know what he meant when he said it wasn't just him. But, I didn't know what time he had to get up and get ready for his day. So, I went to the gym instead. I wasn't sure what to do with the majority of the equipment that was in there, but I knew what a treadmill was and spent my time on that. It's definitely not like running the trails back home, but it served its purpose. My body and mind were tired enough to push away my invading curiosities.

My next objective was to see if Erin and Tara were in the café, but they weren't. Just a middle aged woman named Mabel. She wasn't much of a talker, so I grabbed a blueberry muffin and banana and ate in my room before my appointment with Dr. Keller.

Finally knocking on Dr. Keller's office door, I entered after she called for me to come in. To my surprise, both Dr. Keller and Graham were there. Dr.

Keller was sitting in the chair behind her sleek, white desk, eyes fixed on the screen of the black laptop resting on top. Two smoky blue suede chairs sat on the opposite side, one already being occupied by Graham. Dr. Keller gestured to the empty chair next to him, "Please. Have a seat, Heidi."

I didn't know Graham would be here and I have to remind myself not to launch into the questions I had for him. I took a seat next to him. "Good morning, Dr. Keller. Graham."

"Good morning," they both said in unison before Dr. Keller said, "I've been reviewing the EEG readings from your scan last night. Did you get a good night's rest?"

"I did. But you were right, the cap was uncomfortable at first. Once I had fallen asleep, it didn't bother me."

"I'm glad to hear it," she said, scrolling her mouse as if she was searching for something on the monitor. "I've marked the areas of your scan where you experienced REM sleep." She turned the monitor around for Graham and me both to see and placed the mouse near my hand. "When you scroll over, you'll see areas marked with green. Those are periods of your REM sleep cycles."

I scrolled the mouse wheel to view the scans. The areas marked in green were tight zig zag lines, which took up most of the scan, preceded by a short hump with a squiggly line. "These tight, jagged marks are REM sleep? Is that bad?"

"Not at all. Those line are markings of your brain's electrical current and appears that way for everyone who experiences REM cycles." I've noticed

Graham has leaned in closer to examine the scans himself. He looked astounded. "What's unique about your scan is that it appears you experienced a REM cycle about fifteen minutes after falling asleep. You then continue to experience it for the duration of your sleeping period. We typically see the first cycle of REM about ninety minutes after someone has fallen asleep. It comes in cycles, or waves, with NREM sleep. Less than thirty percent of someone's sleep is spent in the REM cycle. You, however, spent approximately eighty-two percent of your sleep in a REM cycle."

Why were my scans so different? I wondered. "Is that bad?"

"Heidi," Graham said, "That's amazing. It's not something we've ever seen before."

His words made me remember what Dr. Keller said at our initial appointment, that recurrence of Connecting, or dream sharing, has never been documented before. I thought on that thought for a moment while Dr. Keller was going on about one thing or another.

If a secondary dream sharing experience had never been documented, she was either keeping her son's ability to Connect a secret, or she didn't know about it.

I set the thought aside for a moment and focused back on Dr. Keller. "...and that's why it's an incredible gift," she concluded enthusiastically.

"I'm sorry," I said, tucking my hair behind my ear. "An incredible gift?"

She walked around the front of the desk and sat on the edge with her ankles crossed. "Your ability to

Connect. You could help people in unimaginable ways, Heidi." She stood with enthusiasm, "I'll be right back; I need to ask Annie to cancel my appointments for the rest of the day." She practically bounced out of there with glee.

Graham was still looking over the scans in amazement when I asked, "Does she know, or have you not told her?"

My question caught him off guard. "What do you mean?"

"Why is she so enamored with my scans? You also have the same ability."

"Oh." He nodded subtly to himself and let out a breath, "I haven't told her."

"Why not?" I would have thought that his ability would be big news for his line of work.

He dragged his hands through his hair. "Because. If she had known, she would have thrown herself into more research and it'd be like my childhood all over again. We do amazing work here and I would hate to see the institute and our patients suffer because she's too preoccupied with researching this phenomenon further. But I have run scans on myself before and mine looked nothing like yours. I do have extended periods of REM but nothing continuous." Still sitting in his chair, he turned his body toward me and rested his hands on my knees. "Heidi, it really is amazing."

Goosebumps erupt over my skin when he said my name. I could feel myself blushing under his brown eyes. "So, last night, in my dream, you were there?"

"I was," he said softly. "Prior to you, we've only seen one other patient who has had scans of extended REM cycles longer than mine. Still, nothing like yours, but he sadly passed away." Before his hand could make it to the top of my thigh, he snatched it back quickly to rest in his lap. The door to the office had widened and Dr. Keller stepped inside. Her sad blue eyes met Graham's. She shut the door and took a seat back in her chair. "Mom, I...," Graham began.

Dr. Keller held her hand up to stop him. She looked hurt, I wondered how much of that she heard. "How long?" she asked, setting her hand down. "How long have you known that you've been able to Connect? Your father has been down there, suffering and you could have been helping him."

Shocked, I turned to Graham, "I thought your dad passed away?"

"I never said that. He's been in a coma for..."

"For years, Graham," Dr. Keller interrupted. "And you could have been helping him." She reached for a tissue to dry the tears that had started to form in her eyes.

Lifting myself out of my chair, I announced, "I think I should go. This seems like a family matter."

"No." Dr. Keller pleaded before I could stand fully, "Please stay. I could use your help."

She looked so sullen. But as a mother, not as a doctor. Her normal, sunny disposition and sparkling smile was no longer evident. It was hard to say no to her, so I stay seated.

"Mom, she can't be a part of this," Graham tried to convince Dr. Keller.

"Well, since you're none too keen to offer help, I have to ask someone, and I think she could do it."

"Do what?" I interrupted, "What the hell is going on here?"

Dr. Keller dried her eyes again and softly cleared her throat. She began, "I would like for you to try and connect with my husband." I raised an eyebrow to her, wondering what the hell she meant. "My husband is in a coma. Has been for a while. Throughout the early years of my dream research, and Connecting specifically, it has been theorized that it's not necessarily dreams that are being connected to, it's the energy from the brain's electrical signals. Because of this theory, I think you would be able to reach him."

"With all due respect, how would me Connecting with him help?"

"His doctors have advised us that the chances of him waking up are nonexistent. But neither of us," she said, looking at Graham, "can pull the plug on him. He was the love of my life, I'm not ready to give him up."

Graham scoffed. "Love of your life. You didn't act like it." Dr. Keller looked at him pointedly. "Don't give me that look, Mom. All either of you ever did was argue with each other. You were the love of *his* life. Yet, you didn't have any time for him. Or me for that matter."

"Sometimes, we realize things after it's too late. You don't know how heavy it all weighs on me now. I took him for granted, I took our *life together* for granted, and I regret it. I need to know that he's at peace. The last time I spoke with him, we had that horrible fight." She pulled a new tissue from its box and sniffled into it.

Graham turned to me, like he knew I was wondering what happened to his dad. "It was my parents' anniversary. My mom made reservations for dinner at dad's favorite Italian restaurant. Reservations she never showed up for. She was here in the office still working."

"It's not like I did it on purpose. I forgot. It was an honest mistake," Dr. Keller began.

How can she forget a reservation that she made?

"Or at least I thought it was. He called me from the restaurant. He was so upset with me. We got into a fight. He told me I was selfish and thought we needed to separate. He said that since I clearly had no intention of slowing down at work and prioritizing our relationship, it was the best thing for us to do." She paused to wipe the tears away from her eyes again. "And I didn't fight for him. I told him that maybe we should. Next thing I knew, an officer from the Sherriff's Office was calling me to inform me that my husband was in a terrible accident."

"And you're wanting to know if he forgives you," I concluded. I understood the kind of help she needed from me. Tears welled back up in her puffy, red eyes as she nodded yes.

Graham stood to his feet, "Mom, I don't want Heidi trying to Connect with him. It's not a good idea."

Looking up at him, I asked, "Why not? I want to help."

"Because. It's not just me." I drew my eyebrows together. That's what he said last night. "The paralysis, or the stillness, as you've called it, I've felt it too."

"*Graham,*" Dr. Keller said with realization in her voice, "It's you. You're who Heidi has been seeing in her dreams, hasn't it? You've known all that time that you had the ability to Connect, and you never told me? You've never tried to help him?"

"I have!" Graham's voice raised with frustration. "Every night since his accident, I have tried to Connect with him. I couldn't Connect with anyone until four months ago, when I realized I had been connecting with Heidi."

With hope in her voice, Dr. Keller asked, "Have you Connected with him?"

"No. Like Heidi, I have also experienced paralysis from time to time. I thought it was because my abilities weren't strong enough to Connect. Now that I know Heidi has also experienced the same sensation, I'm not sure what it could be. This is new territory."

"Then let me help," I suggested.

Graham returned to his seat next to me, placed his hands on my knees, and leaned in towards me, "Heidi, we don't know what the paralysis means, if it's detrimental or not. I don't want you putting yourself in harm's way."

Before I could protest his advice, Dr. Keller interjected, "Heidi, I'd be lying if I said we could do this without you. Even with your help, the chances of you being able to Connect with my husband are slim. But I think you're our best shot. I would still be happy to treat you, of course, and free of charge." Her eyebrow raises at Graham's hands on my knees, "But only *I* will conduct your therapy. It appears my son's ability to counsel without emotion may be compromised."

Graham withdrew his hands and sat back into his

seat, "Because you're not emotionally compromised?" His question sounded more like an accusation against his mom.

I couldn't listen to any more of their arguing, "I'll do it," I blurted out. They both went silent and looked at me. Dr. Keller's offer to complete my treatment, free of charge, made this decision almost a no brainer. But I did want to help them. "All I can do is try, and I'd like to at least do that."

"Then I'll go with you," Graham said with determination.

"No," Dr. Keller said firmly. "Only Heidi. We still have to care for the fact that she experiences paralysis. And since she experiences it when you're around, we can't dismiss the possibility that you could be the source of it."

Graham hung his head before giving a reluctant nod of agreement.

"Heidi, are you sure this is what you want to do? I will still be more than happy to treat you if change your mind."

"I'm sure. I want to help. But I'm not sure how exactly."

"That's alright. There are techniques we use in dream therapy that should also help you Connect with my husband. I will go over everything with you, but first, I need to have a word with my son. I will meet you up in your room shortly."

I nodded to Dr. Keller and gave Graham a sympathetic look. I knew what it was like to have opinions that differed from your parents, and I knew the conversation that would follow would not be a pleasant one. I excused myself from her office and made my way back to my room, eager to understand more about this supposed ability of mine.

Chapter 25

"Come in," I called to the door. Dr. Keller entered my room with a notebook, some pens, and a blue folder. Her appearance seemed calm and put together. My mind raced with curious thoughts of what details Graham may have shared about us with her after I left the office.

She made her way to the chair in the corner of the room and took a seat. She stacked everything in her lap. "Let me begin by first apologizing about Graham's conduct. I have never seen him become emotionally attached to a patient before. And secondly, I want to apologize for our behavior back there. Sometimes, when working with family, it's hard to keep your emotions in check."

Don't I know it.

"But," she continued, "I want to assure you, I will continue with your therapy regardless of your decision. It's a big ask, I know that." She paused for a moment, like she was searching for her next thought.

"I'll help," I assured her. "I would be happy too. I'll admit, I don't fully understand how all of this might work, but if you're confident that I can be of any help at all, I'm happy to at least try."

Dr. Keller released a sigh of relief. "I do. I really do think you could be the key to all of this," she said tapping her hands on the pile of materials that rested in her lap. "Recurrence has never been documented before, so no one truly knows for sure. But, it is theorized that Connecting could be possible between REM energy and any non-REM energy.

"Like the type of energy someone has while in a coma."

"Yes, exactly," she confirmed. "Individuals in comas do not experience REM cycles but there are still some basic brain activities happening. Which means, there is energy that could potentially be tapped into, Connected to. My hope is…" Dr. Keller's voice began to crack slightly, trying to fight back the emotion in her voice. "If you're able to Connect with him, with my Martin, you should be able to communicate with him, and he with you." She took a shallow inhale and straightened her posture, "But, we have to first try and assess what's going on with your sleep paralysis." She pulled the blue folder from the pile of things in her lap. "There are materials in here to help you enhance your chances of experiencing a lucid dream. I don't suspect you will need those based on what you've told me about your past dreams, but they're here for you just in case. Also, in this folder, there are some practices to help you navigate your way through your dreams. These are the skills I want us to focus on for now."

She leaned forward in her chair, extending the blue folder to me with her right arm and holding the notebook and pens with her left to keep them from rolling out of her lap and onto the floor.

The folder felt thick and heavier than I expected. I opened it to view its contents. The pockets were filled with several sheets of paper and informational cards.

"Find the page titled Dream Navigation Practices," she said to me, answering the question in my mind. I found it, pull it out, and began to skim over its words. "The most important, or most helpful, practice is listed at the very top – Reality Assessment. This is when you study your surroundings, usually starting with the room where you sleep, in order to take all the details back to your dream and recall it accurately. Being able to distinguish between what belongs, and what doesn't, will allow you to navigate more accurately between your own dream and dreams, or energies, of others you can Connect with."

"Like the scenery outside a bedroom window that should be woods but is actually a park?" I asked. I was curious if that could be what she was referring to. It was strange to see the waterfront park outside my bedroom window instead of the wooded area that was normally there.

Dr. Keller raised her eyebrows in surprise, "Yes. Exactly that. Although, it could be something much more subtle than that. Is that something you've experienced before?"

"Last night. My dream started out at home, and I heard voices from outside and when I looked through my window, I noticed the scenery was different. So, I walked outside and was no longer at home."

"Amazing." She shifted forward in her seat, eyes locked on me. "Have you experienced anything like that before last night?"

I had to search my brain before I remembered, "Michael." Dr. Keller's eyebrow shot up in curiosity. "The bird watcher that I dreamed about," I reminded her. Her eyebrow softened as she recalled the details. "I saw a backpack float downstream from me. When I turned my head in the direction it came from, I saw boots on the bank. I started to walk that direction and eventually found him."

"You might be a natural after all." Her hopeful tone weighed heavy in my chest. I hoped I wouldn't let her, or Graham, down. "You could also try to meditate before bed to achieve a stronger Connection. Have you ever meditated before?" I shook my head. "That's alright. It's fairly simple and beneficial in more ways than one. It's something I recommend all my patients continue after they've complete therapy. There's a website listed there," pointing to the page I held in my hand, "that you can visit for virtual meditation videos." She looked down at the remaining contents in her lap and handed them to me. "I want you to journal."

My eyebrows pulled down in confusion. "Like, about my feelings or…"

Dr. Keller smiled, "Your dreams. Write down what you see, what you hear. Places where your dreams begin and end, and any places in between. Write down your feelings, any sensations, fears, and joys, that you experience. Your journal will serve as a log. This will also help us recall on things you experience so we can hopefully find a source for your sleep paralysis."

"Okay. Yeah, that makes sense."

"Any questions?"

"Yeah." I sat everything down beside me on the bed, "How do I find someone while I'm dreaming? Before, it just kind of happened. I wasn't looking for anyone, or at least, I wasn't aware that I was looking for them."

"That leads me to the next thing I wanted to talk

to you about. Since this is not the typical situation, Connecting to a non-REM energy, I think it would benefit your chances of Connecting with Martin if I took you to see him. Would you be up for that?"

"I think so." Nodding my head, "Yeah."

"Great!" Dr. Keller's voice, filled with hope, "I will come get you around five this evening."

"I'll be ready by then."

"Perfect. Before I leave, did you have any other questions for me?"

"Yes." Graham mentioned the patient with scans better than his, died. I guessed now was as good a time as any to bring it up. "The patient who died. Did he have the same ability as me?"

"Oh. Uh…" She hesitated. "I'm not sure. His scans looked promising, but he unfortunately passed before we could explore his ability."

"So, you didn't get to ask him to try and Connect with your husband?"

"Nope. Like I said, he passed. Are these the only questions you have? I really should be going."

For someone who cleared her schedule, she sure seemed to be too busy to answer my questions. I wondered if my questions were making her uncomfortable. I would have to find out later. The nauseas feeling had returned and I could use a nap. "No. I don't have any other questions."

"Wonderful. I'll see you this evening then." Dr. Keller flashed me a polite grin and left my room quickly.

I took the folder, notebook, and pens and set them down on the side table next to my bed before kicking back and stretching out in it. I was exhausted. After last night's dream, this morning's appointment, and this sick feeling in my stomach, I was spent.

***

I'm sitting on the bank of lake Jericho, the park behind me is noisy and full of people. I get up and look around for Amanda, but she's nowhere to be found. Next, I search for Graham. No sign of him either. I begin to stroll down the pathway, taking in the views, until I notice a small child crying. She doesn't look to be older than two or three years old.

When no one made their claim as her caregiver, I ran to her. I kneeled, keeping my hands in my lap so I didn't scare her away. Before I could ask if she's alright or where her parents might be, the scenery around me changed suddenly and the little girl was no longer in front of me. I heard her cries, but I didn't see her. Where there was once grass under my knee, there was now dark green shag carpet. And where there were several happy families playing in the grassy field, there was a black futon folded into a couch in front of me.

Sitting at the edge of the futon, I saw the profile of a man hunched over with his elbows on his knees and hands in his hair, rocking back and forth. Without standing, I craned my neck back and forth, taking in this new environment.

I saw beer bottles everywhere. On the floor. On the futon, and on the coffee table in front it. On the ledge of the rectangle opening in the wall across from me, leading to what I assumed was a kitchen. All covered in beer bottles. I could still hear the little girl crying but I didn't see any doorways of where she might be.

Careful not to startle the man, I gently said, "Sir?"

Jerking his head up to turn in my direction but not meeting my eyes, I noticed that his cheeks were damp with tears. "What do you want from me," he yelled.

Now I'm the one who's startled.

I searched his face, trying to determine if he was talking to me or not.

He looked familiar.

"My name is Heidi. What's your name?" I waited, but no response.

I tried again. "Sir?" I said carefully, "Is she in trouble? I can help her, and you. Will you let me help?"

His eye locked onto mine, "No one can help me."

Goosebumps rose along the back of my neck and fear started to bloom in my throat. I remained frozen by his gaze until he looked down at the floor. And that's when I remembered where I knew him from. He's the young man that I passed in the hallway yesterday on my way out of the institute.

The beer bottles. It makes sense now.

Gaining a little of my confidence back, I finally responded with, "I can try. If you let me." Reluctantly, he nodded in agreement. A silent sigh of relief left my chest. "What's your name?"

"Eric."

"Hi Eric. Do you think we could find the little girl? She's crying hard."

Shaking his head, "She's not here. I'll never see my little girl again!" He reached forward towards the coffee table and forcefully flipped it, causing beer bottles to shatter as they hit the wall. To avoid getting hit with glass, I moved quickly to the right near the futon. "Fuck!" His anger was pushing me closer to the edge of panic. "Why can't I get my shit together already!"

Now was a bad time to question if I could get hurt or not.

Eric's anger turned into sobs. I slowly made my way onto the futon and sat next to him, placing my hand on his shoulder. "Shhh. It's okay. Everything will be okay," I tried to console. "Can you tell me what happened here?"

Eric used the bottom of his shirt to wipe away his tears, "Isn't it obvious? I'm a mess and unfit to take care of my own daughter."

The sound of crying from the little girl had started to fade. "Is she safe?"

"Much safer now that she's away from her fucked up dad. I don't know how I could do that to her," he said through sniffles.

My heart's beat pounded a little harder in my chest, "What did you do to her?"

I hope I don't regret asking.

Blowing his nose with the same part of his shirt used to dry his eyes, he leaned back on the futon. "It was my weekend. My ex drops my daughter off to me on Fridays after work. I had a shit day and really wasn't in the mood but when I saw my daughter's smiling face, I thought "This is exactly what I need. Some quality time with my precious girl. Everything will be fine." But she had a hard time getting to sleep. Crying and wanting me to hold her. By the time she finally fell asleep, I was more irritated than before she got here. So, I grabbed a beer. I knew her mama didn't like me drinking when she was here, but what could one beer hurt?" He rubbed his eyes and took a few breaths before continuing. "One beer turned into two and before I knew it, my door was being kicked in by local police. Standing behind them was my ex. My daughter was screaming from her room, and I had been passed out cold, right here on this futon. It was almost noon when they got there." His voice cracked when he said, "Only God knows how long I left her crying and calling for me."

My heart was heavy for him. I couldn't even begin to image the turmoil he felt. "How old is she?"

"She's three now," he said with a smile. "She's so smart and beautiful. And has the sweetest little laugh. It's the best sound in the world. But uh," he cleared his throat, "when this happened, she had just turned two. I so badly want to get better so I can be there for her. I even checked myself into some dream rehab or some shit. It feels like it's my only hope since traditional rehabs haven't worked for me in the past."

I look around at the mess of beer bottles and the now flipped over coffee table. "How about we start with cleaning this place up? Maybe that can be the next step. That way, the next time she comes over, she doesn't have to see this mess."

He thought on that for a moment then nodded his head, "Yeah. I can do that." As he stood, a doorway appeared on the wall with the rectangle opening. He disappeared for a moment before returning with a trash bag. He shook it opened and began to clear the ledge of the opening. I started to pick bottles up from the floor to take to him...

My eyes fluttered open to the sound of my cell phone vibrating. Realizing I was awake, I reached over for it. Through my hazy eyes, I looked to see the name illuminating across the screen. Duncan Johnson. I answered.

"Hello?" I rasped softly.

"I'm sorry, did I wake you?"

"Yeah," I finished with a yawn. "But it's okay. I needed to get up. What time is it anyway?"

"Almost four. Is everything okay?"

"Yeah, everything's fine. This morning was a little chaotic and I was too exhausted to go out and explore the city. Figured a nap would do me some good. So, what's up?"

"I uh...I just wanted to call and check on you. And apologize for yesterday."

"Yeah. I'm sorry too. But I talked to Olivia and we're okay now. She didn't understand why I would keep something like this from her, but she understands now. She promised she wouldn't say anything to Ronny. Or your folks," I added.

"I appreciate that." Silence danced between us for what felt like several minutes. I don't normally talk to Duncan over the phone. His voice sounded different. It almost made me miss him. His sudden words pulled me away from my thoughts. "Heidi, do you think we should continue to do this?"

"Talk on the phone? It is a little different, huh?"

"No. I mean *us*. Do you think it's smart for us to keep going like this?"

And there it is.

"Umm…" This felt too familiar. He was just telling me that he cared about me. That I was the one he wanted to settle down with when the day comes. The nausea returned. How could I have been so stupid? Of course he didn't really want me.

"Before one of us gets hurt."

It was too late for me, but I didn't want to hurt him. "We can still be friends, right?" I was not ready to completely lose him.

His chuckle met my ear, "Yeah. We can still be friends."

Chapter 26

After hanging up with Duncan earlier, I headed over to the café for a quick bite to eat. Erin and Tara were already there working. Erin, still in a much better mood than Tara, they both were up for small talk with me while I ate. Nothing deep like yesterday, but they gave me ideas of things to do while I was in the city. Now I was back in my room waiting for Dr. Keller to take me to meet her husband.

I still hadn't heard from Graham. I thought that maybe he would have come by at some point today. Whatever he and Dr. Keller discussed earlier must have scared him off. I hadn't decided yet if that was a good thing or not. But it would have been nice for him to at least stop by. I could have told him about the dream I had earlier.

Oh shit, the dream journal. Grabbing the notebook and a pen, I took a seat in the chair and quickly jotted down what I could recall from earlier.

Think.

I started at the park. Then I saw the little girl, crying. Once I got to her, I found myself in a beer bottle cluttered apartment with the guy I saw in the hallway yesterday.

My heart weighed heavy for him. It was apparent that he loved his daughter, and that he was in so much pain. I hoped he would be able to heal and be there for his little girl.

A knock at the door ceased my thoughts. I closed

the notebook and set it and the pen on the end table and made my way to the door.

"Good evening, Heidi. Ready to go?" Dr. Keller greeted.

"All set."

"You might want to grab a sweater. It gets chilly down there."

Down there? "O-okay." I grabbed my sweater from the closet and walked to the elevator with Dr. Keller. Once the doors closed behind us, she pressed the button marked with a B. "He's here? Your husband?"

"Mhm. I spend most of my time here at the institute. I thought if he was here, I could check in on him at any time and visit with him. The nurses upstairs also help with his care."

The elevator door opened to a dim, grey room. There were a few chairs and a couch lining the wall to the right of the elevator. There are two doorways on the wall directly in front of the elevator. One was labeled Patient Records, the other was labeled Storage. Once out of the elevator and into the room, there were two more doorways. One was for the stairwell and the other one, on the left-hand side of the room, had no label.

"Right through here." Dr. Keller led me through the unmarked door.

It was much brighter in this room, more inviting. Black framed pictures with floral subjects adorned these walls.

"This is my husband, Martin." She took his hand as she introduced me to him. He was tucked neatly into his hospital bed. Several of the machines hooked to him let out various sounds of hisses and beeps. His face was freshly shaven, and his dark black hair looked trimmed and washed. At least he was being taken care of.

There was a single chair and a rolling table next to his bed. A framed five by seven photo of Dr. Keller, Martin, and Graham sat on top. Graham favored his dad, with their matching dark hair and brown eyes. Judging by the smiles they were all wearing, they looked like a happy family, but based on what I heard this morning, I don't think they were.

"Can he hear me?"

"Yes. His EEG scans have shown that he is able to detect sounds. He can't process the information into words, and the chances of him remembering anything if he were to wake up are slim, but in the moment, he can hear you."

I looked back to the frail man lying in the hospital bed, thinking how devastating it would be if I ever saw my own dad in this condition. Not just for me, but for my mom and sister too. "Hi Martin. My name is Heidi. Your wife has asked for my help to Connect with you and I'm going to do my best to find you."

I could see the tears well up in Dr. Keller's eyes, "Thank you, Heidi."

"Of course." I took a mental note of everything I saw in the room. The machines, the chair and table, the pictures hanging on the wall. The family photo. Even the color of Martin's sheet and blanket. That was all that was in there and should be easy to search for tonight. "Is there anything else I should do to increase my chances of Connecting?"

"Other than becoming familiar with this room,

that's pretty much it." Dr. Keller placed Mr. Keller's hand back down on the bed. "Let's have a seat outside and we'll chat for a few minutes." I followed her back to the main room where we both took a spot on the couch. "Unfortunately, Connecting isn't an exact science. Or not yet anyway," she said with a smile. "Before you go to bed tonight, try to meditate and keep his room in the back of your mind. If you're not successful tonight, please don't worry. This could take some time before you achieve an intentional Connection. And remember to write any details you can remember in your journal. You'll bring it with you to our sessions for us to discuss. Through those details, we should be able to identify the reason for the paralysis you sometimes experience."

"Oh! Speaking of the dream journal. I took a nap earlier today and I think I saw one of the patients here. His name was…Eric." My words came out like a question. Dr. Keller's eyebrows raised in amazement. "He misses his daughter and seems like he really wants to get better for her."

"What else did you see?" she asked excitedly. "Wait, just take me from the beginning, if you can, please."

"My dream started with me at the park. It was filled with people. But I noticed a little girl, by herself, crying. I approached her to try and help but suddenly I wasn't at the park anymore. I was in an apartment with beer bottles everywhere. And I mean everywhere. I could still hear the girl crying and asked where she was. He was very emotional but eventually told me he lost custody of his daughter because he had drank himself to sleep and didn't hear her crying for him the next morning. He seemed so lost, and I didn't know what to do so I told him we should probably clean the place up for when she's able to come back. We started to clean but then my phone rang and woke me up." I paused, trying to think if I was forgetting anything. "Something that was strange though, there weren't any doors anywhere. Not until I asked if he wanted to clean. Then a door to what I'm guessing was a kitchen appeared for him to enter."

"Heidi," she says excitedly, "that is amazing!" Dr. Keller stood to her feet and began pacing the floor in front of the couch a few times before stopping and turning to me. "You have such an incredible gift, and it seems to get stronger with each dream. Not only could this be a breakthrough in the field of Dream Study, but you could be a real asset here," she exclaimed with her hands.

"Here? How do you mean?"

"You could help patients. For someone with your abilities, you could Connect with patients and help them heal. Help them overcome their addictions. Help them overcome their fears and anxieties." She sat back down beside me before saying, "But no pressure. I understand this is a lot of information all at once."

"Yeah. Kind of."

"So," gently clasping her hands together, "let's focus on how your dreams go tonight and worry about everything else later. Whether you Connect with Martin or not, journal your dream and we'll talk tomorrow."

"Okay." With a smile, I said, "I can do that."

"Great." She gave my arms a friendly squeeze. "I'm going to visit with Martin a bit longer, but you can go on and head up."

"Have a good night."

"You too, Heidi."

I took the elevator to the first floor, curious if Graham was still here. I found his office further down the hall from Dr. Keller's, but the lights were off, and the door was closed. He must be gone already. Maybe I would find him tonight in one of my dreams.

I took the elevator back up to the second floor. Dr. Keller felt that Graham could be the cause of my paralysis. I wasn't convinced though. I've seen him plenty of times, including last night, when I didn't experience any paralysis.

Confused, my thoughts twisted between Duncan and Graham again. For just a moment, I allowed myself to get lost in delicious thoughts of Graham. I stepped out of the elevator and turned towards my room, barely noticing the tall figure standing in my doorway.

"Hey." A smooth and low tone startled me.

Graham. "Hi," I said meeting his eyes. "I just went by your office looking for you."

"Great minds think alike," he said behind a playful smile. "Can I come in?"

"Please."

I unlocked my door quickly, hoping Dr. Keller wouldn't catch us out here in the hallway.

"Did she take you to see dad?" He asked once we were safely inside.

"Yeah. She might still be down there." I kicked off my shoes and took a seat at the foot of my bed.

Graham took a seat in the chair and nervously pat his knees. "Is everything okay?"

"Listen, I don't want to interfere with your treatment, but I don't think I'm the cause for your paralysis," he finally said.

"I don't think so either. But I'm not the expert in all of this, your mom is. And she seems convinced that you're the reason."

He shook his head back and forth, "It doesn't make sense though. I have also experienced paralysis. And like you, it's not every time I dream either. Unfortunately, I haven't paid any attention to the variances between the times I've experienced it and the times I didn't. But I don't feel good about you going in and looking for him by yourself. I don't like the idea of you dreaming at all when we still don't know what's causing it." Staring off at nothing in particular, he arched his eyebrow and rocked his head from one side to the other, like he's wrestling with a thought. "On the other hand, I would hate to go in with you and my mother turn out to be right." His gaze met mine, "I think that's why I always seek you out. I want to protect you. I don't know from what, but I can't help but feel like you need it."

Not breaking eye contact, I kneel on the floor in front of him and place my hands on his knees. "Hey," keeping my tone soft, "I'm going to be okay. It's just a dream, what's the worst that can happen?" I asked, not expecting him to answer.

"That's just it, Heidi, we *don't* know. This is completely uncharted territory."

"Well, you can Connect too. Has anything bad ever happened to you?"

"I have only been able to Connect to you."

"Oh." Letting my head dip, the reality sunk in that all the theories they have about Connecting are just that. Theories. Was I out of my league thinking I could actually help them? What if I *could* get hurt?

I felt his fingers glide under my chin as he tilted my head back, so my gauze met his, "You don't have to do this. Honest. I can keep trying." His beautiful brown eyes burned into me, causing me to swallow hard. I lusted for the feeling of his lips on mine.

Snap out of it, Heidi. I wanted to do this. Even if I failed, I had to try. "I-I can do this. I want to do this, Graham. Here," I stood up to grab my phone and the business card Dr. Keller left with Graham's number. I entered it into my phone quickly and sent him a text so he had my number now too. "Tomorrow morning, you can call me to check on me. Maybe that will put your mind at ease," I smiled.

He removed his phone from his pocket and saved my number. "Heidi Miller." He smiled as he said my name, "I will call you first thing tomorrow morning." He slid his phone back in his pocket and stood to his feet. "Be safe in there." He gently stroked my temple with his thumb. "You won't be able to find me tonight."

Chapter 27

I sat, rocking in one of the rocking chairs at the store, while Mom and Dad were fussing over something. They're standing near the mailboxes in the back. Dad had the news blasting so loud from the tv that I could barely hear myself think. I glanced around for Olivia, but I didn't see her. I guess I'll ask Mom and Dad what's going on. With my luck, I was probably the reason they were arguing.

"What is Annette going to do?" I hear my mom say as I approached them. She placed her hand over her heart and closed her eyes, "Oh, I just can't imagine what she must be going through right now."

My Dad pulled her in for a hug.

They're not arguing, they're hurting.

"What's going on?" I asked, "What's wrong with Mrs. Johnson?"

My mom wiped her tears and faced me, "Honey, Gerald was diagnosed with stomach cancer. Stage three."

The letter.

My heart sank then shattered for Mr. and Mrs. Johnson. Ronny and Duncan too. They have been friends with my parents for forever, but really got close once Olivia and Ronny started to date. "I am so sorry." I hugged my parents. "He came in the other day to get his mail. He didn't seem his usual chatty self and was quick to get out of here. I wonder if that's when he found out."

"Possibly," my dad said softly. I could tell he was keeping his emotions in check. My mom was already a wreck, he's standing strong for her.

The tv is still blaring. Some story about a car accident was playing over and over again. "I'm going to turn the tv down and then maybe we can go pay them a visit."

"That sounds nice honey. I think they'll like that," Mom said before blowing her nose into the crumpled-up tissue in her hand.

"The accident happened just here, along these streets of this suburban neighborhood." A reporter advised from the screen as I approached the tv. The camera paned to a two-way street with trees lining either side.

A car accident. Like the one Martin Keller was in?

"The victim is forty-eight-year-old Martin Keller. He has been transported to Easton City Medical for his injuries. The family has been notified," the reporter continued. I push up onto my tip toes to turn the volume down. As soon as I reached the button, the tv was no longer in my reach. Falling back to my flat feet, I looked around, seeing that I was no longer in the store. I'm on an elevator. But it didn't feel like I was moving.

The three buttons on the panel let me know my options were the second floor, the first floor, or B... for basement. I must be at the institute. I pressed the button identified as B and started my descent.

The doors opened to the same plain grey room I just visited with Dr. Keller earlier this evening. The only difference was that now, fear had forced itself *inside me. My heart was pounding so hard that I could hear it in my ears. I cast my gauze around the room, looking for any sign of Graham. But nothing.*

He said I wouldn't be able to find him tonight. I thought I wouldn't need him but maybe I was wrong.

Trying to steady my pounding heart, I took a deep breath in and a full exhale out. Wanting to improve my chances of Connecting with Mr. Keller, I watched a few of the meditation videos before bed. The instructor said deep breaths were good for calming our inner stressors, but nothing calmed the anxiety rising in my throat.

I saw the door to his room. My steps towards it felt heavy and slow but I could tell I was getting closer. An echoing beep grew loud and fast.

I finally reached the door and open it. The pictures hanging on the wall begin to come to life. The flowers, stretching towards the floor and ceiling, became darker, almost like shadows.

Now, standing in the middle of the room, unsure how I got this far in, I didn't see Mr. Martin. The only thing in here was me and the now morphed flowers that had begun to curl from the ceiling down towards me.

I screamed.

No sound escaped.

"Mr. Martin!"

Again, no sound.

The stillness was starting to take hold of me.

The door to his room started to slowly shut with me still inside. The view of the grey room became narrower with each second.

The grey room.

The beeping.
The fear.
The stillness.
The flowers on the wall.
I see it now.

This is where I've been, all those times the paralysis struck.

I've got to get back! If I can just get back to the elevator.

The flowers were still reaching down towards me, blocking my vision to the now narrowing view of the doorway.

"Graham!"
"Dr. Keller!"
"Mr. Keller!"
"Duncan!"
"Anyone!"

No sound. And even worse than that, no response.

Sounds of beeping and my heart pounding rang deep in my ears.

It's deafening.

I placed my hands over my ears hoping it'd stop. It didn't.

I squeezed my eyes shut, willing myself to move, to get back to the elevator but my feet don't comply. Tears streamed down my cheeks as I felt the fear bury me.

A sliver of light danced across the floor as the door got closer to closing.

If that door shuts, I fear that I'll be stuck in here forever.

"Help!"
"Help!" I scream, finally hearing the sound of my

voice.

"Heidi, you're safe. I've got you." I felt an arm wrap around my back and a hand press into the back of my head, causing me to fall into something warm and firm.

Instinctively I pushed away, "Help!" I could feel my arms flailing around me, like I'm trying to rid myself of a spider that had fallen on me. My eyes were still squeezed shut, too scared to see the flowers finally take me completely.

"Shh shhh, open your eyes. It's me. You're okay now." His voice sounded familiar. I still my arms for a second, considering if that was true. If I was okay now.

I took a deep breath in and was immediately met with a soothing fragrance. Something clean and fresh. I took a quick peak through one eye to see who was with me.

"Graham!" I squealed as I leaped towards him and curled up in his lap. I felt the EEG cap crash against his shoulder as I squeeze my arms around him.

"Yeah. You're okay now. I've got you," he said as he rubbed my back to sooth me. "Your heart is pounding like crazy. What happened?" he asked. But when I didn't answer, he held me tight. "I tried to call you but when you didn't answer I rushed over as quickly as I could. You were out cold when I got in here. I thought if I set you up it would help you wake up, but even then, it took me a few minutes."

So relieved to finally be awake, I sobbed uncontrollably into his chest. That is a fear I hope I never had to experience again.

I heard the door open. "I knew you took the

master key, Graham. You can't be in here." Dr. Keller said outraged.

I felt Graham's body shift and neck flex, probably to look back at his mom and shoot her a pointed look.

"What happened here," Dr. Keller walked over to us. "Oh, Heidi, what happened?" She started to work around my sobs and removed the EEG cap from my head. "She's clearly upset, Graham. Maybe you should go and let me handle this since you already shouldn't be here."

I squeezed my arms tighter around Graham in response to Dr. Keller's cold words to him. I didn't want him to go. I was not ready for him to leave yet. My sobs had yet to calm down. And they wouldn't if he left.

"Heidi, would you like for me to go?" he asked.

I shook my head, still buried in his chest, not giving a shit how Dr. Keller might feel about seeing me curled up in her son's lap.

"Heidi, I really am better equipped to help you through this. My son is not thinking clearly." She rested her hand on my shoulder, and I quickly shrugged her off. "Heidi," her tone sounded shocked, "I …"

"Just go!" Graham ordered.

"Fine," she huffed. "Heidi, when you're ready, let the nurses know and I'll clear my calendar for you." And with that, she finally left us.

Graham delicately took my face in his hands and dried my tear-soaked cheeks with his thumbs. "What can I do for you?"

"Nothing," I croaked through my sniffling, wiping my face on the long sleeve of my sleep shirt. "I – I," I started, trying to keep the sobs down, "was so scared." I climbed off his lap and back onto the bed, bringing my knees to my chest and hugging them. "I didn't believe you when you said I wouldn't be able to find you. How were you able to stay away?"

"I set an alarm for every twenty-three minutes." My eyebrow arched curiously. "I didn't want to fall into a REM cycle. My EEG scans show that my REM cycles occur anywhere from twenty-seven to thirty-three minutes after each non-REM cycle begins. Twenty-three minutes felt like a safe amount of time to sleep," he finished with a smile.

"Yeah. Makes total sense," I teased, making us both laugh. I took my legs from my chest and sat crisscross, releasing a cleansing breath. A term I learned last night during meditation.

"Do you think you can tell me what happened?" His tone was soothing and protective, like his embrace.

Inhaling deeply, I nodded my head. I reached for my journal so I could write down the details as I told them to Graham.

Graham's thumbs anxiously thumped against his knees as he listened to me recall my dream. "I knew I should have been there. I had a feeling something like this would happen."

"I didn't recognize it last night when your mom took me down to the basement to meet your dad, but it's the same place in our past dreams. The same place where I've experienced paralysis. Do you think that happens because we're trying to Connect with someone in a coma?"

"That's one theory, but because there is absolutely

no data on this type of occurrence, I have nothing to substantiate it."

"I'm sorry I failed."

"Hey now," he placed his hand on my knee. "There's nothing to be sorry for. I'm sorry for not being there with you."

"But, if you were there, we wouldn't know what we know now; that *you* aren't the reason for my paralysis."

He shut his eyes and sighed, like a wight had been lifted from his chest, then a smile spread across his handsome face. "You're right. If there's an appreciation I've gained from your unfortunate experience, it's the knowledge that I'm not the cause of your anxiety."

"But, Graham, I don't think I can go back there. I can't try and Connect with him again. I'm sorry."

He scooted closer and wrapped his arms around me, "That's alright. And to be perfectly honest, I don't want you to try again. We can work on ways for you to identify links to him and the basement so you don't have to encounter the paralysis again."

I sat up and away from him, unable to look in his eyes when I said, "No, that's not necessary. I think I've decided to go home."

"Oh."

"Yeah. I just – I think, um. I think I just sort of want to be home. In a place that's familiar and safe." I missed my sister more than I thought I would.

And Duncan. Even though he's made it clear that we're just friends now.

But my heart ached at the idea of not being able to see Graham, like this, again. The details of his face were more radiant in person than they were in my dreams. His smoothed chiseled jaw. The slight dimple in his chin. The way his forehead wrinkled slightly when he showed concern for me. The way I felt when I stared into his eyes, like I knew everything and nothing all at the same time.

"So, I guess I need to go talk to your mom about all of this," tapping my fingers to the top of the notebook that contained the details of two of the four dreams I've had since arriving at the Keller Institute. The first two dreams, where I Connected with Graham, unfortunately weren't in the notebook.

"Yeah, you should. I'll go let the nurse know you're ready for Dr. Keller." Graham stood and walked to the door.

"Graham, wait." I called. He turned to face me. "The patient who died. Can you show me the room he stayed in?" I have a hunch and am curious if I'm remotely close.

Graham pulled out the master key from his pocket and looked at it in thought before answering. "Yes. I'll show you."

Graham unlocked the door for room two and we entered. The set up was the same as the room I was in except for the decorative aspects. Most notably, the framed photos on the walls. They were photos of flowers. Instead of them being black and white or in full color, they were all a monochromatic shade of purple.

Chapter 28

"Come in." Dr. Keller called after I rapped a few light knocks on the door to her office. "Please, come in, have a seat," she said with a smile. I took a seat in one of the plush chairs in front of her desk, holding the notebook to my chest. "You seemed to be out of sorts this morning when I saw you. How are you feeling now?"

"I'm okay."

"Good. Please, let me apologize, again, for Graham's behavior."

"No," I cut her off, "he was a big help this morning. There's no need to apologize."

She cleared her throat, "Alright then," she said. She crossed her hands and placed them on her desk, "are you up for some questions?" I nodded.

"Great. First, did you experience a dream last night?"

"I did. It was pretty bleak."

"Can you elaborate on that?" She slid a pad in front of her and picked up a pen.

I took a deep breath and opened my notebook to the page where the details were scribbled. "It started out as a normal dream. I was in the store with my parents when I noticed a news report blaring from the tv. The report was in a loop, telling the same story over and over. It wasn't until I went over to turn it down that I paid attention to the details. It was Mr. Keller's accident. The next thing I knew, I was on the elevator down to the basement. But when the doors opened, I was overcome with fear. I kept walking towards his room anyway. But, when I made it there and opened the door, I was pulled inside with the beeping sound. Then, the flowers started to morph into these growing shadows. I didn't see Mr. Keller in there but the flowers started to hang down from the ceiling, reaching towards me while the door closed slowly. But when I decided to head back to the elevator I couldn't. The paralysis had already set in. Instincts kicked in and I tried to yell for help, but no sound came out. So, I was standing there, unable to move or speak as these creepy morphed flowers stretch to take hold of me. Eventually, Graham was able to wake me up. It has definitely been the scariest experience I've ever had." I closed my notebook, "It felt sinister."

Dr. Keller finished with her notes and set her pen down. She looked over to me, then back to her notes.

"Something I didn't realize when you brought me down to meet Mr. Keller was that it's the same place I'm always at when I experience that fear and paralysis. In my dreams, I mean. The grey room, the beeping, the flowers on the wall. It's the same place every time."

"How could you get there if you…" She stopped mid-sentence and nodded her head as if she had just figured something out. "Graham," she finally said. "You must have Connected with Graham as he was trying to Connect with Martin."

Graham. I didn't think about that, about him Connecting with his dad and how he seemed to be in pain the night I helped him. I make a mental note to see him one more time before I left.

"Dr. Keller, do you think this is happening because I'm trying to Connect with someone in a coma?"

"It's possible but we'd need to follow up with more studies to be sure."

"More studies?"

"Yes. I'd like for you to try to Connect with other coma patients."

I felt a wrinkle between my eyebrows form as I narrowed my eyes at her, "I'm sorry. You want me to try that again?" Graham was right. She threw herself into her work and didn't seem to care about the wellbeing of others. "Didn't you hear me earlier, it felt sinister. It's a fear that I don't want to experience again."

"I understand it was a scary experience, but nothing can happen to you in there. You're safe."

"How do you know? You said there's literally no data, or evidence, or anything for this type of occurrence. Or recurrence or whatever the hell you call it!"

"I suppose that's true…"

"Is it? Is it true?" Dr. Keller looked at me bewildered. "Is that what you told the patient in room two?"

Her jaw dropped. "I-I- I don't know what you're talking about. What patient?"

"The one who died. The one who's murder I witnessed." I crossed my arms and waited for her response. The pictures of the purple flowers hung in the room he stayed in was all the evidence I needed. But to be sure, I needed Dr. Keller to confirm. "I told you about it during one of our appointments.

She let out a gruff. "Fine. But he wasn't murdered. He just simply passed away. His autopsy showed he died of a heart attack. He wasn't murdered."

Could that be true? I wondered. I guess there was no way for me to truly know, and not a way I could report this without sounding like I made it all up. "Why didn't you tell me you knew who I was referring to? I have been suffering for weeks, trying to find out that man's identity. I told you about the field of purple flowers and him grabbing his chest. You didn't think to maybe let me in on the fact that you knew the person I was referring to?"

"How was I supposed to know for sure that the two were the same individuals?"

As much as I hate to admit it, she had a valid point. But still, something seemed off. "You didn't ask him to Connect with your husband?"

"So, what if I did? What's the point you're trying to make here?"

"The point I'm trying to make here is that you are withholding. I trusted you. I believed you. I allowed myself to seek your husband because you told me it would be safe. Yet, you've been sitting on information that could possibly prove that not to be true. And you still allowed me to think I was completely safe."

"Heidi, please, let's not lose our cool here. This could be the breakthrough we've needed to truly understand Connecting. Your gift could turn the study of dreams on its head. Think of all the good that would come from it. All the people you could help."

Infuriated that she was not listening to me, I stood from my chair. My hands balled into fists and fell to my side, "You lied! How could I continue to work with someone I can't trust? In fact, I'll be packing my bags and getting the hell out of here." I stormed out of her office, not meaning to slam the door behind me, causing the pictures hanging on either side of the doorframe to rattle.

I looked down the hall to Graham's office, the light was off. I needed to find him and tell him not to try and Connect with his dad. I ran down to the lobby, he wasn't there either. Just the sweet faced receptionist who shot me a strange look after poking my head out for a quick glance at the waiting room.

He was not in the gym or the little garden slash outdoor area either. I made my way back to the elevator, repeatedly pressing the Up arrow to hurry along the descent. Ding! It finally rang as the doors opened for me. I pressed the button for the second floor and impatiently waited until the doors finally opened again to let me out.

He wasn't in the café or the nurse's office.

Dammit. The last place to check was the basement.

I wasn't sure I was ready to go back down there. I headed back to my room for my cell phone. I quickly typed a message to him asking that he didn't try and connect with his dad again. There was no way to be sure if John Doe died from a heart attack or something else from his dream. I didn't want Graham to suffer the same fate.

Without taking the time to fold my clothes, I shoved everything back in my bag haphazardly, not caring about the wrinkles that would definitely be formed once I unpacked. Lastly, I needed to grab everything from the bathroom.

My shampoo and body wash bottles sat in a ring of water on the shelf within the shower. I didn't bother to dry them before tossing them and my toothbrush in the bag with my clothes.

I took another scan around the bedroom before I zipped up my duffle bag. My phone charger was still plugged into the outlet behind the nightstand. I unplugged it and coil it around my hand before packing it up too.

Okay, I think that's everything.

I zipped my duffle bag and threw the strap over my shoulder. I checked my phone for a response from Graham, but he hadn't even read the text yet. Looks like I have to make the dreaded trip down to the basement after all. I couldn't leave here until I knew he wouldn't try and Connect with his dad again.

I shut the door of room number four behind me, got on the elevator and made my way down to the basement.

"Heidi?" Graham called to me as he shut the door to his dad's room behind me. "I figured you'd out of here by now."

"I'm on my way," gesturing to my duffle bag, "but I wanted to ask you a favor before I left."

"Sure. What is it?" He walked over to me, close enough that I smelled his sweet, clean scent. I almost forgot what I came down here for.

Swallowing hard, I refocused. "Please. Please, don't try to Connect with your dad. Your mom is hiding something. I can feel it. The patient from room two, I watched him die. Yet she repeatedly tells me that nothing bad can happen to me when I Connect? I can't believe the stillness and the patient's death are a coincidence.

Graham looked as if he had something to say but I didn't give him a chance. I had to get this all out.

"You even said it yourself. His scans looked promising. Your mom didn't confirm or deny if she asked him to Connect with your dad, but I think I already know the answer to that. So, please," I plead, not only with my words, but my eyes as well, "don't try to Connect."

"Okay." He slid his hands into his pockets.

"Wait, really? I thought I was going to have to fight you on it."

"Nope. I agree that it might not be safe to Connect with him, so I won't. I have been suspicious of Wyatt's death too. And I think you're right. It feels like my mom is hiding something."

"Wyatt? Was that his name?"

"Yes."

After all this time of searching for him, I had finally found him. I felt both relieved and sadden at the loss. What I witnessed had finally been validated, but a man had lost his life. A life that may never get the justice he deserves. "I've been searching for him, for so long. Ever since I saw him die in that field of purple flowers. I – "

"Purple flowers?" Graham asked.

"Yeah. Weeks ago, I saw this man die in one of my dreams. That was the first time I felt the stillness. The first time it felt like someone was watching me in my own dreams."

"That's because someone was watching you. Me."

"So, it *was* you! I couldn't make out the details, but I saw someone standing, just off in the distance. And if you were there, you must have watched Wyatt die too."

Graham shook his head, "I only saw you. And the flowers. I saw you scream and run for help, but I couldn't get to you." My face bunched into confusion, ready to unleash a string of questions when Graham answered them before I could speak a word. "I probably couldn't see him because I was Connecting to you and not Wyatt. My abilities were not as strong then as they are now, so that could also be a factor in why I couldn't see him then."

"That makes sense... I think," I said, still trying to wrap my mind around all of this. "I'm sorry I wasn't able to help your family."

"Your efforts were more than enough, Heidi. Thank you."

"Yeah, of course." I tucked my hair behind my ear, "So, I guess this is it." I pointed with my thumb over my shoulder to the elevator, "I'm going to take off now."

As the elevator doors begin to close, Graham dragged his right hand through his hair and locked his deep brown eyes on me one last time, "Bye, Heidi."

Chapter 29

It's close to noon when I finally fly down the main road of my hometown. Passing by the store, then my parents' house, then the rest of the small business that also sat on the main road. I hoped I had made it through there without anyone noticing. Once I came to the hook in the road, I knew there were just seven more miles before I got to turn down the short dirt road that led to my house.

All I could think about was showering then curling up on the couch to catch up on some of my shows. This has been a long few days and I just needed to clear my mind before I told my mom that I was back from therapy. She's going to want to throw this in my face and I'll need to be at full strength to be able to handle her.

Finally pulling into my driveway, I felt a sense of bliss wash over me. I know I didn't do anything, other than get my nails done, buy horrible tasting food, and sit and stare at Lake Jericho while I was in the city, and maybe this isn't a fair statement but, it wasn't as exciting as I thought it would be. Maybe I'm not missing much adventure after all.

Putting my car in park, I mulled over that last realization a little longer. Maybe the city wasn't as exciting as I thought, but the possibilities of doing something worthwhile were. I could go back to school and get a job doing something meaningful. I could help people at the Institute as Dr. Keller suggested. Well, maybe not anymore after what happened last night, but the idea did set a spark of joy ablaze in my heart.

But, on the other hand, my family was here. My sister. *Duncan*. And I missed them more than I thought I would.

I jingled my keys in the lock of my front door and opened it before heaving my duffle bag on the floor of my living room. I shut the door, set my purse down on the console table, kicked my shoes off, grabbed my toiletries from my bag, and made a beeline to my shower, eager to wash last night's dream off of me. I still couldn't believe Dr. Keller had the nerve to think I'd try and Connect with another coma patient. I couldn't believe she lied to me. I couldn't believe I fell for her caring mother act.

I stuck my hand under the streams of water to test the temperature. It was perfect. Turning the nozzle of my shower head to the massage setting, I stepped inside, letting the burn of the hot, forceful water beat down on my neck and shoulders. The water soothed my body, but only fueled my mind.

Wandering back to the morning I left for the Keller Institute, I replayed Duncan in the shower with me, his hands traveling hungrily down my body. Wishing he had got to touch me before we were interrupted. How good it would have felt to feel his fingers slip inside me, stretching me before filling me with his cock. Water rained down over my nipples as I turned into the water, sending an unexpected jolt of pleasure through me. It made me crave Duncan even more. It didn't matter though, he had called off our…'benefits'.

I couldn't say I blamed him, now that my sister knew, it felt like more people could know, and someone *could* get hurt. Whether he was talking about us, or our families, I didn't know. I forgot to ask him to explain what he meant when we talked yesterday, I was too thrown off by his suggestion. I didn't know what else to say except to agree with him.

I dried myself completely off before hanging up my towel. I kicked my dirty clothes out from in front of the door and walked naked to my dresser to grab a pair of panties and an oversized sleep shirt to slip into. I grabbed the burnt orange knitted throw blanket draped across the corner of my bed and settled into a comfortable spot on my couch. Wrapping the blanket snuggly over my feet, legs, and torso, I reached for the remote and turned on one of my shows. This one was a reality competition show where teams of two complete outrageous and adventurous challenges for a shit ton of money.

After a couple of episodes, I felt my eyelids grow heavy. I positioned one of the decorative pillows between my head and the armrest of my couch and settled in for a nap. My eyelids fluttered shut, and I could feel sleep coming to carry me away.

Flashes of black floral shadows evade my mind, forcing my eyes to open. I took a few breaths and reminded myself that I was home, and I was safe. As long as I didn't seek Mr. Keller, I would have enjoyable dreams. I needed to think about something else, something that brought me peace.

Think.

Kingsman trail has always been a place I go to

clear my head. Feeling the breeze cut through the trees, watching the wildlife scurry around me, hearing the crunching sound of dirt, leaves, and gravel beneath my feet silenced my mind. It helped calm all the thoughts that wrestled around with one another.

My breaths were deep and rhythmic as I allowed my mind to drift to the trail, picturing myself walking along the tree line.

This is helping.

Sleep came for me again and I went peacefully.

***

The breeze whipped my long hair around my face, forcing me to gather it, twist it, and pull the wound strands in front of my left shoulder. I strolled peacefully for what felt like several minutes until I approached one of the benches and decided to take a seat. As soon as I did, Duncan appeared on my right.

"Enjoying your walk, Heidi?" he asked.

"It certainly is a nice day for a one," a second voice to my left said to me. I turn my head and saw Graham.

What is happening right now?

"It is, isn't?" Duncan closed his eyes and lifted his face toward the sky, allowing himself to bask in the sunlight.

I stood quickly and faced them. Duncan on one side, leaned back, knees apart, allowing him to sit comfortably as his calloused hands rested atop his thighs. Graham on the other, his right ankle resting on his left knee, his right elbow resting on the back of the bench. I looked back and forth at them, noticing how different they each look.

Duncan's mysterious green eyes, thick and short wild curls adorn his head. A neatly groomed beard covered the lower half of his face. A black tee shirt stretched across his chest, under a long sleeved, unbuttoned, plaid shirt. Jeans wrapped snug around his burly thighs and his feet took up residency in dusty, tattered work boots.

Graham's deep brown eyes, short almost black, styled hair. Smooth skin along his strong jaw. His style of dress was as clean cut as his hair style. A white collard button up shirt, neatly tucked into navy blue slacks, held by a belt. Caramel colored laced loafers completed his outfit.

Both a stark contrast to each other in looks.

But they both made me feel something. Even if I'm not completely sure what exactly it is they make me feel, I could say with confidence that they're both special to me.

I looked up and then down the trail for any sign of another Graham.

This must be my dream. I doubt Graham would be napping in the middle of his workday.

"Why are you both here," I decided to ask them.

In unison, they respond, "To help you choose."

"Choose? Choose what?"

"The life you want," Duncan said.

"And who you want to spend it with," Graham concluded.

Nope. I am not doing this right now.

I turned and walked away from them.

This is my dream, I'm in control.

"We'll be here until you make your decision,"

their voices rang in unison again.

I didn't turn to look back at them, I just kept walking. But I can't help but hear their words rattle around in my brain. They're right… or am I right since this is my dream? Eh, it doesn't matter either way, I will have to make a decision eventually. I can't continue to live my life allowing my actions to be dictated by my dreams and thoughts.

Looking further down the trail, I saw a mailbox. Just, a single black mailbox resting on a wooden post in the middle of the trail. I took a deep breath, trying to decide if I wanted to approach the mailbox or not. Once I did, I knew I'd be transported to someone else's dream.

I eventually decided to approach it and hoped for the best. I opened the lid and noticed I was no longer on Kingsman Trail, but in a bright room. There were several reclining chairs along three of the four walls, each with a privacy curtain hanging from above. Only one chair had someone sitting in it. An older man with grey and rusty colored hair rested with his eyes closed. It's then when I noticed all the lines hooked to his arm lead to a series of machines beside him.

Mr. Johnson.

The first part of last night's dream replayed in my head. My parents were emotional for him and Mrs. Johnson. Does this mean he really is sick?

I need to get to Olivia. I need to wake up.

Before I could turn to try and find my way out, Mr. Johnson called to me, "Heidi?"

I raised my hand in a small wave and offered a sympathetic smile, "Hi, Mr. Johnson. How are you feeling?"

"Please, Gerald is fine. And I'm feeling as strong as an Ox!" A series of coughs erupt from his chest. He used a handkerchief to wipe his mouth. "The doctors are going to fix me up good as new. You'll see." A warm smile spread across his face.

That's the kind of person Mr. Johnson is, always so positive and caring. "I'm sure you'll be back and at 'em before we know it."

He laughed, "That's right. You all can't get rid of me that easily." Another cough escaped his chest. "Do you think you could do me a favor?" He reached for my hand.

"Of course," I said, taking his hand.

"Will you tell Duncan not to worry so much?"

Confused why he'd ask me and not Ronny, but I'm not one to disregard a kind man's wishes. "Yeah. Of course."

"He cares for you, you know? He's a stone wall when it comes to letting others see his emotions, but we can tell." I couldn't stop my lips from curling into a subtle smile, but I didn't respond. "So be patient with him. I don't think he's ever healed from being abandoned by his birth parents."

He was abandoned. I knew he was adopted but didn't know the circumstances. Duncan was pretty tight lip about it all and so were his parents. Except when they're dreaming apparently.

Mr. Johnson closed his eyes and pat the top of my hand with his free hand, "Thanks for the visit, dear. Duncan is wise to have his sights set on you." He dropped my hand and folded his to rest over his belly.

Now, I need to wake up.

Chapter 30

Uncurling my body, I stretched my arms above my head and my legs towards the opposite end of the couch, letting out a purr. I sat up, rubbed my face with my hands before getting up to dig my phone out of my purse. It was almost five o'clock.

Damn, I napped longer than I expected.

I headed to my room to get dressed. I needed to see Olivia to figure out if Mr. Johnson was actually sick or if it was just a dream. Her car wasn't in her driveway when I pulled up earlier, which means she might be finishing up at the store. I hoped Mom wasn't there too, I still was not ready to deal with her.

Sliding into a pair of jeans, leaving the same oversized sleep shirt I pulled on after my shower, I grabbed my purse, pulled on my sneakers, and headed out the door.

Olivia's car still wasn't at her house, so I made the trip back down the main road. Not hauling ass this time since I need to keep an eye out for her white sedan.

Approaching the store, I saw my dad's blue pickup truck parked out front. No sign of Oliva's car. She must be at Ronny's house. After passing the store, I turned right, down the only other paved road in this town. This road led to more houses and eventually dead ended to Ronny and Duncan's lumber business.

Ronny's house sat about a mile off the road, but I

could still see Oliva's white car parked up near his house. I turned onto his gravel driveway, driving slowly not to kick up any rocks with my tires, and parked next to Olivia's car.

Ronny answered the door shortly after I knocked. His surprised look told me he was definitely not expecting to see me. "Hi," I started, "I wanted to stop by and check on you. May I come in?"

"Yeah, of course," he stepped aside as I entered and shut the door behind me. Oliva came from the hallway to the right and stopped when she saw me.

"I didn't expect you to be back home already," she said, closing the gap between us and wrapping me in her sisterly embrace. "Is everything okay?"

"We'll, that's kind of why I'm here. But yes, I'm okay," I said to her before turning to Ronny, "I wanted to stop by and check on you. How's your dad?"

Perplexed, he looked over at Oliva then back at me. "How did you know?" Oliva asked, before Ronny could get a word out.

"It doesn't matter," I said softly, hoping she would move past this line of questioning. Saying "I had a dream" would make me sound like a lunatic in front of Ronny. I was hoping I could confirm with Olivia first before confronting Ronny and Duncan but, here we were. She gave me a look that said she understood exactly how I knew.

Ronny cleared his throat and made his way to the brown recliner sitting near the middle of the living room. Olivia and I followed and took our seat on the couch next to it. "He's been better. But you know my old man, always has a positive outlook on things. He said a little bit of cancer can't keep him down. It's Mom and Duncan that I'm mostly worried about. Mom of course is crushed. Hasn't stopped crying since we found out yesterday evening."

"And Duncan," I said, trying to keep the heart ache out of my voice, "how's he holding up?"

"He hasn't said a word since Dad sat us all down. He just nodded and sat there while Mom bawled her eyes out." Ronny leaned forward in the recliner, rested his elbows on his knees and started to pick at his left hand with his right. "When my parents adopted Duncan, he didn't speak for nearly a year. Not because he couldn't, but because he wouldn't. The doctors said that it could have been caused by some sort of trauma, but Duncan never told anyone anything about his time with his birth parents. He was only six when the adoption was finalized, and he was slow to warm up to us. But us Johnsons, we're persistent," he smiled, glancing at Oliva. She giggled. "We weren't going to give up on him and eventually, he came around." He sat back in the recliner and rubbed his eyes, "Dad's worried his diagnosis has triggered that same non-verbal response in Duncan."

"I didn't know that about Duncan. I can't imagine what it must have been like to start a life with strangers. And I'm so sorry about your dad. Are his doctors optimistic?"

"Apparently, he has known about this for a while, but decided it was best to keep it to himself. He received a letter a few days ago, letting him know that his case was reviewed by a specialist and that he was a great candidate for a clinical trial. His doctors are optimistic he'll be cancer free within the next eighteen months. Once he got news that there was hope, he decided to tell us. He started treatment this morning. Mom is with him at the hospital now."

"I'm happy to hear that. I think with the fighting spirit of your dad, that cancer doesn't stand a chance," I said with a smile, trying to lighten the mood.

"I appreciate it, Heidi."

"Well, I should get going. I don't want to take up too much of your time. I just wanted to come by and check in on you. Please let me know if there's anything I can do for you or your parents." I stood, ready to head back out to my car.

"You could do one thing for me," he added.

"Sure. Anything."

"Can you go by and check on Duncan? If there's anyone he'll talk to, it's you."

Tucking my hair behind my ear, I looked down at my feet and thought back to what Mr. Johnson said to me in my dream. It pained me to know Duncan was hurting. His dad, and now his brother, thought I could somehow alleviate his worry. I'm not sure they're right, but I'll do my best to help. "Of course," I said with a sympathetic smile. "I'll head over now."

"I'll walk you out," Oliva said.

"Thanks. See later, Ronny."

"See, ya," he said as he waved his hand. "Thanks for stopping by. I'll let my folks know you send your best."

"Thanks." Olivia and I stepped outside, shutting the door behind us, before walking to the bottom of the porch steps.

"So, what happened? Why are you back so

early?" she asked quietly and quickly. "Not that I'm not happy to see you, I missed you quite a bit," she concluded with her arms stretched out towards me for another hug.

"I missed you too," I said as I hugged her back. She released me from our embrace and held me by my shoulders, examining me, waiting for me to answer her. "It's a lot, and I don't really have time to discuss it all now. Want to come over tonight? I could tell you everything then."

"Yeah, I'll be there around seven. But let me ask you this before you go; did you learn about Gerald's diagnosis through your dream?" I nodded. "I knew it!" She snapped her fingers like she discovered something important. "How do you do that?" She asked more out of amazement than actually expecting a response. I shrugged my shoulders at her, her guess would be as good as mine. "Alright, go check on Duncan and I'll see you later."

"Okay. See you in a bit." I drove my car towards Duncan's house, which was about ten miles past his brother's house, and closer to the lumber yard. Duncan's house didn't sit as far back from the road like Ronny's did. As I pulled into Duncan's driveway, I could see him gently swinging in his wooden porch swing. When he heard the sound of gravel crunch under my tires, he looked in the direction of my car, stood and waited for me to pull up behind his black truck to park. Shutting my car door, I looked up at him, still standing and watching me from the porch. He didn't utter a single word. Not even a wave.

"Hey," I said, suddenly feeling nervous and a little embarrassed. If I had known I was going to see

Duncan, I would have put something more flattering on. But instead, here I stood, in this oversized tee shirt and jeans. I was nervous because the last time I spoke to him, he said we should stop seeing each other… in *that* way. That was only yesterday afternoon, before he was told about his dad's diagnosis. And now I was here, strictly on a friendly basis, trying to help my friend process some upsetting news. "Are you up for some company?"

Duncan walked back over and sat on his porch swing and stared out into his yard. I wasn't sure if that was an invitation or not, but I decided to take a chance and join him. Criss-crossing my legs in the seat of the swing, Duncan rocked from the heels of his feet to his toes, causing us to swing gently back and forth. We sat in silence for a while as I picked at the frayed hem of my jeans. The late afternoon breeze danced around us.

Deciding to break the silence between us, I said, "You haven't told me to go yet. Is it okay that I'm still here with you?"

Duncan took a deep breath, closed his eyes, and nodded his head.

"Is it okay if I talk?" Again, he replied with a nod. Not the verbal confirmation I had hoped for, but it was better than nothing. "I wanted to come by and tell you that I'm sorry to hear about your dad." Duncan's large hands interlocked as he tapped his thumbs together. "I talked to Ronny; he said your dad's doctors are optimistic about his treatment plan. That's something to be hopeful for, right?" Enthusiasm filled my tone. I had to remain optimistic if there was any hope of helping Duncan through this. "Ronny said the treatment time is eighteen months. When you put that into perspective, it's not all that long of a time."

Nothing. No response at all.

I was terrible at this. Why Ronny and Mr. Johnson thought I could help was unbeknownst to me. We sat in silence once again. Duncan's thumbs had stopped their dance and his hands laid in his lap. I went back to picking at the hem of my jeans. I didn't want to give up on him, but I didn't think I was what he needed right now. Maybe he just needed space to process everything.

I decided to ask one last question before throwing in the towel. "Is there anything I can do for you, Duncan? Anything at all?" I wanted him to know that I was here for him. Regardless of the nature of our relationship, I still deeply cared for him.

Duncan flattened his feet against the porch to stop us from swinging and stood up. I guess he needed me to go now. I uncrossed my legs so I could stand and leave too, but before my feet hit the porch, he turned to face me, extending his hand. His green eyes burned into me with a familiar intensity. I thought I must be mistaking his expression but took his hand anyway. He pulled me to my feet, and in a single motion, he lifted me up, cradling my ass with his large hands. I wrapped my legs around him to steady myself in his grip.

Without breaking eye contact with me, he carried me into his house, then into his bedroom.

I wish I knew what he was thinking.

I wish I knew what he needed.

Well… maybe this *is* what he needed.

He laid me on his bed and quickly undressed me,

not allowing his eyes to leave mine until I was completely naked. His eyes traveled slowly down the length of my body, then back to my eyes. My bare chest rose and fell in anticipation of his touch, hungry for him. I thought he had started to regret his decision until he removed his own shirt and straddled me. He planted a deep, longing, desperate kiss on my lips. Our mouths parted, allowing him to gently tug and suck on my bottom lip before he moved to my neck then chest. My nipples grew hard as he neared my breast.

I swallowed hard, worried this wouldn't do him any good. "Duncan," I pant, "you don't…" He looked up at me and brought a single finger to the center of his full lips, mimicking a shushing gesture, allowing a devilish grin to appear behind it. He then moved that finger from his lips to between my thighs, seeking my slick center.

Inserting two fingers, he stroked my core as his green eyes stay locked in on me. His expression was effortless, yet determined, as his fingers worked faster, pressing firmer against my insides. Using the palm of his hand, he created friction above my clit, finally coxing me to orgasm around his skilled fingers. He removed his fingers from me and quickly moved down my body, spreading my legs wide and aligning his mouth with my folds. He moved his tongue up and down my soaked slit until I felt my insides tightening again. My body trembled as he flicked his tongue quickly over my clit. My hands reached towards him, tangling my fingers in his thick hair, guiding him up and down in the way my body demanded.

Duncan let out a muffled hum, shooting his eyes up to mine.

He wanted to taste me. He wanted to taste the pleasure he elicits. The pleasure that belongs to him.

My hands steady him, signaling to him that he's hit my sweet spot. My legs squeezed together around his head as I let out a restrained yelp, covering my mouth with my hand, trying to quite my response to the second orgasm he caused. Duncan used his entire tongue to lap up all my juices.

He watched me through satisfied, green eyes as he used his hand to dry his mouth and beard, still kneeling between my spread thighs. He eyed my swollen lips and unbuttoned his jeans.

I could barely contain my squeal when his erection was finally released from his denim prison. After our conversation yesterday, I didn't think I'd ever get to feel him inside of me again. Expecting him to kneel between my thighs again after removing his jeans, he surprised me by flipping me over on my stomach. My arms and legs spread out like an X across his bed.

His calloused hands left delicious scratches in their wake as they ran up my calves, across my thighs and finally over my ass and hips. He gave each cheek a squeeze before pulling my hips up and back towards him. He pulled me closer to where he was standing at the foot of the bed. My knees were resting on his bed, my shins are hanging over the edge of the mattress, and my ass was high in the air.

I could feel the head of Duncan's penis tease my opening, sliding my slickness up and down my folds to prepare me for his length. Finally, he entered, hitting all the best spots inside me. His hands firmly gripped my hips as he rocked me back and forth on his cock. This time I couldn't suppress my moans and whimpers. I didn't want to. I wanted him to hear how bad I wanted it, how I craved him.

We went a couple more rounds in various positions, causing me to have one orgasm after another after another, before he crashed beside me on the bed and pulled me into his arms. Our bodies were sweaty and his chest heaved against my back. Part of me hated how right this felt, being wrapped securely in his arms. The other part of me wanted to stay wrapped in them forever.

Just another confusing thought I had been wrestling with lately.

Duncan exhaled and gave me a tight squeeze, "Thank you."

Shocked, I turned to face him and propped my arm under neath me. "You spoke!" I couldn't stop the ear-to-ear grin that developed on my blushed faced.

Duncan tucked a wild tendril behind my ear, "Yeah." He stroked my chin with the back of his finger. "I think I... shut down. Or something. I felt like I was lost inside my own head." I gave him a sympathetic look because I could absolutely relate. "I know everyone dies eventually, but I wasn't prepared to hear that it could be sooner rather than later for my dad." He rolled onto his back and dragged his right hand from his forehead into his hair and let out a huff. "I thought I was healing from my life before they adopted me, but I guess I'm not as healed as I hoped. I mean, I know I still have a lot to work through, I just thought I was stronger."

"Hey," I dipped my head down to kiss the inside of his left bicep, "This doesn't mean you're weak. This means you love your family. We all process grief differently." I placed my hand on his chest. "If that means you have to stop talking until you fuck me senseless, then so be it. You give me a call anytime you need help," I teased.

He laughed then rushed his left hand in my hair and held the back of my head as we shared a brief tender look. He cleared his throat, "So, you're back already huh? Something must have happened."

My eyebrow arched at his assumption. "What makes you think something happened?"

"You wouldn't have given up an opportunity to prove your mom wrong unless it was absolutely necessary."

Damn, maybe he did know me. "Yeah, uh…" I stared absentmindedly at his chest as I stroked the soft chest hair that was beneath my hand, "something happened." I was just now noticing that the sun was starting to sink low in the sky. I needed to be home before Olivia got there. "But, I actually do have to get going. Olivia is coming over tonight. Was all of this," gesturing between our naked bodies, "what you needed?"

"In a sense, yes. I needed to feel safe." His right hand held my hand that was on his chest and locks eyes with me, "And that's how I feel when I'm with you."

Holy. Hell.

Duncan Johnson knew how to make a girl wet, that was for damn sure. The heat rose up my neck and to my cheeks. He could tell. He offered me a boyish grin before lifting up and planting a swift kiss on my forehead.

"Better get going. I don't want Oliva to get upset with us again. I'll talk to you later."

"Or if not," I shrugged playfully, "I'll know just how to *help*."

Chapter 31

"You want a full pour or half?" I called from the kitchen to Oliva.

"Oh, what the hell, give me the full."

"You got it," I chuckled. Holding two stemless glasses, with full pours of red wine, I walked over to the couch and took a seat next to Oliva. We were both sitting cross-legged, but facing each other. We clinked our glasses together before taking a sip.

Olivia's eyes went wide as she looked at my hand holding the glass to my mouth. "You got your nails done! I love them!"

Already gotten used to them on my hand, I forgot that I had them done my first night in the city. "Oh yeah!" I said, examining my nails. "Eh, they're alright. They make my fingers feel heavy."

She raised her eyebrows and slightly nodded her head to consider my point. "So, tell me everything. I wasn't expecting for you to get home until next week, so I *know* some shit had to have happened."

I took another sip of my wine and sighed, "I don't even know where to begin."

"Start at the beginning."

I puffed my checks before exhaling air dramatically between my lips. First, I started with the institute and what it was like. I told her about the little gym, the café, the twenty-four seven nurse's station. The photographs on the walls, how chic and cozy Dr. Keller's offices were. What my bedroom looked like.

I told her about the terrible tasting food I got from the little coffee shop and that I was pretty sure that's what made me sick.

Next, I told her what Dr. Keller and I talked about in our sessions, about the EEG and what my results were and why It was supposedly a big deal in the world of dream science. I told her about the dream I had with a patient, and how I felt when I got to talk to him and help clean his apartment. How it felt like I was doing something that could help him in his recovery. It felt meaningful. I told her Dr. Keller even said as much about it.

Then I told her about Graham.

"*Olivia*. He's *the* guy – from my dreams." Her eyes went wide and her mouth fell. I took another sip of wine. "Yep! And I *freaked*. Literally high tailed it out of there."

"And you're sure it's the same guy? Not saying that I don't believe you, but you have to admit, it's a little wild. Maybe you two have met each other before."

I shook my head and told her about Connecting. I told her about the dream he had when he was younger, how he had a similar experience to me when I dreamed about Michael. "In fact, that's what first triggered Dr. Keller's interest in dream study. It's how she came up with her idea of dream therapy." I paused to take another sip of my wine. "Not only does she counsel her patients in a traditional way, but she also pairs it with dreaming. She teaches techniques that help patients have lucid dreams, and to dream about their triggers or their vices, then, in their dreams, they can practice being sober, or unafraid, or whatever it is they need to be healthy and to heal."

Oliva didn't look convinced. "And that's supposed to work? The *dreaming* part of it all," she clarified.

"Dr. Keller, and Graham, stand behind it. And to me, it makes sense. She was explaining to me how lucid dreaming is like practice." Oliva's expression told me she was lost. Her eyebrows were pulled down and her eyes were squinted at me. "Okay, here's an example. Remember when I was a kid, and I couldn't ski for the life of me, I just kept falling over and over? Well, that night, I had a dream about skiing, and eventually, in my dream, I was able to ski without falling down. The next day I asked Mom and Dad to take us back up…."

"Oh yeah! I *do* remember that. I thought you were kidding about the dream and was just trying to convince Mom and Dad it wouldn't be a wasted day to go back up there."

Taking another sip of my wine, I shook my head. "Nope. I learned in my dream. Pretty wild right?"

"Definitely." We both took another sip of our wine. "So, anything else I need to know about this Graham guy?"

A small smile curled up at the corner of my lips, "He's beautiful." I leaned my head to one side and looked up at nothing in particular, remembering his features. "He has these deep, get lost in me, brown eyes. The cutest little dimple in his chin. An amazing jaw line. And, we're drawn to each other in a way that I can't explain."

"Did anything happen between you two?" She

shot me a suspicious look.

"Um. Almost" She raised an eyebrow waiting for me to spill it. "I had a dream. It felt so real….and intimate."

"Wait. If it happened in your dream, doesn't that mean it actually happened?"

"No. I do dream my own dreams. Dreams where I don't *Connect* with anyone. It was the middle of the day when I dreamed this dream. I doubt he would be catching a nap in his office when he should be with patients."

"Did you ask him if him about it? Like, did he confirm he wasn't napping during the day?"

"I did… but, he never answered," I suddenly remembered. "I asked him the night I got sick but completely forgot all about following up with him about it." Olivia arched her eyebrow again. "But the day of the dream, something came up and he had to go. So, I'm pretty sure it was just my dream."

"Yeah, I guess that makes sense." Taking another sip of her wine, she asked, "Is that all?"

Feeling guilty about it now, I told her how we almost hooked up. "Coincidentally enough, it was the same night I got sick. In fact, that's what stopped us." Her eyes grew wide. "Not my proudest moment but it felt like a force dictating my actions." Which led me to bring up Amanda and how he broke up with her because he started seeing me in his dreams. Then I told her about how I saw them in the park, then later dreamed about them in the park and how there were two of Graham. She took steady sips of her wine, trying to process all the information I was throwing at her.

I then told her about the dream I had about Duncan, before I left, about the house and being pregnant, and how Graham was there. I told her about how sad he sounded when he asked about Duncan and if I had feelings for him.

"We'll circle back to that tid-bit there, but I still haven't heard why you left."

I tapped my fingers on my wine glass. There was a lot to unpack there. "His dad, Dr. Keller's husband, Martin, is in a coma. He and Dr. Keller got into a big argument one night. She apparently spent more time with work than her family because she forgot about their anniversary dinner. One *she* planned for them. He got into a car accident on his way home and has been in a coma ever since."

Oliva's hand shot to her mouth, "How awful."

"His doctors are saying the chances of him waking up are slim to none and they might need to pull the plug on him soon. Dr. Keller was hoping I could Connect with him and basically ask if he forgives her. But when I tired, I got…stuck. I became paralyzed." I dismissed the fear built behind the memory. "It was terrifying and sinister. It felt like something bad could happen to me. Like something was coming to get me. She then asked me to try and Connect with other coma patients to see if that was the reason for my paralysis. Which is why I sought help to begin with. It pissed me off that she would ask me to do it again, in the name of science." I took a big gulp of my wine this time, finishing off the glass. Oliva took it from me, refilled it, and brought it back. Her glass had also been topped off. "She said a recurrent Connection has never been documented before so the science behind it all is just theoretical at best. Originally, she thought Graham was the reason for my paralysis, before I knew who he was, I mentioned to her I would always see the same guy in my dreams."

"Wait, if her son can also Connect, how come she thought recurrence hadn't happened before?"

"He never told her."

"Oh shit."

I nodded to her and took another sip of my wine. A buzz was starting to tingle through me. "Yep. He said he had experienced the paralysis before too but thought it was because his skill just wasn't strong or developed enough. He made sure he wasn't around the night I tried to Connect with his dad to rule out if it was him or not causing the paralysis. Thankfully, it wasn't him. He and I think it's because we've tried to Connect with a patient in a coma but can't confirm because – well, because I left."

Oliva reached over and grabbed my knee, "That all sounds scary and difficult, Heidi. I'm sor..."

"Oh!" I blurted. "I can't believe I almost forgot. He *is* real! Well, was, real." Olivia looked confused again. "The man from the field of purple flowers. The one who I saw die. That happened."

Olivia's hand covered her mouth, and her eyes grew wide.

"He was a patient there. Apparently, his scans showed a promising ability to Connect. Not as great as mine, but better than Graham's. Dr. Keller says he died of a heart attack. I can't prove it wasn't, but her behavior when I asked her makes me suspicious. I think she's hiding something.

"So, what do you plan to do about it?"

"I don't think there's anything I can do about it except to stay as far away from her as possible. She's intelligent and has a lot of money. If I make an accusation against her that I can't prove, she could destroy me. Our family.

Olivia squeezed my knee, "I'm so sorry I didn't believe you. And I'm sorry you had to go through all of that without me."

"Thanks. And at least now, I have a better idea of how to avoid Mr. Keller if I get any indication of him in my dreams. If I avoid them, I should be okay. I've also learned to trust my dream instincts, my dreamstincts, if you will." We both laughed at the ridiculous term. "Besides, I missed everyone. The city wasn't at all what I thought it would be. Not that I really got out and explored, but maybe I don't need to be away from home."

"I'd be lying if I said I didn't miss you too. And while I hope you find something that gives your life meaning, I do hope it's here. I hope you know that I will always support you and any decision you make."

I leaned forward towards her and gave her a quick hug, "Thanks, Oliva."

She smiled. "Now. Let's talk about Duncan," her eyes narrowed at me, wanting to get back to what I mentioned earlier about the dream I had.

I sighed before smiling giddily, "It's nothing really. We were married, I was pregnant with a little boy. We were building a house and trying to decide on which shade of blue we should paint the nursery." Olivia squealed with excitement before taking another sip of wine. "Calm down," I laughed.

"I'm surprised it didn't freak you out."

"Yeah. Me too honestly. It felt nice."

"Could you see yourself with him?"

I stared down into my glass, searching for my thoughts that were getting lost in a wine haze. The thought of a life with Duncan made me feel all warm and tingly inside. But it was hard to deny my attraction to Graham. It wouldn't be fair to either of them if I didn't let myself figure it out. "I think Duncan and I would be happy, yes. I think we'd have a beautiful life. But he and I both are still trying to figure things out in our own lives. Things that have to be sorted out before we can give ourselves to someone else. I also can't help but think that if there were more woman to choose from, he might not choose me. And on top of all that, I can't just sweep Graham under a rug like he only exists in my dreams. But his taste in women is far different from me. You should have seen Amanda, she's stunning. Petit, beautiful, silky, long black hair, and a sense of fashion that is beyond jeans and tee shirts."

"Either of them would be lucky to have you, Heidi," Oliva said in true sisterly fashion, and while I didn't believe her, I appreciated her words anyway.

"I don't know," I said before finishing the last bit of wine in my glass and setting it on the coffee table. "Enough about me, how were things here while I was gone?"

"Not uh, not so fast. How did things go with Duncan this afternoon?"

I was hoping she wouldn't ask but knew she probably would. I immediately felt heat tease the back of my neck, threatening to rise to my cheeks if I didn't stop thinking about the hours we spent fucking.

"Oh my gosh! Are you blushing," Oliva squealed.

Too late. I fanned my face in an attempt to cool myself, but it did no good. "Well, if you must know – " She nodded emphatically. "It went well. He was talking before I left," I said proudly. Not that I did anything other than let him have his way with me.

"Uh huh," she smirked. "And how'd you manage that," she teased. I could tell she already had an idea.

"When I first got there, we just sat on his swing as I talked. I tried to be positive and encouraging but still, he didn't respond. Just kept swinging us. – Oh!" Startling Olivia with my loud voice again, "I can't believe I almost forgot to tell you this too. Yesterday afternoon he called me. First to apologize about how you found out about us, then to basically break off our," I cleared my throat, still not sure how to classify our relationship, "*relations*. His reasoning was to avoid anyone getting hurt. I didn't protest because he's probably right."

Olivia raised an eyebrow and pursed her lips together, telling me she was not buying the excuse.

"So, today, when I thought I had overstayed my welcome I tried to leave. Instead, he carried me inside." My cheeks were starting to burn red again, so I decide to skip the details, she got the picture. "Before I left, I asked if that was really what he needed. He said he needed to feel safe, and that's how he feels when he's with me."

Olivia jumped to her feet and pressed her free hand to her cheek in excitement. "Heidi, that boy *loves* you."

'That is *not* what he said, Oliva. You're starting to

sound like Mom," I said rolling my eyes as I poked fun at her reaction.

"Heidi, maybe that's not what he said, but I bet that's what he meant."

"I'm not sure about that, but that's not the point. The point is that I was helpful. I helped," I said with a proud and drunken grin.

Throwing her hands up in surrender and grinning at me, she said, "Whatever you say."

"Good. Cause that is what I say." Oliva took a seat back on the couch next to me. "Can we change the subject now? How were things around here?"

"Fine." She finished off her glass of wine and set it next to mine on the coffee table. "Things were the same ole same ole around here, except Gerald's diagnosis. The whole town is taking it pretty hard. Even Mom has been in tears."

"You remember that day he came into the store to check his mail and then left without saying much? I think that's when he got the letter Ronny was talking about."

"Yeah, I think so too." She shook her head in disbelief, "It blows my mind how he could keep news like that from his family."

"It doesn't sound all that crazy to me. Maybe he just didn't want to hurt them."

"I guess. I know I wouldn't be able to keep something like that from my family."

"Speaking of family, I didn't hear from Mom or Dad while I was in the city."

"I think they trying to keep their distance and just let you be. Have you told them you're back yet." I shook my head. "Are you coming to the store tomorrow?"

"Yeah. I don't want to sit around here all day."

"Alright, I'll be in in the morning too." She looked at her watch, "guess I need to get home, it's pretty late."

We both stood and walked to the front porch. "Good night," she said as she pulled me in for one last hug. "I'll see you in the morning."

"Night" I waved her off as she headed down the steps and cut through my yard on the way to her house. I waited for her to flash her porch light twice to let me know she made it inside.

I tidied the living room and placed the glasses in the sink before heading off to bed. I needed all the rest I could get if I was going to face my parents tomorrow.

Chapter 32

Pulling into the small gravel parking lot of the store, I pushed my bike to the side of the building, propped up its kick stand and made my way inside. It was such a nice morning, I thought the bike ride to work would do me some good. Based on the cars already in the parking lot, I knew Olivia, Ronnie, and at least my dad was here. But chances are Mom was here too dropping on her freshly made breakfast sandwiches.

I braced myself before opening the door to the store. The bell rang above my head, signaling to anyone already inside that another patron had entered. Except, I wasn't a patron. I was an employee… owner… prisoner… whatever you'd want to call it.

"Heidi?" My dad called from his rocking chair before standing to come wrap me in a hug. I squeezed him back. "What are you doing back so soon? I mean, I'm happy to see you, I just thought we wouldn't see you for a few more days at least."

"Heidi!" My mom came around from the back and nearly pushed my dad out of the way to wrap me in her arms. She hugged me like she hadn't seen me in years, almost suffocating me. "I'm so happy that you're home," she confessed.

Of course she is. I had to suppress my eyeroll. I'm just not buying it. I don't want to start with an attitude this early in the morning, so I held my tongue – for now. "Hey mom," I dramatically gasped.

She laughed as she released me, "I'm sorry. I really missed you."

"Mom, it was two days." And she basically said I'd have a bad dream and come running back home. Which I did. I knew she wanted to gloat.

"Oh, I know," she flicked her wrist. "But I've seen you every day since you were born. Not being able to see my babies' faces each day pains me." She clutched her chest.

At first, I thought she was being dramatic, but then I noticed her eyes welled up with tears. Was she being sincere? I glanced over to Dad to try and get a read on the situation. He offered me a small reassuring nod that said she was genuine. My absence had been hard on her. I pulled her back in for a hug. "Don't worry. You can't get rid of me that easily. I'll be around." I didn't know why I said that. I still wasn't sure what the hell I was doing with my life, but for some reason, I didn't regret saying it.

Mom dried her eyes and squeezed my shoulders with her hands. "There's an extra sausage, egg, and cheese croissant in the basket waiting for you."

"Thanks, Mom." Offering her a thankful smile, I retrieving the tin foiled wrapped sandwich. Before I took a bite, I noticed Ronny and Olivia standing near the middle of the store. Olivia was tucked in under Ronny's left arm as they each sipped from their coffee, observing my reunion with my parents.

"There's nothing better than being surrounded by your family. You never know how long you'll have each other for." Oliva shot Ronny a sweet, sympathetic smile as she rubbed his back with the arm she had wrapped around him. "I wanted to thank you, Heidi," Ronny continued. "Duncan seemed to be back to his old self when he stopped by last night."

"No need, Ronny. I was happy to help." The look on Oliva's face said "Yeah, I bet you were." as she tried to hide a teasing grin. I shot her a look. I didn't want Mom to catch on.

Ronny raised his coffee in the air slightly, "We'll, I ought to get going." He leaned down and gave Oliva a kiss before telling her, "I'll be home for supper." She said okay and he left the store.

"We ought to get going too," Dad said. "We're going to hit some trails with Ed and Marge later this morning and need to get back and gather our supplies."

"You'll come over for supper tonight?" Mom looked at me then at Olivia, waiting for us to respond. Her tone made it sound like a command instead of an invitation. We nodded to comply. Satisfied with our response, she said, "Good. Supper will be ready at seven thirty."

She and Dad gave us each a hug before leaving the store and continuing on with their day.

The sound of gravel crunching signaled that it safe to speak freely. I looked at Olivia who was walking towards me at the counter. "What's with Mom? I feel like she was ready to disown me before I left. And now she's all lovey dovey?"

"I told you; everyone is taking Gerald's news hard. I think she's realized how silly she's being and just want's her youngest daughter happy and home."

I shrugged. I guess I could see that. She took a seat on the stool next to mine. "Hey, I wanted to ask you last night, but it completely slipped my mind; do you know anything more about Duncan's life before he was adopted? Has Ronny ever said anything to you about it?" With this new ability of mine, I wanted to try and respect the privacy of his dreams. If I knew some details, maybe I could avoid any identifiers that could be related to his past.

"No. I've never asked but the few times anyone mentions it, everyone gets pretty hush hush about it. It's obvious the Johnsons don't want to talk about it."

The thought saddened me. Thinking about Duncan as a child, enduring only God knows what at such a young age, something that ultimately left him abandoned and alone. Something that he was clearly still carrying with him.

Oliva must be able to tell I'm getting lost in thought and changed the subject. "So, did you see Graham last night?"

It took me a moment to realize she was asking if I saw him in my dream. She still seemed uncertain about Connecting. "You know, I didn't actually." I wondered why, after Connecting with me in the previous dreams, he didn't last night. I mean, he had an alarm set every twenty-three minutes to make sure he wouldn't interfere with my attempt to Connect with his dad. He must have figured out how to avoid indicators of me in his dreams. And I didn't seek him out in mine.

"Did you dream about anything?"

I chuckled at the memory of last night's dream. "I did. I dreamed I was a contestant on my favorite reality competition show. I was crawling through mud, running across ropes courses suspended in the air above water, falling off said ropes course," I laughed. "The falling woke me up. I hate falling in dreams. It feels a little *too* real."

"Could you image actually doing those things? I would be a ball of nerves every time."

"Yeah. I'll stick to observing others compete from the safety of my couch. I…" my words got cut off from my cell phone ringing. KELLER INSTITUTE flashed across the screen. I rolled my eyes and silenced the ringer.

"Who is it?" Olivia gestured with her chin towards my hand that held my phone.

"Dr. Keller. Probably to beg me to come back and Connect with more coma patients. I'm not interested in being her science experiment."

"I don't blame you." We stood in silence for moment before she drummed her hands on the top of the counter, "I'm going to head back to the office for a bit. I need to finish placing a few orders. Holler if you need anything."

I nodded and Oliva made her way to the office.

***

It was almost noon and we had several tourists stop in and pick up snacks and fill up on gas. A group of highschoolers from White Plains, a city about five hours from here, came in with a couple of chaperones earlier. They were here on their senior trip and the excitement was split fifty-fifty between the group. Some kids asked me several questions about the best trails and areas to camp. They were in awe of our small-town charm and beautiful scenery of trees and surrounding mountains. Others stood around the front of the store and huffed as they held their phones above their heads in the air, desperately searching for stronger cell service. I recommended my favorite trails and camping spots as well as some of my favorite homemade goodies from Mrs. Trudy. They loaded up on homemade cookies, chocolate covered popcorn, and a few bundles of fudge before heading on their way.

Dr. Keller had also called me eight more times throughout the morning, and I refused to answer a single one. She never left a voicemail, so I didn't truly know what she was calling for. Around the fourth call, I wondered if it could possibly be Graham, but ultimately thought if it was him and he needed to get in touch, he would call from his phone.

Olivia and I were both standing behind the counter, playing a round of M.A.S.H when the bell above the door jingled. Duncan entered, holding a paper sack, and approached us at the counter.

He sat the sack down on the counter and pulled out two Tupperware containers and something wrapped in foil. "Mom wanted me to bring you ladies some lunch. It's pot roast, carrots, potatoes, and gravy. She also threw in a few slices of cornbread." He turned his attention to Oliva, whose mouth was already watering. "Mom knows how much you like to crumble your bread on top, so she made sure you had plenty to share."

"Oh, I just love her to pieces! Thanks for bringing this to us," Olivia said with a smile.

"Sure thing," Duncan nodded in a gentlemanly way before turning his attention to me. His green-eyed gauze warmed me, causing me to tune everything around me out. I was reminded that Oliva was sitting next to me when she cleared her throat.

"I'm uh… I'm going to go warm this up for us, Heidi." She grabbed the containers and foil wrapped cornbread and disappeared through the threshold of the office.

I returned my attention to Duncan, taking in his charm. "Ronny said you went over and visited with your family last night. How was it – all things considering, I mean."

"It went well. My mom was the most relieved to see me. I feel guilty for putting her through that, recoiling back into my fear."

I reached across the counter and held the top of his hand, "She's your mom and she loves you. I'm sure she understands."

Duncan opened his mouth to say something else but stopped when we heard gravel stir aggressively outside followed by a car door being slammed. The door to the store flew open. I was met with sad blue eyes. Her blonde hair was slick and straight like it has been every other time I've seen her, but her overall appearance was disheveled. Mascara stains were present just under her eyes and her lashes were clumped together. It was apparent she had been crying. A lot.

Instinctively, my grip around Duncan's hand tightened. I was not expecting to see this woman ever again. How dare she show up here. "Don't bring your crocodile tears here. There's nothing you can say to get me to go back there."

Her voice cracked as she said his name, "Graham. It's Graham." Tears fell quickly from her eyes and my heart sank just as quickly. "He – he," she chocked back more tears, "He isn't waking up."

My eyes went wide and tears begin to gather as fear took its hold on me. What did she mean he wasn't waking up? Oliva had emerged from the office due to the commotion. She approached the front of the store. "What does that mean," I plead. I noticed that Duncan had caught on to my emotions and he stood there, looking unsure of what to do. He couldn't leave because Dr. Keller was blocking the door, he was forced to watch our interaction.

"He's breathing, but unconscious and unresponsive," she finally answered through her tears. "I need your help. Please, I don't know what else to do. I can't lose him too. I just can't." She looked down at my hand on Duncan's then back to me. Something nefarious flashed across her face before producing more tears. "I know you care about him too. You have to help me. Help, Graham."

How do I know she's telling the truth? She has fooled me before. But if she was being honest, Graham was in real danger. I narrowed my eyes at her then plucked my phone from my back pocket with my free hand. I called Graham. The line rang and rang until his voicemail finally picked up.

Shit.

I know what she needs me to do, she needs me to Connect. I looked at Olivia and concern stretched across her face. I looked at Duncan, his expression perplexed. His eyes searched mine for an understanding, unsure of what was happening. I didn't get a chance to explain yesterday, and I didn't have time to explain now. Dr. Keller's emotions might be fake, but I think Graham could really be in trouble. I just had to go with my gut on this one.

I squeezed Duncan's hand and offered an apologetic shrug. I grabbed my backpack, tossed it over my shoulder, and looked towards Oliva. "I'll be back as soon as I can." I rounded the counter to stand face to face with Duncan, my back to Dr. Keller. "I don't have time to explain now, but I will." His green eyes pierced me. His lips part slightly like he wanted to kiss me but didn't. He wrapped me in a hug and told me to be safe. "I will," I assured him, even though I wasn't sure at all. I turned to Dr. Keller, "I have to go get my car, I rode my bike today."

"We don't have time. I'll drive."

Chapter 33

"Your approach was pretty tactless back there."

Through her forced sniffles, she said, "I'm not sure I know what you mean."

Bullshit. "You just had to include the bit about me caring for Graham after seeing me holding Duncan's hand."

"Ah, so *that* was Duncan." She shrugged her shoulder, "Was I wrong? It's obvious you care for my son."

She wasn't. But I refused to answer her. I should have just kept my mouth shut.

"Doesn't matter anyway." She pulled a tissue from the center console and blew her nose. "My son is too good for you. He deserves someone with class."

Again, she wasn't wrong. But it hurt to hear someone else's words confirming my own thoughts. How could she be so callous while shedding tears for her son? "No," I surprised myself, feeling overcome with anger and hurt. "He's too good for *you*. You're the one who doesn't deserve him."

She scoffed at my assessment.

"It's a wonder he has any sense of compassion at all with a mother like you. I'm sure he wishes you were trapped in a coma, tucked in that bed. Not his dad."

Damn. Maybe that was a bit too far. Neither of us had any words for my emotionless comment. Tears started to stream down her cheeks.

Dr. Keller and I continued our drive to Easton City in silence. She softly cried on and off until we were about thirty minutes out. I had to say, if this was an act, she put on one hell of a show.

She eventually informed me that she was taking me to Graham's apartment instead of the institute. "I didn't want to transport him to the institute and have people questioning what was going on. I have stationed nurses in his apartment for constant care and observation. There are two EEG machines there also. One has already been connected to Graham, the other will be connected to you."

She also tried to apologize again for how we left things, but I held my hand up to stop her. That's not why I was here. And as far as I was concerned, it was water under the bridge. We needed to focus on Graham right now.

Dr. Keller went through all the possible medical reasons this could have happen to him but explained that he didn't display any symptoms to give her reason to believe he was experiencing anything life threatening.

"So…" I tried to wrap my mind around what she just told me. "He's just *asleep*?"

"That's how it appears, but I can't explain why or how."

I was impressed with her worry for him. Graham has voiced his frustrations with his mom, that she was always too focused on her work than to give him, or Mr. Martin, any real nurturing. Maybe she was realizing the importance of family after all.

"I'll have to cover all of his appointments for today. And since you couldn't bother to answer any of my phone calls, I've lost too much time coming to get you. My patients need me. I will drop you off at his apartment and then I have to immediately head back to the institute. The nurses there will fill you in on anything else you might need to know."

Well, so much for my last thought. I guess she still very much worried about her work and to hell with the health of her only son. "You're going to work? You've been a blubbering mess for almost two hours, and you think you'll be able to focus on your work during a time like this?" I asked, flabbergasted that she was thinking about work at all. "You don't think you should be there with your son?" I couldn't keep the contempt from my voice.

She scoffed in my direction before turning her eyes from me and back to the road. "I don't think you understand the importance of the work we do. The lives we change, Heidi. The lives we *heal*. If I'm not there to make sure everything stays afloat, who will?" It was a rhetorical question. "My son is a big boy and can take care of himself."

"Now he is," I mumbled under my breath and rolled my eyes.

"Excuse me? What is that supposed to mean?"

Shit. I needed to stop with those passive ass remarks. It really wasn't any of my business. "Forget it. It's not my business."

"You're right. It's none of your business. Why don't you worry about what you came here to do – help my son."

She had me irritated by the time we pulled into the parking lot of Graham's apartment building. And while I'd love to give her a piece of my mind, it's not the place or the time to get into this with her. I can't worry myself with other people's issues when I have my own to deal with.

"Sixth floor, apartment 605. The nurses are expecting you."

I got out of the car and faced the building as Dr. Keller peeled out of the parking lot. The building was impressive. There was a total of seven floors, the first floor being the lobby. It appeared that each floor was its own unit, each with floor to ceiling windows on the exterior of the building facing out to the center of the city. The building looked like it was made completely of glass. It wasn't until I walked into the lobby that I could see that the building wasn't a giant glass box.

The lobby had a clean and contemporary flow to it. A well-dressed attendant stood at the long marble topped counter in the far side of the lobby, he smiled politely as I entered. I saw the elevators on the left hand wall and made my way to them.

The directory posted on the inside of the elevator identified where the gym and spa were located. It appeared that I was on the ground floor and the first floor was actually the floor above me. That floor was where I would find the gym and spa. *Fancy*. We didn't even have a gym and spa in my whole town and Graham had one in his apartment building. The remaining floors were residential units. I pressed the button for floor six and waited for the elevator's ascent.

On the way up, my heart began to pound nervously. My mind started to race with thoughts.

What happened?

I hope he's okay.
I hope I can find him.
I hope I stay safe.
I didn't tell Mom and Dad that I was leaving again.
I hope Duncan doesn't worry.
What the hell is my life?

The elevator dinged as the doors opened to a small waiting area in front of a single door. There was no hallway or anywhere else for me to go except to the black door with the numbers 605 fixed in gold.

I didn't have the chance to knock before the door swung open. A familiar and kind face appeared behind it. "Heidi, come on in. We've been expecting you." It was Beatrice, the same nurse that helped me remove my EEG cap the first morning at the institute. I felt better being here with a familiar face.

My jaw dropped as I entered Graham's apartment. His furnishings looked like something out of a home design magazine. The expansive view from inside, from this high up, allowed you to see the entire downtown area. The restaurants, the shops, the hustle and bustle if it all. I was beautiful.

The kitchen was nestled against the same wall as the entrance. Stainless steel appliances, a six-burner gas stove, and the ocean blue subway tile back splash, were a few of the first things I noticed about it. The nurse led me from the main living area down a short hallway that led to another series of doors.

Through the door on the right was a bedroom. A king-sized platform bed sat centered in middle of the back wall. I didn't look further than that because in that bed lied Graham. He looked peaceful. Even with the EEG cap around his head, he looked unbothered.

"I'm sorry, but I'm afraid there's not another bed in the apartment. You'll have to lie in here with him. Dr. Keller asked us to keep the both of you under observation," Beatrice announced from behind me.

"That's alright," I turned to look at her. "I understand."

She extended her hand, "I'll take your backpack for you. Please take a seat on that side of the bed," she pointed with her eyes, "and I'll get your cap in place."

I handed her my bag and took a seat on the empty side of the bed. Beatrice moved in front of me and got busy putting my cap in place. I couldn't help but think back to my failed Connection with Mr. Keller. Panic started to bloom in my chest.

What happens if I can't find Graham.

"You're all set. Go ahead and get comfortable. Do you need anything to help you get to sleep?"

Swiveling my legs onto the bed and finding a comfortable spot, I settled in, "I don't think so. I've been able to nap easily here lately. But I'll let you know if I have trouble falling asleep."

I closed my eyes and started with deep breaths. Focusing on inhaling through my nose and exhaling through my mouth. With each breath, I thought of Graham. I tried to hold his image in the front of my mind, forcing all my energy to Connect with him. I had never intentionally Connected with him before, so I hoped it would work.

Chapter 34

I'm in the lobby at the institute.

I'm alone.

The receptionist's post was empty behind the desk. I entered the hallway and made my way towards Dr. Keller's office.

Empty.

Then to Graham's office.

Empty.

I checked the gym, the outdoor area, the nurse's station, the café, then all the rooms upstairs. All empty.

I noticed nothing out of the ordinary as I looked around the institute. Nothing that would indicate a pathway for a Connection to him, or anyone. Everything here at the institute was in its place. The last place I need to look is the basement.

Fuck. I was hoping I'd never have to go down there again. In my dreams or otherwise.

I steadied my breathing, trying to calm my nerves before getting on the elevator and making my way down there.

When the doors opened, I found myself in the grey room. Everything looked as it did on the day I left. I checked the supply closet and then the room of records. Everything looked in its place. I swallowed hard, acknowledging I'd have to go in there, to Mr. Keller's room.

I turned the doorknob, but nothing happened. I

*tried again but still the door doesn't budge. I pound
my fist on the door. "Graham! Are you in there?"
When I didn't hear anything, I pounded again.
"Graham!" The door still didn't budge.*

*I backed away from the door as my eyes dart all
around the room, trying to find another way in. I
check the records room and storage for vents or loose
ceiling tiles. With no luck, I went back to Mr. Keller's
door.*

*"Graham! Please, if you can hear me, say
something." I slammed my fist against the door
again, "Graham!"*

*"Heidi!" a muffled voice finally sounds from
behind the door.*

*"I'm coming to get you, okay." My heart pounds
heavy behind my chest, anxious to help him but
terrified of what I'll find behind this door once I'm
able to open it. Deliberating on how to get the door
open, a thought occurs to me. If I can't open it from
out here, maybe he can open it from in there. "But I
need your help, Graham. What do you see?"*

"Nothing. It's pitch black."

"Can you move? Can you follow my voice?"

"I can't."

*I swallow hard remembering the fear I felt the last
time I was in there. Alone. The only difference is that
this time, we're here together. "You have to try."*

*When I didn't hear him, I called his name again.
"Graham... Graham!" Panic took hold of me, I
began to pound on the door harder, causing my fists
to ache.*

*"Heidi." His voice sounded much closer now.
"I'm here, I feel the door."*

"Graham," I said softly. My forehead pressed against the door, relieved to finally hear his voice again.

"But the doorknob, it's stuck."

"Let's try and turn it together." I took hold of the knob, "Ready? On the count of three."

"Ready."

"One... two... three!" I turned the knob as hard as I could. Suddenly I was falling through the door jam and into Graham's arms.

"Heidi, are you okay?" Graham caught me and tried to steady me on my feet. We're in Mr. Keller's room, but it was still dark.

Without answering him, I used my hands to feel around his arms, making my way to his face. Once I felt the smoothness of his jaw, I moved my thumb down to his chin. Down to where the slightest little dimple laid. It really was Graham. Thankful to have finally reached him, I pulled him in for a hug. He wrapped his arms around my back and pulled me in tighter. My eyes started to adjust in the darkness that surrounded us.

"Why are you here." Graham asked, holding my face in his hands.

"Your mom. She came to get me. She said that you weren't waking up." Suddenly, it felt like the air had been sucked out of the room. Pressure began to push around my chest, like I was being squeezed too tightly, causing my breaths to become jagged. I thought the pressure was only affecting me until I felt Graham's hands fall from my face before he fell to his knees. "Graham!" My plea was barely audible. I dropped to the floor with him, squinting my eyes

*trying to make out his expressions and gauge his
pain.*

*Graham gasps for air as he falls completely to the
floor clutching his chest.*

Flashbacks of Wyatt appear in my mind.
Hopelessness falls over me. I failed him. I can't fail
Graham too.

*Turing to face the darkness, to the pressure that
continued to build, I mustered any strength I had left
and screamed at the top of my lungs. "You're killing
him! Please, don't hurt him!" Kneeling beside him on
the floor, I scooped his upper body off the floor so he
could rest in my lap. I could feel the short and
incomplete movements of his chest as he tries to
breathe.*

*My head started to feel lightheaded as my own
breathing became more labored. Unable to fully
expand my chest, it was challenging to stay up
straight. "Please!" I attempted to scream but it came
out as a whisper instead. Tears rolled furiously from
my eyes when I noticed Graham's chest had stopped
heaving.*

I've failed. Again. I couldn't help Wyatt. I
couldn't help your dad. And I couldn't help you.

*I begin to choke. There's no more oxygen. Only
pressure.*

*My eyes fell to Graham's lifeless body in my lap
one last time. With my last breath barely audible, I
told him, "I'm sorry." I felt my upper body fall
backwards into the shadowy abyss.*

*Just as I accepted my fate, the weight of
Graham's body shifted from my knees and light began
to flicker above me.*

This is it, isn't it? This is the light people talk about seeing when it's your time to go.

I'm not ready.

I didn't tell my family goodbye.

I'll never be able to see Duncan again.

Never start a family of my own – no – of our own.

I felt an arm slide under my neck, then another arm under the crook of my knees. I'm being raised in the air. The light was getting brighter, and air slowly returns to my lungs, "God?"

I heard a chuckle from above me. My eyes fluttered open and I peered up at the person carrying me. He looked familiar but I couldn't place him until he looked down at me with a slight smile. Except this smile wasn't cheerful like the one in his picture, it's apologetic.

Before I had a chance to jump out of his arms, he sat me on something low to the ground. Graham was sitting beside me, trying to regain his bearings. I looked around us and realize we're not in the basement room anymore, but on the side of a street. Looking further down the street I saw a crumpled car smashed into a tree.

This must be where the accident happened.

Graham still hadn't realized where we were, he's doubled over with his head between his knees trying to fill his lungs with the air that was stolen from him. Finally, I raised my gauze to meet Mr. Keller. Concern warped his face as he looked at his son. Graham finally lifted his head and focused his attention on me, but once he followed my gaze, he jumped from the curb we were sitting on.

"Dad!" Graham cried before the two of them

embrace in a hug.

"How are you, Son," Mr. Keller said with tears in his eyes.

Graham held his dad by the shoulders, at arm's length, and looked down at me, "We did it, Heidi!"

I stood, tucking my hair behind my ear, still trying to process how we got from the darkness to here. How we were freed from the stillness.

"We've been trying to reach you, Dad." Graham gestured between us with his hand.

"I'm sorry," I extend my hand towards Mr. Keller for a handshake, "We haven't been introduced, I'm Heidi." He accepted my handshake. "Your wife asked for my assistance with trying to Connect with you." His hand tightened around mine and his eyes grew dark at the mention of his wife. Graham notices that I withdrew my hand quickly from his.

"Woah, Dad. Take it easy."

Mr. Keller shook his head and blinked away the anger that formed in his eyes. "Sorry. That woman has caused me so much pain. So much anger. All that time, longing for her to make time for me, for our family, but never following through." Mr. Keller dragged his hand down the lower part of his face. "I knew she'd try to do something like this, to use me as some sort of science experiment. And you," he pointed to Graham, "my sweet boy. How could she rope you into it?"

"Rope me into what, Dad?"

"Your mother always theorized that a Connection could be replicated between any two unconscious energies, not just between two concurring REM cycles, but she's never had the means to test it." He

reached out and held Graham's face in his hands, *"You've aged,"* his eyes were filled with sorrow, *"which tells me I was right; I'm not simply dreaming, but in a coma. And from the looks of the fine lines of wisdom forming at the edge of your eyes, I'd wager to say I've been this way for a while."*

Technically, she roped me into it, *I thought, as Mr. Keller continued speaking.*

"Once I concluded that I wasn't dreaming, my anger grew into something uncontrollable. All I focused on was building a wall to prevent her, or anyone, from Connecting with me. I didn't want to give her the satisfaction of validating her Connection theory if there was any possibility of it being viable."

"So, you knew you were causing paralysis?" Graham shot his dad an accusatory look.

"Paralysis? What paralysis?" Mr. Keller questioned genuinely.

"Any time either of us tried to Connect with you, you've caused us to become paralyzed. Hell, this time, it damn near killed us!"

Mr. Keller recoils from Graham's tone, "K-killed you?" His eyes searched Graham's face before turning to me, looking for me to corroborate what Graham was saying.

Nodding in agreement with Graham, I spoke softly. "It's true. We could feel your anger. At the time, we didn't know it was you. We didn't know it was intentional…"

"We thought it was because we were trying to Connect with a non-REM energy," Graham interjected.

"She had asked me to Connect with you to see if

*you were at peace. Claimed it was because your
doctors wanted her to pull the plug. Graham had
been trying to Connect with you long before I came
into the picture, but he didn't want to let your wife
know he had been trying. When I came to the institute
seeking treatment, for the paralysis I might add, she
educated me about my...gift. I was inspired by her
story because I wanted to help, but when I tried, it no
longer felt safe to pursue you." Tears started to form
in my eyes, reliving the terror that danced around me
as the darkness grew. "I left the institute after that."
Mr. Keller offered me a regretful look. "Were you
able to feel us, or anyone trying to Connect with
you?" I asked, hoping to learn the truth about Wyatt.*

*He shook his head. "No. I just focused on keeping
everyone out."*

*My heart sank, knowing I probably won't ever
know the truth about Wyatt. If he really did die of a
heart attack, or if Dr. Keller sent him to Connect with
Mr. Keller and he died like Graham and I almost did.*

*"How did you stop it, Dad? We were literally just
lifeless on the floor of your room, surrounded by,
what honestly felt like a sinister force, to now this,"
Graham swung his arms wide, emphasizing the
change in scenery.*

*Mr. Keller's head hung from grief, "I'm sorry I
caused you both such turmoil. I didn't know that's
what I was doing. I was only trying to put up a
barrier from anyone trying to Connect. But once I
heard someone say, "I'm sorry," I cracked. I couldn't
hold the barrier any longer. The sincerity in those two
little words evaporated my anger. I didn't know who
said those words or to whom they were being said to,*

but I couldn't counter the effects it had on me."

Graham gave his dad another hug, "I'm just so happy to see you again, to talk to you again. I'm sorry this happened to you."

"There's nothing to be sorry for, Son. None of this is your fault. I'm sorry I left you behind."

"I'm okay, Dad, really. I just miss you."

Mr. Keller rubbed the back of his neck, "I miss you too. But I have a favor to ask – I need you to pull the plug. Not just on me, but on your mother too. She's the reason I'm here."

Chapter 35

The low hanging sun cut through the window and across my face, taunting my eyes to open. The sun was successful, but only for a moment before I gave in to the weight of my eyelids and closed them again. I was exhausted.

"Heidi." I heard my name being called and seconds later I felt large hands wrap around mine. I didn't have to open my eyes to know who it was, but his presence confused me. I just saw Duncan this afternoon, why was he here?

"Get Dr. Keller on the phone. They're waking up now." It didn't sound like Beatrice, but my guess was that it was one of the other nurses.

Trying to keep my eyes open and wake up, I felt Duncan let go of my hands as someone rushed to my side. "Heidi, can you hear me?" Her hands moved quickly from my wrist, then to my eyelids. She raised one, shone a light across my pupil, then moved to my other eye and did the same.

That was unpleasant. I was definitely awake after that. "I'm fine," I groaned in protest. My hands wiped at my eyes to erase the assault the flashlight just committed. They then traveled to the cap that was still on my head. My eyes finally opened for good, and I looked at the nurse standing above me, "Can you help me remove this please?" I sat up and the nurse got busy undoing the cap. I saw Duncan sitting on the edge of the bed at my feet. He looked worried.

"What's wrong?"

Duncan opened his mouth to speak but I heard Graham groan beside me.

Graham!

My head jerked in his direction before the nurse could finish taking the EEG cap off of my head. The dream we just experienced came rushing back to me. The darkness, the fear, the anger, Mr. Keller, and… *his request*. "Hey, Graham," I shook his bare shoulder, "We've got to go."

"Not so fast," the nurse stationed on Graham's side of the bed said, "You both need to undergo an evaluation before we can discharge you."

"An evaluation?" Why do we need an evaluation? What the hell is going on?

Graham finally sat up, letting the blanket fall to his waist, revealing his toned chest, arms, and torso. My eyes lingered a second too long and I could feel Duncan's gaze burn into the back of my head. I placed my attention back on the nurse explaining why we needed an evaluation.

"The two of you have been out for almost three days. Dr. Keller…."

"I'm sorry," Graham interrupted, "did you say three days?"

"Well, technically, *you've* been out for about four days," she said to Graham.

Graham and I looked at each other, mentally retracing our steps to our last conscious memory, trying to determine if the nurse was telling the truth or not. When we couldn't confirm on our own, I looked at Duncan, doubt spreading across my face. "Is that true?"

The look on his face told me the answer before he even spoke. "Yes. I've been here since last night." His eyes, still filled with worry, he said "I couldn't wake you up. It's like you were... dead." Duncan's voice cracked, but he maintained eye contact with me, allowing his green eyes to display emotion. Fear.

Lifting onto my knees, I leaned forward toward him, wrapping my arms around his neck, "I'm fine, I promise. I didn't mean to scare you." I leaned away from him so I could look back at his face, "Where's Olivia, or my parents?"

"Your dad hurt his knee during their hike Friday." My face crinkled with worry. "He's okay," Duncan reassured me, "It's swollen, and he has to stay off of it for a little while. Your mom is tending to him, but the store couldn't go unattended, so your sister gave me a call to come be with you."

"How did she know that I was here?"

"Olivia harassed Dr. Keller until she gave up your location. Took her a while but she eventually got the doctor to break."

A smile formed across my lips. *That sounds like Olivia.*

"Graham," I heard the nurse call from behind me. I turned my attention toward the commotion. "Your mom asked that you not leave until you both have undergone evaluation."

Graham was sliding a tee shirt over his head, "I don't give a damn what she's asked. I have things to do." The nurse threw her hands up in surrender and exited the room. Graham grabbed his wallet and keys from the top of his dresser and flashed me a disheartening expression. His eyes were asking me to come with him.

I turned to Duncan, "I've got to go, but I'll be back. I promise."

"Absolutely not." Duncan's tone was firm. "I'm coming with you." He wasn't going to take no for an answer.

"I'll keep her safe. You're not needed here," Graham hissed.

Duncan stood from his chair, "Yeah, because you've done such a great job so far." His tone, sardonic and accusatory, "I'm coming." His brows furrowed above his green eyes, but Graham didn't back down.

"This doesn't concern you," Graham said through his teeth.

"Will you two cut it out. We don't have time for a pissing contest." Swiveling myself off the bed, I pulled my sneakers on and walked to the door of the bedroom. "We'll all go." I turned to see that neither of them had moved an inch. "Now!"

Both Graham and Duncan made a beeline towards me. That was more like it.

We headed down to the ground floor in the tensest elevator ride ever, followed by the most awkward car ride ever.

Once we got outside I sent Olivia a quick text as Graham walked us to his car. A Tesla. Duncan laughed at the sight of Graham's tiny car. "There's no way I'm fitting in that thing," he told Graham. "We'll just take my truck."

Both Graham and Duncan were tall, but Duncan had about three inches and probably a good eighty pounds on Graham. It would be a tight fit for him in that Tesla. Besides, I wasn't sure how I felt about electric cars just yet.

When we finally pulled up to the Institute, the sun had almost set. The three of us filed out of Duncan's truck and headed towards the front door. Graham, leading the way, Duncan and I followed behind, entering the lobby. The receptionist, whose name I never learned, looked surprised to see us. "Graham, Heidi. Dr. Keller was not expecting to see you two so soon."

"That's good. We're not here to see her." Graham charged through the door to the hallway. The lights in Dr. Keller's office were on, but her door was shut. We passed the hung photos on the way to the elevators and Graham repeatedly pressed the down button. The elevator chimed as the doors opened. We stepped inside and he pressed the button to close the door.

"Graham! Wait!" Dr. Keller called as she ran toward the elevator.

Graham pressed the button faster. The doors were almost shut as we saw a flash of Dr. Keller's blonde hair appear between the closing gap.

"So, what is it that we're doing again?" Duncan asked. The atmosphere around him and Graham had been tensed to say the least. None of us spoke until now.

When Graham didn't respond, I said, "We have to kill his dad."

They both looked down at me, flabbergasted. "We're not going to *kill* him, Heidi." Graham scrunched his face at me before shooting Duncan a reassuring look. "He's in a coma. He asked us to pull the plug. Apparently, he had a living will asking that in such an event, he didn't want to remain on life support. I wasn't aware of it and my mother has intentionally ignored his wishes."

"Oh. Okay. I started to regret coming along for a minute."

A secret smile curled at my lips at my attempt to get them to talk without tension.

"Wait. He *asked* you?" Duncan asked as the doors to the elevator opened to the basement.

"I take it that she hasn't told you then?" Graham had a hint of gratification in his voice, that he knew a part of me that Duncan didn't.

I could feel Duncan's gaze fall from Graham to me, but I didn't meet it. The tension was up again. Now wasn't the time for an explanation.

The doorway from the stairs opens and Dr. Keller entered, huffing and out of breath. "Graham," she tried to approach him calmly. Her hand was up in a manner meaning to disarm him. "What's going on?"

"We know what you did, Mom." Graham stormed toward the door of his dad's room. Dr. Keller stepped in front of him, preventing him from reaching the door. "Move." His voice was laced with disgust.

"Not until we talk about what's going on." She looked from Graham to me, "We're you able to Connect? The two of you have been out for quite some time. Tell me, were you successful?" There was an excitement in her voice that certainly didn't match the energy in the room.

"You're unbelievable. Work is all you've ever cared about. How could you do that to him?"

"Do what, sweetheart." The word sounded strange

on her lips. Like she had never said them in her life. Now that I knew who Dr. Keller really was, I felt dumb for ever believing her motherly love act. Because that's all it was, an act.

Graham threw his head back in disbelief and let out a manic laugh. He started laughing so hard that I feared he was about to snap. I couldn't let this woman destroy him too.

"Drop the act, Dr. Keller. You know what you did. Don't make him say it. Just do us all a favor and step out of the way."

"Oh, Heidi," she tisked her tongue at me. "All you've done since your arrival is distract my son and be nothing but a selfish bitch."

Simultaneously, Graham yelled, "Mom!" and Duncan said, "You better watch your mouth, lady."

Dr. Keller finally noticing the handsome lumberjack accompanying us, "Ah, Duncan. Sorry I had to skip the introductions when I came to borrow Heidi away from you."

Graham turned his head toward Duncan, giving him a *you stay out of this* look. Just as soon as he turned away, Dr. Keller dropped something shiny from the arm of her blazer into the palm of her hand. She reared back ready to strike Graham.

I rushed to him and pushed him out of the way. I felt a piercing pain in the back of my shoulder before Graham and I crashed to the floor.

"Heidi!" I heard Duncan yell as his heavy footsteps raced towards me.

"Freeze!" A deep and authoritative voice filled the basement. "Everyone put your hands up, now!"

I heard the clatter of something metal fall from

behind me, but I couldn't turn to see who's yelling or what has dropped. Duncan's feet had stopped in their tracks, complying with the man's request. Graham was pushing himself into a seated position in front of me. His eyes moved to where I felt pain in my shoulder and his eyes went wide. I tried to lift myself up too but the sharp pain in my left arm didn't allow me to.

"Please help her, she's hurt," Duncan's voice boomed from above me.

An officer quickly approached and knelt beside me. She reached for her radio attached to her shoulder and spoke into it, "We need a medic to the basement. One injured and needing medical attention." She released her radio and spoke to me, "I'm Officer Thandy. I'm going to help you sit up now." She touched my left arm gently, "Don't put any pressure on this arm, okay?" I nodded as she helped me sit up. My back was still towards the commotion.

While waiting for the paramedic, I heard a male officer tell Dr. Keller that she was under arrest. Graham eventually moved from his spot on the floor in front of me and joined the stir of activity happening behind me.

After the paramedics arrived and bandaged me up, I declined immediate transport to the hospital. I overheard one of the officers saying they needed to get my statement. I will go to the hospital afterwards. "Heidi, I'm Detective Reid. Is it okay if I get your statement now?"

"It is."

Detective Reid took a seat next to me on the couch and flipped open the notepad he pulled from the inside pocket of his coat. "Please begin whenever you're ready."

I took a deep breath in to steady my nerves. I wasn't nervous because I did anything wrong, I was nervous because I wasn't sure how to explain how I knew what I knew. "We, Graham, Duncan, and I, came here to say our final goodbyes to Mr. Keller. From my understanding, he's been in a coma for quite some time and his doctors have been urging his family to make a decision on his quality of life. Graham, Mr. Keller's son, decided that it was time to, um..."

"Discontinue life support," Detective Reid offered.

"Yes. But Dr. Keller stopped us. That's when she tried to hurt Graham."

"It appears she hurt you instead. How did that happen?"

"I pushed Graham out of the way." Officer Reid continued to take notes as I retold my account. "I didn't see what she had in her hand, but I knew it wouldn't end well if it came into contact with Graham. It looked like her hand was heading for his neck."

"Okay. And why did you text your sister to have the police meet you here at Keller Institute?"

I took another breath, "Because, we believe Dr. Keller tried to have Mr. Keller killed."

Detective Reid stopped writing and cast an inquiring expression my way. "What makes you say that?"

"The night of the accident, Dr. Keller made dinner reservations for their anniversary, to show she was still committed to their marriage. Except she didn't show up. Mr. Keller saw one of Dr. Keller's current patients hanging out by the bar. He didn't think anything of it. Once he realized Dr. Keller was late, he glanced up at the bar to see if she had maybe come in without him seeing her and helped herself to a glass of wine. That's when Mr. Keller noticed that the patient was watching him, but still, he didn't think too much of it. He called Dr. Keller, to see how much longer she was going to be. She told him she wasn't going to make it, and that's when he and Dr. Keller got into an argument."

"What as the argument about?"

"About how she never made time for him, and that her missing their anniversary was the last straw. He confessed that he would be filing for divorce. However, Dr. Keller had other plans. She told him that they would not be getting a divorce, that she made a promise to him that she intended on keeping – 'Till death do us part.'"

Chapter 36

Olivia stopped by this morning on her way to work and dropped off breakfast for me. I was still asleep, but she let herself in and left me three pancakes, two sausage links, and two boiled eggs in the fridge. I had just set the plate in the microwave to warm it all up when I heard a knock on my door.

After what happened last night, I was sure my mom had called all the residents in Mount Hopewell to tell them her baby girl got stabbed. And with a rusty pair of scissors no less! That's what Dr. Keller hid in the sleeve of her blazer and had planned to kill her own son with them. She believed something had happened when Graham and I were down for three days. She assumed, based on our rush to Mr. Keller, that we successfully Connected with him, and he was able to recall events before the accident. She assumed right and tried to silence us because of it.

After I gave my statement to the detective, about how Dr. Keller blackmailed her patient to cut the breaks in Mr. Keller's car to ensure he didn't make it home safely, he asked how I could prove my claims. I told him to check her personal laptop.

Mr. Keller told us she never went anywhere without it, and he was never allowed near it. She never connected it to the internet either. She said she feared it could be hacked. Which would have made some sense if she didn't have a second laptop she kept at the office, which stayed connected. According to Mr. Keller, the one at the office was the one she was always working on. He always found it strange for her to have two of them but only work on one.

It was a gamble to tell the cops. Mr. Keller's hunch could have been wrong, but Graham trusted his dad's intuition, and I trusted Graham's.

Detective Reid called me this morning, letting me know they found blackmail photos of the patient on Dr. Keller's personal laptop after all. They also found other potentially criminal evidence that he couldn't yet discuss with me. But for the blackmailing of her patient, Dr. Keller had apparently confessed everything almost immediately during the interrogation.

 The patient being blackmailed was a fourth-grade teacher who had a cocaine addiction. When Dr. Keller first propositioned the patient, she threatened that if he didn't help her carry out her plan to kill her husband, she'd tell the school board about his addiction. If she did, he'd be fired.

The patient told her that he'd have her license revoked for breaking doctor patient confidentiality.

She didn't think a fourth-grade teacher would have the gall to threaten her back. To work around her oath, Dr. Keller then decided to follow him one night after one of their sessions. She caught him buying. She took photos of him and said they would be sent to the school board anonymously. The patient felt as if he didn't have any other choice. If his cocaine problem got out, he'd lose a lot more than his job.

Dr. Keller then told the detective that she first devised the plan when Mr. Keller gave her an ultimatum about a month prior to his accident. He told her that if she didn't take the time and plan something for their anniversary, he was going to divorce her. The thought of him getting half of everything, when he didn't work for it like she did, made her livid. She decided then that he wouldn't get half of anything.

She thought the anniversary dinner would be the perfect time. He'd go to the restaurant, realize he was being stood up, then fly off in a fit of rage and wreck his car on the way home. She asked the patient to cut the brakes in Mr. Keller's car to ensure he didn't arrive alive. When Mr. Keller fell into his coma, she thought it was a better outcome than she could have imagined. Sure, she'd have to pay for years of medical expenses, but at least this way, she could test her Connection theory on him.

Dr. Keller evaluated every patient for the ability to Connect during their session. All with plans to ask them to Connect if they had the potential to do so. Patients like Wyatt and myself. She would use the ruse of asking for forgiveness from her dying husband to get the patients to feel sorry for her and feel obligated to partake in the experiments. An experiment she didn't get to attempt until she met Wyatt. But his untimely death threw a wrench in her plans. Until she met me. At the time, she thought I'd be able to Connect with what was currently happening in Mr. Keller's comatose brain, not with an energy formed prior to the coma. Which is why she didn't have concerns with asking either of us to Connect. But that all backfired. And now we were here.

I opened the door, surprised to see Graham standing on my front porch holding a small vase of flowers. "Graham," I said with a smile. "What are you doing here?" I stepped aside and opened the door wide to allow him inside.

"I wanted to come and check on you." He leaned down and pulled me in for a hug. "I'm so sorry you were caught in the middle of all this."

Wincing at the pain dwelling deep in my wound, Graham released me and apologized. I gave him a smile and told him it was okay. We walked over to the couch, and I took the vase of flowers and set them on the coffee table.

We both took a seat. "I wanted to call you last night, once I got home." I fiddled with my blue nail polish, picking at them with no avail. "But I thought you might need some time." After the detective collected our statements and after the crime scene was released, Graham had to say his final goodbyes to Mr. Keller.

"Thanks," he said appreciatively. "It was difficult, but I took comfort in the fact that it was what he wanted. I mourned my dad for months after the accident. I knew the prognosis wasn't positive, but I couldn't give up hope. That's when I started to conduct my own research into Connecting. I unfortunately had not uncovered anything that my mother hadn't already. The only thing I had, that she didn't, was experience. I had Connected once before, I just needed to try and do it again. However, it took me longer than I had expected. I had almost given up hope, until I saw you for the second time in my dreams. That was when I knew I was making progress." He took a hold of my hand and stared into my eyes. "You renewed hope within me, Heidi."

A flurry of butterflies and guilt built in my stomach. I couldn't find the words to respond to that declaration. I tucked my hair behind my ear with my free hand and offered a sweet smile. Before the moment became too awkward, I tried to change the subject. "Hey, can I ask you a question?" Not understanding the guilt I felt, I released his hand.

"Yes. Anything."

"Why did you try and Connect with your dad after I left? You said you wouldn't."

"I didn't mean to. As I waited for sleep, I forced my brain to drown you out. When you left the institute, it felt like you were leaving me behind too."

I dropped my gaze to the floor. H wasn't wrong, I left with the intention of never seeing him again. I knew it would be a challenge for me to avoid him at night too.

"I tried to think of things that were total opposites of you. Things that would put me the farthest away from you. But I couldn't. I just kept thinking about the dream that made you leave. I was so upset that I wasn't there with you. When my own dream started, it felt like I started where your dream left off."

I shuddered at the thought. I had hoped he wouldn't have had to experience the fear I felt that night.

"But I have to confess. I may have another motive for coming here today." Graham swallowed hard and took my hands again. "I want you to come back to the city with me." He gently squeezed my hands, "The thought of not being near you pains me."

I stared at his beautifully sculpted face and allowed myself to think about what that might look like. My life, in the city. Without my family. Without a j…

"You could help me at the institute, too. You'd be employed there if that's what you want," Graham said, answering the question I was just about to ask myself. "Now that my ability is growing, we could Connect with patients together. To help with their therapy."

The potential of a meaningful job was tantalizing, I would admit. But could I be without my family? And what about Duncan? When I thought I was dying, he was the one I thought of. He was the one I wanted in that moment. There were still so many unsure thoughts surrounding Duncan and I's relationship. I hadn't had a chance to sort through them all.

Graham looked longingly at me holding my face and stroking my cheek with his thumb. I didn't stop him. His brown eyes pulled me deeper into him, unable to turn away. He leaned in closer to me. Our eyes closed with anticipation of our lips meeting again.

Finally, our lips were pressed ever so lightly together when another knock rapped from my front door.

I pulled my face from Graham's and cleared my throat. "I um, I should get that." Part of me felt relieved to be interrupted.

He looked disappointed.

I found Duncan on my front porch, also with flowers, once I opened the door.

"Duncan, hi." *This might get awkward.*

He held the beautiful bouget of fresh flowers out towards me. "I wanted to bring these to you." I took the flowers from his hands and inhaled their subtle scent. "I also wanted to let you know I'm here for you. Especially while you're healing. You need a light bulb changed? I'm your man. You ne...."

Graham cleared his throat from the couch, causing Duncan to look past me into the living room.

"Oh. I didn't know you had company already this morning." That was when I noticed Graham's Tesla wasn't parked outside. The trip must have been too long for his electric car. "I'll come by later."

I was getting ready to stop him when a chime sounded from behind me. It was Graham's phone. He checked the screen for the notification before standing up and returning his phone to his front pocket.

"That's alright. That was my rideshare, its circling around and on its way back." He walked towards me, still standing at the door, "Think about what I said?"

I nodded because I would. I just didn't know what my answer would be yet.

He leaned down to give me a kiss on my cheek before moving his lips to my ear and saying, "And to answer your question, I *do* nap on the job."

My breath caught in my throat. It wasn't just *my* dream that afternoon.

He smiled longingly at me. Finally casting his gaze to Duncan, he offers a hardened nod as he passed him on the porch then down to his rideshare which had now arrived.

"I'll get going too then." Duncan turned on his

heels.

"No, Duncan, please come in." I pushed Graham's words from my mind for the time being. Duncan looked hesitantly at me as I waved him inside. Shutting the door behind him, I set the flowers he got me in a vase. When I returned from the kitchen, I found Duncan lingering in my entry way. "What's wrong?"

"Heidi," he rubbed the back of his neck, looking for his words. "Am I getting in the way of anything here. Between you and Graham?"

I wasn't sure how to answer his question. "Between us how?"

He shortened the distance between us with a few wide strides, "Do you have feelings for him?

My lips parted to say something. To say *anything,* but no words came out. There was an attraction for sure, but feelings? I selfishly couldn't answer until I knew where Duncan and I stood.

Duncan took another stride, completely closing the gap between us now. His green eyes poured into me, causing my heart to race with desire. He had that effect on me. "Do you love him?"

That one was easy, "No."

"Good," he proclaimed and picked me up, wrapping my legs around him. He held me steady, careful not to bother my wound, and sat down on the couch with me still in his lap. He kissed my lips gently, pushing my hair behind my shoulders before moving his tender kisses to my neck. "I was so scared," he spoke between kisses as he pulled me closer to him. "I thought I was going to lose you."

"Hey," I leaned slightly back to catch his eyes

with mine. His lively green eyes had darkened with despair. The sight of him nearly broke me. He hid much of his life and his emotions in those eyes of his, only this time, I could see. I could see what he wanted. I could see how he felt.

Fuck.

I had forced myself to not think of Duncan in any way other than a *friend*. All so I would never again have to confront what I had recently been feeling.

Love.

He said he'd wait for me, but I think it's I who will have wait for him. He wasn't ready, I knew that, but he wants to be. And finally, I wanted that too. Running my right hand up the back of his neck into his hair, I kissed him once then tilted my head slightly towards the hallway. There are no words to tell him how I felt so I would show him instead.

Duncan's eyes flashed blissfully at me. He carried me down the hall to my room. He carefully undressed me before undressing himself. I motioned for him to lay beside me. I straddled him when he did. He looked like he was about to protest, but I kissed his words away. I was okay. I continued my slow and teasing trail of kisses across his neck and chest as I eased my wet center down his erect cock.

From my knees, I pushed myself slowly up and down his length, holding his gaze with mine. I wanted him to feel how I felt. I wanted him to know that I was his and I wasn't going anywhere.

We continue like this for a few strokes before he carefully rolled us over to where I laid on my back. A single tear rolled from my eye as he leaned down and kissed me hard. He rocked me tenderly in his strong arms until a wave of ecstasy rushed through me, causing me to gush around him.

He locked his lips with mine, grunting against my mouth as he unloaded inside me.

He pulled himself out of me and slid his right arm under my neck. I turned my back to his chest and backed up closer to him. His fingers traced the bandage over my left shoulder before planting a kiss right above it and wrapping his arm around me.

Graham was right, he and I would forever share something that Duncan and I could never, but that was all. Sitting here wrapped in Duncan's arms, there was nowhere else I'd rather be. No one else I'd rather be with.

I thought about Graham's offer to work at the institute, nothing would make me happier.

Except starting a life with Duncan.

Can I do both?

Epilogue

Since I never got to eat the breakfast Oliva left for me, Duncan whipped us up something to eat for lunch. As we sat and ate, I told Duncan everything that happened while I was at Keller Institute. I explained what Connecting was and that Graham also has the same ability. I went over all the details of the dream we had when Connecting with Mr. Keller. I also updated him on what the cops told me earlier in the morning. Dr. Keller would be charged for blackmailing her patient, and two counts of attempted murder. One count for me, one count for Mr. Keller. The patient she blackmailed would also be charged with one count of attempted murder.

I also decided to tell him that Graham and I shared several dreams together before I met him at the Institute. I told him that I didn't know he was a real person or that it was even a possibility at the time. I explained that all of this is part of what drew me to Graham, and why my feelings had been so confused. I decided to keep the sexual details to myself for now. I would tell him later if I had to.

Lastly, I told him about the offer Graham gave me – for me to come back to the city and work at the institute. And while I've decided that I don't need to live in the city, or any city for that matter, I would like to take him up on the job offer. Having a meaningful job was still important to me and something I'd like to pursue. The idea of me working there had me feeling the most excited I had been in a long time.

I would have to talk to Graham too. I hoped the offer wasn't contingent upon me living in the city, or contingent upon the possibility of a relationship between us, because both were off the table. But I knew I could help patients at the institute. I could go back to school, get my degree and be a real asset. If Graham agreed, I'd also have to figure out the logistics of it all. It was a two-hour trip from here to Easton City.

Duncan wasn't thrilled about the idea of Graham and I working together but he understood and supported my decision.

We decided that we would tell Olivia and Ronny about our relationship, but they would be sworn to secrecy. With everything going on with Mr. Johnson right now, we didn't want to cause any fuss. But more importantly, I wasn't ready to tell my mom.

Detective Reid called me later that evening to give me a heads up. Even though Dr. Keller confessed during her interrogation, she could choose to recant her statement and plead not guilty. If that happened, Graham, Duncan, and I would most likely have to testify against her. He also inquired how Graham and I knew the information we gave. Our statements were identical and since Mr. Keller couldn't physically tell us the details of the crime, Detective Reid wanted to sit down with us again for another interview.

It seemed, regardless of if Graham offered me the job, he and I would still have to see each other until Detective Reid was satisfied with our explanation, and potentially through the end of a trial.

Acknowledgments

A special thanks to my circle of support.
Matt
Paige
Peggy
Courtney
Kacie
Barbs
Arlene
Y'all have encouraged me and cheered me on from
the beginning. Thank you for supporting my dreams.

To my readers, THANK YOU for taking a chance on
my first novel. I hope y'all enjoyed it as much as I
enjoyed writing it. For a long time, the thought of
becoming an author lived in the back of my mind,
guarded by doubts. For a long time, I allowed those
doubts to prevent me from taking a chance. You
reading this book, making it this far, is a testament to
why we shouldn't let doubt, or fear, gate keep our
dreams. If you have a dream, a goal, or a passion that
you want to follow, do it. Let your efforts and
accomplishments speak louder than your doubts.

I'll see y'all in the next book.

With love and appreciation,
Olivia Pelar

About the Author

Olivia Pelar is a first time Indie author. Her love for creative writing, good mysteries, and romantic stories has inspired her to write her very first novel. When she isn't working on her next project, she's spending time with her family, snacking, and reading through her ever-growing TBR.

Connect with me on Instagram @
Instagram.com/Oliviapelar